THE MAN WITH TWO LAST NAMES

A Novel

By

WF Waldrip

WF Waldrip

The Man with
Two Last Names

WF Waldrip is an attorney, adventurer, and novelist. Since childhood Waldrip dreamed of writing stories that readers would enjoy. He is the author of *The Man With Two Last Names*, *The Guards Themselves*, *Honor Among Thieves* and *The Float.*

BOOKS BY WF WALDRIP

The Man with Two Last Names

The Float

Honor Among Thieves

The Guards Themselves

The Man with Two Last Names

WF Waldrip

FIRST PHARAOH Paperback EDITION

NOVEMBER 2018

In memory of my buddy, Ray Hagist.
Pura Vida

Thou hast clothed me with skin and flesh, and hast fenced me with bones and sinews.

   Job 10:11

Wherever there is a carcass, there the vultures will gather.

   Matthew 24:28

ONE

Some people actually believe that lawyers, doctors, and flight attendants have glamorous jobs. This conviction arises from watching too much television. Television lawyers are caricatures typically depicted as young and beautiful, wearing $2,000 suits, driving Teslas, and sitting around polished conference tables gravely discussing such socially ennobling causes as battered women, homelessness, and climate change. None of them actually work, which leaves plenty of time for them to fuck like minks. Alternatively, television lawyers are utterly corrupt, seedy hustlers. In reality, lawyers are just like everybody else: scratching out a living, paying their taxes, raising their kids, and trying to stay under the radar. Similarly, if anybody bothered to pull back the curtain, flight attendants would be revealed as little more than glorified waitresses. And doctors have far more in common with auto mechanics than with Hippocrates, Galen, or Avicenna. Although practitioners of the foregoing vocations might choose to be offended by such a pedestrian assessment of their esteemed professions, what is, is. It's the same with private detectives.

Since nobody reads Raymond Chandler, Dashiell Hammett, Richard S. Prather, or much of anything anymore, the public's knowledge, such as it is, of private investigators is derived from watching Humphrey Bogart movies and TV shows like "The Rockford Files" and "Magnum, PI," the latter two presenting stereotypes even more fanciful than the usual panoply of television characters comprised of cops, doctors, spies, and business tycoons.

Handsome, suave, quirky, and wise-cracking, television PIs invariably have dubious backgrounds, a colorful assortment of friends, and at least one trusted ally, *always* a detective, on the local police department, the rest of whose members distrust, if not roundly despise, them. About the only credible aspect of television PIs is that most of them are portrayed as having once been cops. Private detectives across the country are highly regulated and must be licensed by passing a state-administered examination. A further prerequisite is that aspiring PIs must tender a documented history of bona fide investigative experience; this *sine qua non* can ordinarily be acquired only through having worked as an actual cop at some point in their lives. Contrary to depictions on television, Joe Six-Pack can't simply hang out a shingle and call himself a "Private Investigator." At least not legally.

If you were to ask Lyman Henry, that's what he'd tell you, anyway.

He got into the PI biz more-or-less by default. Henry departed the Phoenix Police Department after a twenty-five-year career with two things: half a pension and an ex-wife. Half a pension because the court gave the other half to her in the divorce. He'd quickly discovered that half a pension is about as useful as half an arm. Needing income, middle-aged, but possessing no readily marketable skills, Henry had successfully taken the requisite test, submitted his dossier of investigative experience, and been duly awarded his license, printed on heavy-stock paper suitable for framing or for giving as gifts, as an official 'Private Investigator.' All he needed now was a secret decoder ring.

Rather than track down missing billionaires or expose international jewel smuggling operations like the TV PIs do, Henry had thereafter farmed himself out to various collection agencies to perform skip-traces and Internet asset searches on deadbeats who didn't pay their cable bills or credit cards. Occasionally, lawyers he'd met in his former incarnation as a cop would hire him to locate people: potential witnesses in nickel-and-dime civil trials who were dodging subpoenas.

Henry was finding life as a private investigator to be about as far from glamorous as it was possible to get, but that's pretty much what he expected. It would be nice to score one of those missing billionaire/jewel smuggling cases like on TV. Which is why he was surprised when he received Williams Smoot's call.

"Mr. Henry?"

"Speaking."

"Mr. Henry, this is Williams Smoot and I'd like to schedule an appointment with you at your convenience."

He paused before responding. He'd never laid eyes on Smoot and had no idea whether the caller was really him. Besides, Henry couldn't afford a secretary and worked out of his apartment. He had no intention of meeting a potential client there, even if that client was Williams Smoot.

"Sure," Henry finally responded, cautiously. "I can come to you or we can meet somewhere. What works for you?"

"I'd prefer to meet somewhere. Have you any suggestions?"

Henry generally rendezvoused with clients at Denny's but figured that Smoot probably had more elevated tastes. "What about the Los Cielos Grill? Do you know it?"

"Of course," the caller unctuously replied. "It's one of my favorites. What day works best for you? Frankly, the sooner the better."

"Well, I had an earlier cancellation," Henry lied, "so I'm free for lunch today. Or is that too soon?"

"Not at all. I'll meet you at the Grill at 11:00 today. We should have more privacy then, before the lunch crowd arrives. Just ask the hostess to seat you at my private table."

The guy had a private table at the "Grill." Figures.

"Will do. I'll see you at 11:00, Mr. Smoot."

"I look forward to meeting you, Mr. Henry." The call abruptly terminated.

Henry slipped his cell phone back into his pocket. He stared off into space, thinking. Williams Smoot had more money than God. So why was he calling him? More to the point, how had Smoot even learned of him? Aside from some printed matchbooks that he periodically distributed around to local taverns, Henry did no advertising because he couldn't afford to. He didn't even have a website. All of his business came by word of mouth. How would a high-roller like Smoot even know of his existence? And, having obviously learned of it, why would Smoot want to talk to him? With all of Smoot's scratch, he could afford to hire any private investigator on planet earth.

He glanced at his watch, leaned back in his chair, and lit a Kool. If nothing else, he'd get a good lunch on Smoot's dime.

TWO

Smoot was already seated at his private table when Henry arrived at 10:50. He was wearing a powder blue suit, light pink shirt, and a tie with diagonal blue-and-pink stripes. Smoot extended his hand without standing as the detective, escorted by the hostess, approached. As he perfunctorily shook his hand, Henry noted that Smoot wore a gold pinkie ring with a diamond in the center. His hand was soft, cool, fleshy.

"Candice will be your server today, gentlemen," the hostess informed them once Henry was seated.

"Thank you, Phoebe," Smoot smiled. "It's nice to see you again."

"Likewise, Mr. Smoot," she blushed before departing.

Smoot turned his attention to Henry. "Thank you for agreeing to see me on such short notice."

"Like I said, I had a cancellation."

"Perhaps their loss was my gain," Smoot remarked.

"Yeah, maybe. What did you want to see me about?"

"A man who gets right down to business," Smoot replied with admiration. "I genuinely respect that, Mr. Henry."

A young man materialized and began filling their crystal water glasses from a matching pitcher.

"Hi, Mr. Smoot. I'm glad you could join us today. It's always a pleasure to see you, sir," the ingratiating water kid greeted him.

"Thank you, Carlos. It's been a while, hasn't it?"

"Too long," the kid assured him. He gracefully handed each man a lunch menu. "Candice will be right with you." Smoot nodded wordlessly as Carlos turned away to service other tables.

"While we're on the subject, no one calls me 'Mr. Henry' except my ex-wife," the detective said without emotion. "'Henry' or 'Lyman' will be fine."

Smoot raised a quizzical eyebrow. "As you wish."

Henry took a sip of water as he mentally evaluated his host.

Smoot was scion of an old Mormon family that followed Brigham Young, the "American Moses," to the Salt Lake Valley following the 1844 assassination of the Mormon prophet, Joe Smith, in Illinois. His ancestors had subsequently migrated southward, to remote northern Arizona, where subsequent generations of Smoots had prospered by homesteading vast tracts of land where they established profitable cattle and sheep ranches. Some family members cast their lot with the railroad that finally reached the area around 1881. Other Smoots built flour and lumber mills, mercantiles, and hotels. Later generations of Smoots ultimately spread throughout Arizona, especially to the population centers farther south, where they invested in trucking companies, automobile dealerships, wholesale distributors, even funeral parlors. As their pecuniary fortunes thrived, so did the Smoot family's power and influence within the Mormon Church, which was already a formidable social and economic force throughout the state.

Smoot, himself, was physically unremarkable: short, pudgy, pasty skin, thinning light brown hair with a comb-over, watery blue eyes, wire-rimmed bifocals. Henry briefly puzzled over the man's Christian name, "Williams," finally concluding that it was probably his mother's maiden name.

"Do you eat here often?" Smoot benignly asked, interrupting Henry's silent musings. He unconsciously tipped his head slightly backward to scrutinize the detective out of the lower half of his bifocals.

"Rarely." The detective felt it unnecessary to add that he only ate at the Los Cielos Grill when someone else was paying.

"No matter. I've long been a customer." Smoot vaguely smiled, his gaze never wavering. "If you will permit me an indulgence, may I suggest that I order for the two of us? The Grill's lamb chops are superb." Smoot laid his menu aside, rested his wrists on the edge of their table, and laced his plump fingers together, as if in prayer. He smiled again as he looked expectantly at the detective.

Although seemingly intended as a courtesy, there was an underlying air of menace in Smoot's suggestion. He was obviously a man accustomed to being obeyed.

Henry immediately realized it would be necessary to establish some ground rules.

"Thanks, but I'll order for myself." He looked up as a liveried female, presumably Candice, approached.

"I'll have a burger, fries, and a Diet Coke," he informed Candice, somewhat brusquely, before she had a chance to parrot the customary 'have-you-lunched-with-us-before?' greeting. He handed her his menu and looked at Smoot.

The older man was clearly displeased by the detective's failure to display the anticipated deference but remained silent.

"Would you like cheese on your burger?" Candice asked, sweetly.

"Absolutely."

"Lettuce, tomato, and pickles okay?"

"It wouldn't be much of a burger without them."

"And how would you like that cooked?"

"Medium well."

"Very good." Candice turned to the older man. "And for you, Mr. Smoot?"

"How are the lamb chops today, Candice?" he inquired.

"Excellent, as always," she beamed.

"In that case, I'll have one with a little mint jelly on the side."

"Of course. And to drink?"

He gestured to the glass before him on the table. "Just water will be fine." He took a sip as if to confirm his decision.

Candice smiled, nodded, and departed.

"Now, where were we?" Smoot broke the ensuing silence.

Henry decided to take another tack. "How'd you find out about me, Mr. Smoot?"

"Find out about you? A friend referred me to you, Lyman."

"A friend of yours or mine?"

"Yours, I think. I doubt whether any of my friends ever had need for a detective."

"I don't think you'd be likely to know any of my friends."

Smoot shrugged. "If not one of your friends, perhaps it was one of your enemies. Experience has taught me that it's often difficult to distinguish one from the other." Smoot took another sip of water and smiled again. "Does it matter?"

A server arrived with Henry's Diet Coke. He deposited it on their table and wordlessly departed.

"I'd just like to know who to thank."

"Perhaps you should save your thanks for me. After all, I'm the one who's paying for your lunch and may end up retaining you."

Henry nodded slowly. "Fair enough. Retaining me for what?"

"As I said, as a businessman myself, I genuinely respect a man who doesn't waste time," Smoot reiterated before taking another drink.

"I couldn't agree more, Mr. Smoot. Exactly what is it you want?"

"I want you to find the man who murdered my son," he abruptly asserted.

Henry managed to mask his surprise. "Your son was murdered? When?"

The older man's face grew stony. "What! Do you pretend to be unacquainted with my son's murder?"

"I don't pretend to be anything, Mr. Smoot. My question was asked in good faith because I know nothing of your son's murder."

"You don't read the newspaper?"   Smoot appeared incredulous.

"Actually, no." Henry responded, matter-of-factly. "People claim they read the paper to know what's going on but, frankly, they couldn't find a worse guide because most of what's written in the paper sooner or later turns out to be false. Even if it isn't a deliberate lie, newspapers intentionally manipulate their readers through selective reporting. So, no, I don't read the paper. Or for that matter, watch the news on television...it's even worse."

"You're quite cynical, Lyman."

Henry's response was interrupted by the arrival of lunch. He was gratified to note that his hamburger actually resembled one of those hamburgers in TV commercials rather than the fast food burgers he generally ate, which look as though a car had backed over them.

"Cynical or realist, take your pick," he said following Candice's departure. "All I know is that I didn't realize that you had a son who was murdered. I'm sorry for your loss, Mr. Smoot."

The older man stared at the lamb chop reposing on the china plate before him beside a mound of vegetable medley. A lonely sprig of parsley rested atop it. "Three months ago. The police believe that one of Freddie's acquaintances killed him. In fact, he's apparently already confessed."

"Which 'police'? Phoenix?"

"Yes, the Phoenix Police Department."

"And they've already arrested a suspect?"

Smoot nodded resignedly, still transfixed by his lamp chop. "He's incarcerated as we speak."

"So, what am I not hearing? Why do you need me if Phoenix PD already has the perp in custody? Your tax dollars at work."

Smoot finally looked up from the forlorn lamp chop. "Because Danny didn't kill my son."

Henry needed a few seconds to digest Smoot's revelation. He grasped his unwieldy burger and took a bite. It wasn't medium well. Disappointed, he returned it to his plate and ate a French fry.

"Danny's the suspect?"

The other man nodded.

"What makes you think he's not the guy who killed your son? The cops don't go out and arrest people just for the hell of it, you know. More to the point, you said that he's already confessed. What am I missing?"

The French fry was better than the hamburger, so Henry ate a second one.

Smoot lowered his voice and glanced around furtively before answering. "I know Danny didn't kill Freddie because Danny was with me that night."

"What do you mean 'with' you?" Henry paused momentarily, thinking. "Wait...you mean he was *with* you?"

"Yes, Lyman, that's precisely what I mean. Danny and I were together the night Freddie was brutally murdered."

"Where?"

"Is it important?"

"Yes, it's important."

Smoot wrinkled his brow in thought. "Someplace downtown in an old warehouse. I can't immediately recall exactly where it was, but it was clearly some sort of impromptu establishment. I suspect it was what young people call a 'rave.' It was Danny's idea to go there."

"A gay party?"

"I suppose you could call it that." Smoot was becoming testy. "As I said, Danny suggested it."

"What you're telling me makes absolutely zero sense. If you're convinced that your friend, Danny, didn't have anything to do with the murder of your son, why did he confess to it? That defies logic. That thorny problem aside, if you want to help him despite his confession, go to the cops and tell them what you just told me." Henry had another French fry. Smoot hadn't touched his lamb chop.

Smoot sighed deeply. "Who can say what motivates people to do what they do? I certainly don't have to tell you that innocent people routinely confess to crimes they didn't commit. But to respond to your suggestion directly, I'm LDS, the bishop of my ward. If I go to the police, as you glibly suggest, to provide Danny an alibi, it would prove extremely awkward, both personally and professionally. The inevitable scandal would ruin my marriage, my professional reputation, my entire life. That is out of the question." Smoot pushed the plate containing his untouched lamb chop away and tossed his wadded cloth napkin onto the table.

"You find it preferable that your friend, Danny, take a needle for a murder he couldn't possibly have committed? Problem solved?"

"I don't appreciate your impertinence," Smoot heatedly responded. His face grew red and his pale blue eyes flared. "Were that the case, we wouldn't be having this conversation, would we?"

Henry finished eating his small pile of French fries. "No, I suppose we wouldn't, Mr. Smoot. But, then, it all comes back to the question I asked when I first sat down today. What, exactly, do you want with me?"

"I told you. I want you to find who killed Freddie. Having done so, Danny's inexplicable confession will be exposed for what it actually is: a fantasy."

"Why me?"

"Are you LDS?"

"Nope. I'm like Honest Abe, 'When I do good, I feel good. When I do bad, I feel bad. That's my religion.'"

"But you used to be a police officer?"

"Most PIs used to be police officers."

"As I told you earlier, you were recommended to me."

"But you don't remember who recommend me."

Smoot shrugged without responding.

"You realize that if I have exculpatory evidence, I'm obligated to convey it to the cops, right? What you just told me, in other words."

Smoot smiled humorlessly. "You're also obligated, under the canons of your profession, to respect client confidences."

"You're not my client."

"True, but even if you go to the police about Danny, I'll deny that we ever discussed the matter. If the police question me, I'll simply tell them that our meeting today was merely a social visit."

"What if I just get up and walk out of here right now?" Henry challenged.

"That's your decision, Lyman. I'm certain there are other private investigators who will prove less squeamish about taking my money." Smoot smiled again.

"You realize that, if I go to the cops, the first thing they'll do is talk to Danny about the gay *soiree* you went to. Somebody who was there that night will be able to identify him and confirm that you two were there. There goes your secret."

"As I said, the '*soiree*,' as you call it, was clearly an extemporaneous affair. Even if the police are able to locate it, I'm sure the venue where it occurred is once again vacant. Furthermore, there were a number of notable Phoenicians present that night who will prove very reticent about speaking to the police. That, combined with the fact that most everyone was under the influence of drugs and alcohol, will render my exposure most unlikely."

Henry surveyed the innocuous-looking man with a combination of dubiousness and contempt.

"But may I suggest a compromise, Lyman?" Smoot blandly continued.

"What's that?"

"I'll retain you to find Freddie's actual murderer. If, for whatever reason, your efforts prove unavailing, I will personally go to the police and exonerate Danny."

"And, in the meantime, he'll just sit on his butt in jail for a crime he didn't commit? You don't have a problem with that?"

Smoot sighed. "Although Danny didn't murder Freddie, he's far from what anyone would consider a model citizen, Lyman. He has engaged in a multitude of rather unsavory activities so, frankly, no, I don't have a problem with it. It isn't as though Danny will be tried and convicted any time soon; as you and I both know, the wheels of justice grind very slowly. Nothing will happen to Danny while he's in jail. He'll simply be off the streets for a time while you conduct your investigation. 'Three hots and a flop,' as the expression goes."

Henry silently pondered Smoot's unorthodox proposition while the other man watched his discomfiture from across the table with an expression akin to bemusement. Although he found the man repellent, Smoot basically had him over a barrel. If he declined Smoot's offer, there was no assurance that the old man would, in fact, hire another detective. In that event, Danny What's-His-Name might find himself convicted of a murder he apparently didn't commit. Besides, there was probably no other PI in town dumb enough to even consider accepting Smoot's offer. Alternatively, if Henry went to the cops with the information Smoot had imparted to him, the self-righteous bastard would undoubtedly deny everything and the poor schlub would sure as hell find himself on the receiving end of a lethal injection. If Henry agreed to Smoot's terms, there was at least a chance that he'd be able to clear an innocent man. Even if he failed to find Freddie's killer, he had Smoot's promise that he'd go to the cops himself. For what *that* was worth. But Henry also feared that he might be over his head, PI-wise. Although he had plenty of experience from his years as a cop investigating car accidents, his background was in traffic control, not homicides. He'd never investigated an actual murder. The detective rapidly concluded that Smoot, although slimy, apparently had more money than good sense. There was, accordingly, nothing to be lost by nosing around for a few days simply to mollify his hoggish lunch companion and relieve him of a few sheckles. Besides, hunger never saw bad bread.

"What's Danny's last name?"

"Lightfoot," Smoot replied.

"Did he know Freddie?"

"It's possible."

"I realize 'it's possible.' *Anything* is possible. Did Lightfoot know your son or not?"

Smoot scowled. "Yes, I think they were acquainted."

"How?"

"I think Danny may have supplied marijuana to Freddie. Maybe more." Smoot was clearly uncomfortable responding to Henry's questions.

"Although I already know the answer, I'm gonna ask anyway: have you talked to Lightfoot since he was arrested?"

"Don't be absurd," Smoot scoffed. "Even if the police, or his lawyer, allowed me access to Danny, what reason could I possibly give for wishing to engage the confessed murderer of my son in a *tete-ta-tete*? For reasons I've already explained, it is essential that I distance myself from Danny."

"I don't like it, but I'll tell ya what," Henry finally said. "I'll nose around for three days, max, to see what I can find out about your son's murder. If I don't find anything, you agree to voluntarily go to Phoenix PD, tell them everything you just told me, and take your lumps." He paused. "You'll pay me $10,000 today, in cash, and after three days I'm done." Henry pulled the $10,000 figure completely out of the clear-blue figuring that, if Smoot balked at it, he'd been bullshitting all along. "That's the deal, take it or leave it. And, just so we're clear, I agree to your terms only to help the guy who's in jail for killing your son, not to help you perpetuate your double life."

"Understood," Smoot beamed, clasping and unclasping his fat hands, the diamond in his pinkie ring sparkling. "Under the circumstances, I'm sure you can appreciate that absolute discretion is required with respect to this matter. If you wish to accompany me to my office, I'll pay you immediately."

"Where's your office?"

"Central and Fell. Smoot Funeral Chapel."

It figures, thought Henry.

"I don't suppose you know Lightfoot's Social Security number."

"Which one? I'm sure Danny has more than one," Smoot said, indifferently.

"Well, at a minimum, I'll need *your* Social Security number."

"Of course. I am at your disposal to assist in any way I can."

Henry paused. "What happens if, despite everything you've told me, Lightfoot actually turns out to be your son's killer? Do I need to remind you that he's already confessed?"

Smoot gazed thoughtfully into the distance. "Over the course of my life, I've paid professionals a great deal of money for their insight and guidance...architects, surveyors, lawyers, accountants, various consultants. Hundreds of thousands of dollars, Lyman...perhaps millions. It would have been foolish of me to pay such sums, only to thereafter ignore their expert counsel. Why bother to go to the doctor if you don't intend to follow his advice?"

Henry pushed his chair away from their table. "Let's go."

Smoot signaled Candice to indicate they were leaving. She smiled and nodded. The detective surmised today's lunch tab would automatically be added to Smoot's running Grill account. He headed for the door, Smoot trailing him.

At the parking lot, Henry flopped into his eight-year-old Hyundai as his new employer ponderously climbed into a late model Lexus SUV. He slammed the door shut, cranked the engine, flicked on the air conditioning, and lit a Kool. Henry watched as Smoot's Lexus slowly glided from the restaurant's parking lot. Although he drove immediately past the detective's idling car, Smoot didn't glance at him.

THREE

Smoot Funeral Chapel was a handsome colonial-style building located in uptown Phoenix, twenty minutes from the Los Cielos Grill. A large sign on its manicured, almost preternaturally green lawn assured passing motorists of the Smoot family's unwavering commitment to "Helping Your Family in Your Time of Need." Henry swung into the parking lot and left the Hyundai's engine idling, its air conditioning blasting, while he surveyed the area. Aside from a gleaming black Cadillac hearse parked beneath a broad portico on one side of the building, he saw no other vehicles in the vicinity. Not even Smoot's Lexus. There were no discernable signs of life about, though that seemed entirely appropriate given that the place was a funeral home.

Henry sighed, switched the engine off, and clambered out of his car. He figured that the double doors nearest the Caddy probably led directly into the chapel, so he headed around the other side of the building to look for the business office. Skirting a cube-shaped hedge trimmed so precisely that he feared slicing his leg if he accidently brushed against it, Henry spotted a small sign jutting from the side of the building above an unobtrusive steel door: *Office.*

He opened it and stepped inside.

It looked like any other business office. At one end of a waiting area containing a scattering of chairs upholstered in dark green velvet, a well-dressed, middle-aged woman sat at a dark wooden desk, reading a magazine. Soft, comforting music emanated from an unseen source. The woman looked up as Henry padded toward her across the thick carpeting.

"Can I help you?" she was about forty-five, reasonably attractive, unsuccessfully striving to look thirty-five.

"I'm supposed to meet Mr. Smoot," Henry answered. "We just had lunch together."

"Certainly. Let me page him for you." She pushed a button on the phone that occupied one corner of her polished desk. "Mr. Smoot will be right with you. Please make yourself comfortable." She motioned toward the chairs behind him.

To the extent that it's actually possible to make oneself comfortable in a mortuary, Henry complied. The woman behind the desk resumed reading her magazine.

Two minutes later, a door in the far wall opened and Smoot emerged.

"Lyman," he smiled broadly, as if they were two old friends reuniting after a long estrangement. He extended his pudgy, pinkie-ringed hand. Henry shook it. Again. "This way, please." Smoot gallantly stepped to one side and held the door open for the detective to pass.

Smoot led him down a nondescript linoleum-tiled hall to his elegant office. He quietly shut the door as Henry seated himself on a plush settee in the center of the room.

"I didn't see your car in the parking lot," Henry remarked as Smoot eased into a leather wing chair behind a dark wooden desk.

"I always park in back," explained Smoot. "Grieving clients sometimes find it upsetting if they see their funeral director driving an expensive automobile."

"Your receptionist park in the back, too?"

Smoot looked momentarily confused. "Oh, you mean Eileen? She takes the light-rail."

"She must be the only one," Henry observed. He looked directly at Smoot. "So I guess the funeral business must be pretty remunerative, huh?" He indicated the conspicuous opulence of the office in which they sat.

Smoot was momentarily taken aback by Henry's unexpected use of the word 'remunerative' but quickly regained his *sang froid*. "We manage to pay our bills, Lyman."

"Yeah, so it would seem," Henry replied, recalling Smoot's Lexus.

Smoot rocked forward in his chair and rose to his feet by pushing against its arms. He waddled across the room to a small white refrigerator placed against one wall then turned to look at the detective.

"Would you mind helping me, Lyman? It's rather much for me to handle, especially on the carpeting."

Henry rose and walked to refrigerator. "What do you want me to do?"

"Just pull it away from the wall, if you don't mind."

The detective bent and grasped the top of the squat appliance, the palms of his hand resting against its smooth top surface and his fingers pressed against either side. By rocking the refrigerator slightly from side-to-side while simultaneously pulling it toward him, Henry was easily able to wrestle it away from the wall. It was surprising light; judging by its weight, the refrigerator appeared to be completely empty. Cut into the sheetrock behind it was an aperture about ten inches square. Henry wandered back to the settee and resumed his seat.

Smoot stepped around the refrigerator to the previously concealed opening and reached inside.

"Other than Eileen and me, you're the only other person to know about my little treasure trove here, Lyman. My wife doesn't even know about it. You should be flattered," Smoot said over his shoulder. He withdrew from the incongruous hole a canvas bag laced shut with a thin steel cable secured with a disproportionately large brass padlock. Smoot made his way back across the carpeted floor to Henry's settee. He wordlessly placed the bag next to the detective before producing from an interior pocket of his suit a ring bearing a single, small key.

"Your retainer." He handed the ring to Henry and returned to his leather wing chair.

Henry held the lock between this thumb and forefinger and used the key to open it. As he already knew, the canvas bag was full of money: crisp stacks of one hundred-dollar bills in neat bundles sealed with narrow paper bands. He could smell the pungent ink from the stacks of uncirculated cash.

"Your fee was $10,000, was it not?" Smoot blandly confirmed from his seat across the room.

"That was the agreement."

"There is $20,000 in that bag. Remove half and leave it on the settee there, along with the lock. You may use the bag to carry your retainer when you leave." A tiny smile crossed Smoot's smooth face. "No extra charge."

"My retainer agreement..." the detective started to interject.

Smoot stopped him with a dismissive wave of his hand. "Mail it to Eileen at your convenience. We'll take care of everything at that time." He paused. "Unless, of course, you don't wish to take the $10,000 with you today. It's entirely up to you, Lyman."

"I'll write you a receipt while I'm here." Henry nodded toward the refrigerator that had hitherto concealed Smoot's hiding place but was still resting at an angle away from the wall. "Want me to push that back?"

"That won't be necessary but thank you. It's harder to pull out than to push back, and Eileen can help me." He nudged a pad and pen across the top of his desk toward the detective. "Although I'm accustomed to doing business on a handshake, you may write a receipt if you wish. I assure you that your good reputation is perfectly adequate, however.

Henry took the pad and scribbled a receipt for $10,000 before replacing it on the desk. Smoot ignored it.

FOUR

Having learned from Smoot the precise date of Freddie's murder, Henry began, as he always did, with a routine Internet search. According to the three-month-old online editions of local newspapers, 24-year-old Freddie Smoot, "son of prominent local businessman Williams Smoot," was shot in the parking lot of his Phoenix apartment complex at approximately 8:56 p.m. after returning home from work. Police initially suspected a random shooter, but a serendipitous tip rapidly led them to Daniel Lightfoot, a 28-year-old vagrant with a history of petty crime. When Lightfoot was subsequently brought in for routine questioning, he promptly confessed to Freddie's murder, claiming that the victim had cheated him out of some pot. Lightfoot further stated that he'd shot Freddie with a 9mm pistol, a fact confirmed by the coroner. Police divers were, however, unable to recover the murder weapon from the irrigation canal where Lightfoot insisted he'd thrown it after shooting Freddie. Investigators surmised that Lightfoot was high on drugs at the time he shot Freddie and was simply confused about what ultimately became of the pistol. In lieu of flowers, the Smoot family requested that donations be made to the Church of Jesus Christ of Latter-Day Saints. Lightfoot was currently represented by a public defender.

All very blasé. Even so, Henry found it peculiar that Lightfoot would actually kill somebody over some piddley-ass pot. Heroin maybe, meth even, but pot? Hell, *anybody* could buy marijuana legally at the multitude of dispensaries that had sprung up all over Phoenix over the past few years. Why would anyone *kill* somebody over pot?

Henry next undertook to acquire additional personal information on Freddie and Williams Smoot, and Daniel Lightfoot.

According to a confidential website accessible only to law enforcement and licensed private investigators, Williams and Virginia Smoot had a total of six adult children including the youngest, Freddie. Five of the six Smoot children were currently employed by companies owned or controlled by their father, Williams. Freddie was the odd man out. Though he had previously worked in one of the family businesses, Freddie had abruptly resigned the previous year and taken a job as a manager-trainee at Best Buy. It was after his shift ended, and Freddie had driven from Best Buy to his apartment, that he was killed. Other than that, Freddie was a phantom: no college degree, never married, no children, no criminal history, no legal or tax problems. By contrast, Williams Smoot had been, alternatively, either the plaintiff or defendant in a multiplicity of civil lawsuits stretching over the past three decades. Most of them were routine contract matters. Unremarkable, given that Smoot was a businessman with significant assets.

Henry next turned to the county recorder's website, where he learned that Williams and Virginia Smoot were the owners of seven residential properties, as well as a scattering of commercial properties, including the uptown funeral home. Five of the seven residential properties were occupied by a corresponding number of Smoot children and their families; a sixth by the *paterfamilias* and his wife. The seventh was listed as having been Freddie Smoot's previous address, though it was currently unoccupied.

Henry frowned unconsciously. Why did Freddie, unique among the Smoot children, rent an apartment rather than live in one of the several houses owed by his parents, especially since he *did* live there at one point? And why, of all the siblings, had Freddie ended his previous employment at one of his father's businesses?

The detective also found Daniel Lightfoot's criminal history illuminating.

Because of his peripatetic lifestyle, Lightfoot had no permanent address. And, although Lightfoot had been arrested many times in the past, beginning at age 13, it was invariably for something relatively minor: shoplifting, drunk and disorderly, urinating in public, vagrancy, pandering, trespassing...all misdemeanor offenses. Conspicuous by its absence was any record whatsoever of serious or violent crimes ever having been committed by Lightfoot. While not unheard of, Henry knew it was uncommon for a petty criminal like Lightfoot to morph into a murderer, at least over a nickel-bag of marijuana that could now be legally purchased just about anywhere. But if something happens, it must be possible.

It was time to talk to Danny Lightfoot but, in order to do so, he'd have to go through Lightfoot's mouthpiece.

Since he was already sitting at his computer, Henry Googled the number of the Public Defender's Office. He dialed the number on his cell and, when the receptionist answered, politely asked the name of the Public Defender currently assigned to represent Daniel Lightfoot.

Henry waited while the receptionist checked her computer. "That would be Gwen Harp," she finally announced.

"Does she have a direct line?"

"No, but I'll be happy to connect you."

"I appreciate it." Henry hoped that he'd be able to talk to Lightfoot's PD immediately.

After a moment of silence, a recording of a female voice, obviously young, came on the line.

"You've reached Public Defender Gwendolyn Harp. I'm currently away from my desk, but please leave a message and I'll return your call when I return to my office. Thank you and have a wonderful day."

Henry kept his message short. "Ms. Harp, my name is Lyman Henry. Today is May 8th at 3:30 in the afternoon. I'd like to talk to you at your earliest opportunity about your client, Daniel Lightfoot. I have information regarding your client that may prove of interest to you. Please return my call as soon as you receive this message. Thank you." Henry slowly dictated his cell number, twice, before terminating the call.

He had some legwork to do. But first he had to talk to Smoot again. Henry dialed Smoot's cell number.

"Lyman! You *are* diligent," Smoot gushed over the phone. "Have you already found something?"

"I need a photo of Danny Lightfoot. Do you have one?"

There was silence at the other end of the line. Finally, Smoot spoke. "Why do you need Danny's photo?"

"Because I asked for it. Do you have one or not?"

More silence. "Yes, I think I have a photo of Danny on my cell phone. You understand, Lyman, that no one can know where the photo came from. Yes?"

"All I need is a clear head-shot, nothing compromising. Do you have something like that on your phone?"

"Yes, I think so."

"Can you send it to my cell right now?"

"Yes, I can do that."

"Then do it. I need the photo right now, Mr. Smoot."

"I understand, Lyman. I'll send it immediately."

"Thank you." Henry terminated the call. Hopefully, the old man would comply promptly.

FIVE

Irrespective of the specific American metropolis, homeless people habitually congregate at predictable sites in foreseeable patterns. You can set your watch by it. Soup kitchens and flop houses, obviously, but principally where they'll be shielded from inclement weather and won't be hassled by either the public or the cops. Out of sight, out of mind. About the only time homeless people budge from such clandestine "gypsy camps" is when constrained by economic necessity. At such times, they either solicit donations "for gas" from the gainfully employed or bum money from idling motorists on street corners or freeway entrance ramps.

The primary consideration for determining the suitability of any potential homeless encampment in Phoenix and its environs, certainly during the summer months, is the murderous heat. The ideal location must be large enough to accommodate a constantly fluctuating number of inhabitants, shielded to the greatest extent possible from the blistering rays of the sun, yet convenient to street corners and freeway entrance ramps. Henry knew of only one location that satisfied all these criteria: the shores of the large, man-made "Town Lake" in the neighboring city of Tempe.

Expansive, situated near the confluence of three busy freeways, adjacent to Arizona State University, and abounding in lush reeds and a limitless supply of fresh water arising out of its lakeside situs, the haven was none-the-less relatively secluded. Even if he wasn't a permanent resident, it seemed likely that some of its denizens had encountered, or at least knew something about, Danny Lightfoot. Henry intended to buttonhole anybody in the camp who'd talk to him, show them the emailed head-shot of Lightfoot, and pick their brains. He'd promised Smoot three days and the clock was ticking. Lightfoot's public defender had Henry's cell number; even if she called him back that afternoon he'd be able to talk to her while nosing around Tempe.

He grabbed his car keys off their hook near the front door and headed out.

***

Because there didn't appear to be a road leading directly into the homeless camp, Henry had to park his car several blocks away and struggle down a steep embankment to the edge of the lake. As he approached, a malodorous potpourri assailed his nostrils: rotting fish, human shit, wood smoke, stale cooking grease, and marijuana. Several denizens, sitting or lying on flattened appliances boxes, viewed him sullenly. He stopped, lit a Kool, and let the comforting scent of burning tobacco waft over him before approaching the first inhabitant.

"Hey, I'm lookin' for my brother," he explained with as much sincerity as he could muster. "I think he hangs out here sometimes. Our mom died and left him some money." Henry pulled his cell phone from his pocket and clicked on Lightfoot's photo. He held it in front of the guy's face. "Know him?"

"Fuck off," the man grunted.

***

Henry went to one derelict after another with the same question, consistently eliciting responses either blatantly hostile or maddeningly vague. The homeless refuge turned out to be far larger than he'd anticipated and, after questioning what seemed at least a hundred people, the sun finally began to set. Thoroughly discouraged, Henry was hot, thirsty, and sweaty. He headed back in the direction of his car and blissful air conditioning.

As the detective stepped around a recumbent figure lying on the baked earth, he was hailed by a thin, reedy voice.

"You lookin' for Danny?"

Henry stopped to look at the man who had spoken to him. He was sitting on an upturned plastic Home Depot bucket, fifteen feet away. The guy was extraordinarily gaunt, dressed in soiled blue jeans, a diaphanous T-shirt, and a pristine, bright orange baseball cap that said "Cabela's" on it. A grey, braided pony tail hung down his scrawny back from beneath his cap and the leathery skin of his face and arms, furrowed with wrinkles, was deeply tanned.

"Yeah, I am," Henry responded to the man's startling inquiry. "You know him? Our mom just died and left him some money. I'm tryin' to find him so I can give it to him."

"Bullshit," stated the man, matter-of-factly. "Besides, Danny ain't here. He's in the jug."

Henry slowly nodded. "You know him?"

"Yeah, maybe," the guy half-acknowledged.

"Mind if I sit and talk for a minute?"

The man made a show of scanning the area immediately around him. "Only got one bucket. Besides, I generally talk better while I'm eaten'."

Henry chuckled. "Well, I'm kinda hungry, myself. Wanna hamburger?"

"I s'pose I could gag one down," the guy said, standing. "Gotta smoke?"

"As long as you don't mind Kools," Henry replied.

"That'll work," the other man shrugged.

Henry withdrew a crushed pack from his pocket and handed it to him. He withdrew two cigarettes and stuck one in his mouth, the other behind his ear. Henry lit the former for him; the homeless man closed his eyes and took a long, luxuriant drag.

"Took up smokin' when I was in 'Nam 'cause it kept the fuckin' bugs away. Back then, the only grunts who smoked Kools was black. When we was out on patrol, we'd have contests to see which brand of smokes worked best on the fuckin' bugs...you know, Marlboros, Camels, whatever." He opened his eyes and grinned. His teeth were remarkably straight and white. "We'd sit around, smokin' up a fuckin' storm, blowing smoke ever which way...musta looked like the whole fuckin' jungle was on fire! Turns out, bugs hate Kools…wouldn't come anywhere near them black dudes. Must be the menthol in 'em, I guess." He finished smoking and dropped the smoldering butt onto the ground. "Les go," he said after grinding it out beneath his frayed tennis shoe.

Henry and his unanticipated companion clambered up the berm surrounding the lake and walked the several blocks to the detective's car in the scorching early evening heat. He started the engine and cranked the air to "high" while they fastened their seatbelts.

"Any particular place you wanna eat?" Henry asked.

"You're drivin'," the guy laconically responded. He reclined his seat and closed his eyes.

Henry made a U-turn and headed in the direction of a hamburger joint he'd seen on his way to the Town Lake earlier that day.

***

He said his name was "Max," was originally from Alabama, and was a Vietnam veteran. After returning from 'Nam in 1969, Max started having "episodes" that grew increasingly worse as the years passed…he'd black completely out or descend into violent rages. Sometimes he couldn't even remember what had happened to him, or where he'd been, for days at a time. He had a wife back then, but she ended up leaving him. He started drinking too much, using drugs, and eventually ended up on the streets, where he'd been ever since. Max thought he may have had a couple of grown children and maybe some grandkids, too, but couldn't really recall. In any case, he'd not had any contact with his family in a long time.

"The fuckin' VA didn't do shit," Max spat as he devoured his third hamburger. "I went there after I got back from 'Nam but they just kept loadin' me up on all kinds of pills and shit. I finally pulled the plug on the whole fuckin' shitteree."

"Do you think it was Agent Orange, or what?" Henry asked in an effort to establish a rapport.

"God only knows, and He'd only be guessin'," Max retorted. "The government dumped so much fuckin' crap on them poor gooks that it'd make your head spin. And I ain't just talking about bombs. No, sir! It was all kinda chemicals. And it didn't matter that a lot of it got dumped on us grunts in the process." He took a noisy swallow of root beer. "Agent Orange is just the one that made the news and got ever'body's panties in a wad. But there was a shit-load of other crap, too. Motherfuckers," Max growled.

"Well, that sucks big time," Henry commiserated.

"Fuckin'-A," said Max.

The detective decided it was probably as good a time as any to risk changing the subject. "What were you gonna tell me about Danny Lightfoot, Max?"

"Lightfoot? He's a piece of shit."

"How well do you know him?"

"Well enough," Max averred.

"Why do you say that Lightfoot's a piece of shit?"

"'Cause he is."

"It sounds like you don't like him very much."

"Fuck no. Nobody likes him."

"How come?" Henry asked, surprised by Max's obvious enmity.

"Lightfoot's always flashing his nigger wad around in front of ever'body. Actin' like King Shit on Turd Mountain."

"Lightfoot's got money?" Again, Henry was surprised.

"Yeah...more'n me, anyway. He likes kiddie poon tang, which don't come cheap. But I don't go for that kinda shit."

"Interesting," Henry reflected. "Was this just a one-time thing or did Danny seem to have money most of the time?"

"Lightfoot *always* had money, at least ever time I saw him," Max replied. "It weren't just now and again."

Henry fished his cell phone from his pocket. "This is who we're talkin' about, right?"

Max took the phone in a grimy hand and squinted at Lightfoot's picture. "Yeah, that's the prick."

The detective recovered his phone and slipped it back into his pocket. "Did Danny ever tell you where his money came from?"

Max shook his head. "Not directly, but he said that he worked for a mortician sometimes. He thought it was funny."

"A mortician? Doing what?"

"He never said exactly." Max belched before taking another drink of soda. "Just that the mortician paid him good." He glanced surreptitiously about before responding. "But I got a pretty good idea."

"Yeah? What's that?"

"I think he's a damned organ grinder."

"Huh? What are you talking about...like with a monkey?"

Max laughed. "No, not with a fuckin' monkey," he snorted. "I mean that Lightfoot sells stiffs. Parts of 'em, anyway."

The detective was taken aback. "Wait a minute, Max. You're telling me that Lightfoot's in the body snatching business?"

"That's perzactly what I'm tellin' you."

Henry possessed a rudimentary knowledge of the shadowy business of body-harvesting, derived primarily from newspaper articles. For whatever reason, Arizona was one of a handful of states with a thriving cadaver industry. He first became acquainted with the trade when baseball slugger, Ted Williams, died of heart disease in 2002. Williams' lifeless head was removed from his torso then cryogenically frozen in anticipation of some future time when it will be thawed and, presumably, attached to another body and revivified. That was the idea, anyway. As far as Henry knew, the Splendid Splinter's frost-bitten head remained frozen in some high-tech facility in Scottsdale, along with the heads, or entire bodies, of other rich optimists.

Commerce in dead bodies dates back centuries. In the Middle Ages, wars were fought and dynasties toppled over the venerated remains of various Catholic saints, fragments of whose sanctified bodies remain scattered in churches all around the globe. More prosaically, 18th and 19th century European universities required a steady supply of cadavers in order to teach anatomy and developing surgical techniques to aspiring physicians. Drawings and mannequins were adequate to a point but, ultimately, nothing compared to an actual human body. Corpses are still routinely utilized for this, and other less altruistic, purposes. Unfortunately, demand always exceeded supply, which predictably spawned a nascent body-harvesting industry characterized by grave robbing and, inevitably, murder.

The most notorious 19th century "Resurrection Men," as they were derisively termed, were undoubtedly the two Williams, Burke and Hare, who, in 1820's Edinburgh, killed sixteen people, selling the corpses to Dr. John Knox, of the Royal College of Surgeons, for use in his anatomical lectures. In those exceptional circumstances where Burke, Hare, and other Resurrection Men were actually caught and prosecuted, Knox and his associates vehemently protested their utter ignorance of the dubious origins of the remarkably pristine corpses delivered to them.

Today, organ donations in the United States are governed, at least ostensibly, by the 1984 federal Organ and Transplant Act, which regulates commerce in human tissue and organs. Under its provisions, before human remains can be legally harvested, explicit authorization must be obtained from the donor via a living will, for example, or from the donor's next of kin. In the absence of such authorization, the use of human organs or tissue for medical transplant is illegal. The United States Food and Drug Administration monitors, to a greater or lesser degree, the several licensed "tissue banks" that provide such anatomical material to hospitals: skin for burn victims, ligaments and tendons for sports injuries, new heart valves to replace defective ones. Selling a complete, intact corpse for transplant purposes, however, remains illegal under the Act.

In addition to money lawfully generated through the legitimate sale of human tissue for medical transplants, the Organ and Transplant Act also authorizes the recovery of "reasonable costs" arising out of the harvesting of body parts. Thus, human cadavers represent a two-pronged source of revenue: one prong representing the *a la carte* price for the remains themselves and a second prong for processing and transporting the physical remains to the end user.

Notwithstanding the restrictions contained in the Organ and Transplant Act, no federal, and few state, laws prohibit the sale of human body parts, or entire corpses, for use in research or education rather than medical transplant. This loophole led to the creation of a virtual cottage industry in cadavers. Because of the absence of oversight, basically anyone with a Sawzall, irrespective of background or experience, is free to dissect corpses and hawk the resulting parts to the highest bidder. Entrepreneurs who engage in this dubious trade, free from the bothersome scrutiny of the Food and Drug Administration, are referred to as "body brokers" or "non-transplant tissue banks." Modern incarnations of Burke and Hare. The more things change, the more they stay the same.

Henry recalled reading an article that provided a sardonic explanation for the apparent allure of such a repugnant vocation. According to Walter Mitchell, a Phoenix businessman involved in three body brokerage firms, "If you can't make a business when you're getting raw material for free, you're dumb as a box of rocks."

An inexhaustible supply of free raw material, combined with insatiable global demand, insures that a thriving black market in human body parts is alive, well, and prospering. A human body is worth from $10,000 to $100,000, depending on the particular requirements of the buyer and whether the body is sold "as is" or "parted out." Brains are worth $600, hands $850, livers and kidneys $700. A recent investigation by Reuters revealed that, since 2008, body brokers located in the United States have exported human remains to at least 45 countries, including Mexico, China, Italy, Venezuela, Israel, and Saudi Arabia. In Germany, plastic surgeons use the lifeless heads of dead Americans to test new surgical techniques. Entire bodies are utilized at medical colleges located in the Caribbean. Private industries in the United States and abroad, even the American military, use human bodies, or pieces of them, to test everything from ammunition, to hair dye, to hiking boots.

In order to obtain sufficient raw material, body brokers often find it expedient to associate with the compliant director of a funeral home. Because of the staggering profit potential, it generally requires only modest effort to induce the latter to forge the necessary death certificates and consent forms. Having done so, the funeral director either wholesales the entire cadaver to the body broker or, alternatively, removes for eventual sale bones, skin, blood, ligaments, heart valves, various joints, corneas, and other body parts. What remains of the body is then disposed of.   If a conventional funeral has been requested, missing bone is simply replaced with lengths of wood or PVC pipe; excised organs with excelsior, wadded newspaper, or cotton balls.   In the case of cremation, sand or sawdust, or an indiscriminate mixture of ashes, are substituted for the remains.

"Did Lightfoot ever mention somebody named 'Smoot'?"

"Couldn't tell ya," Max shrugged.   "I have a hard time rememberin' shit since 'Nam."   He smiled, mostly to himself.   "The drugs and booze prob'ly didn't help much, neither."

Henry contemplated a moment before continuing.   "How'd you know that Lightfoot's in jail?"

"I guess somebody musta told me.   Like I said, I don't remember too good."

"He supposedly killed somebody," Henry informed him.   "You think that could be true?"

Max shook his head.   "Lightfoot's got plenty of wampum.   What reason would he have to kill anybody?   On top of that, he's a wuss.   He'd rather diddle little girls than thump someone.   If they rousted him for killin' somebody, that ain't the Lightfoot I know."   He drained his Styrofoam cup of root beer.   "But if they cut his balls off while he's in there, I wouldn't cry too much about it."

Henry bought an additional bag of hamburgers to take away before driving Max back to the Town Lake campsite, where he pulled the Hyundai along the same curb he'd utilized earlier that afternoon.   The detective shoved the transmission lever into "P" as Max, his left hand clamped onto his bag of hamburgers, opened the idling Hyundai's passenger door and swung one leg out. Henry reached over to restrain the homeless man before he exited the vehicle and disappeared into the airless night.

"Thanks, Max. You helped me more than you realize." The detective handed him one of the $100 bills he'd received from Smoot at the funeral home.

The retainer he'd received earlier that day was a mixed blessing. Aside from the hand-written receipt he'd left with Smoot, there was no record that any money had ever changed hands. It was completely off the books, at least for now. On the other hand, Henry didn't feel comfortable having that amount of money around but knew that federal law required banks to immediately report to the FBI large deposits of cash, especially in $100 denominations. If he blithely carted a canvas bag containing $10,000 in cash down to his bank and tried to deposit it into his account, all hell would break loose. He could expect visits from the FBI, the IRS, and the DEA and would probably end up on every watch list from here to Siam. Accordingly, until he decided exactly how to handle the situation, Henry had simply placed all the money in the freezer at his apartment.

Max's eyes widened when, in the Hyundai's dome light, he saw the bill's denomination. "Hell, I can't take this," he softly protested. "You already bought me supper and breakfast." He held up the bag of burgers and grinned.

"Naw, take it," Henry insisted. "It'll go on account in case I ever need to talk to you again. Just make sure nobody rolls you tonight while you're sleeping," he smiled.

Max jammed the money into the front pocket of his jeans. "Don't gotta worry about that. Nobody'll even know that I got it." He shook Henry's hand. "You know where to find me." With that, he was gone.

Henry shifted the Hyundai in "D" and pulled away from the curb, heading back to his apartment. Lightfoot's PD never did return his call but it had been a very long day and he was exhausted.

SIX

The Best Buy where Freddie Smoot had been a manager trainee was located along State Route 101 in north Phoenix. Depending on traffic, Henry could get there in thirty-five minutes, so he headed out at 8:30 the next morning in order to get there as soon as the place opened.   He hoped to acquire additional information about Freddie, whether he had any enemies, for example, by talking to Freddie's former boss at Best Buy. Henry briefly considered leaving another telephone message for Gwen Harp, Lightfoot's public defender, before leaving his apartment, but ultimately decided against it. He didn't want to be a pain-in-the-ass, nor give Harp any reason to conclude that he was some kind of nut-job or crank. He snuffed out his Kool and snagged the keys to the Hyundai from their hook.   He figured that he'd simply identify himself to the Best Buy manager as a private investigator hired to look into Freddie's death...what's the worst thing that could happen? The guy won't invite him to his birthday party?

Traffic was worse than he anticipated and Henry didn't arrive at the Best Buy until 9:20. He checked his appearance in the rear-view mirror, popped a breath mint into his mouth, switched his cell phone to 'silent,' and exited the car.

Immediately after stepping through the automatic sliding doors, Henry was accosted by a 20-something male worker, clad in a blue polo shirt, standing behind a lectern.

"Welcome to Best Buy," the sentry greeted the detective with a forced smile. "Can I help you find something?"

Henry handed him his business card. "I'd like to speak with the manager if he's available."

"Of course." The functionary glanced at the card before whispering rapidly, though inaudibly, into a tiny microphone clipped to the collar of his shirt. He nodded slightly as he listened to the response through an earpiece that resembled a hearing aid. "Susan will be right with you," he finally said.

"Thank you." Henry stepped away from the counter and pretended to look at a display of cell phone accessories. Less than a minute later, he spotted a smartly-dressed female heading down an aisle in his direction. When she drew near, Henry extended his hand with a disarming smile. He didn't want Susan to be on the immediate defensive, thinking she was about to be confronted by an irate Best Buy customer.

"I'm Susan Miller," she introduced herself in a detached manner as she glanced at the kid behind the lectern. She shook Henry's outstretch hand like an automaton. "How can I help you?"

Henry's smile never wavered. "My name is Lyman Henry, Ms. Miller. I'd like to talk to you about Freddie Smoot."

A look of puzzlement clouded Susan's face. "Freddie? Are you a police officer?"

"Private investigator."

"A private investigator?" Susan quizzically repeated, as though she could scarcely believe what she was hearing.

"Yes. Is there somewhere we can talk privately?" Henry amiably suggested.

"Yes, of course: my office. Please follow me." She took Henry's card from the sentinel, glanced at it, then turned and headed in the direction of a "Large Appliances" banner hanging along a far wall. The detective trailed her.

They entered a hallway with customer restrooms on one side, four closed doors on the other. Susan stopped at the fourth door and punched a code into its electronic lock. Henry heard a click; she swung the door open and gestured for him to enter before closing the door behind them.

In stark contrast to Smoot's palatial digs, Susan's cramped quarters were Spartan: a grey steel desk with a computer and two monitors sitting on it, a rolling office chair, a few filing cabinets along one wall, a couple of generic client chairs. Two large framed posters on the wall, an aerial photograph of a whale and her calf and a lithograph of a Monet painting, looked like they came from a yard sale.

"Please sit down." She motioned toward one of the thinly-padded client chairs as she slid the rolling chair from beneath her austere desk and sat. "You're here about Freddie? I'm afraid I don't understand."

Henry tried to appear as non-threatening as possible.

"Yes, Freddie's father hired me to look into Freddie's death. Although the police have a suspect in custody, Mr. Smoot felt there were still a few loose ends that needed to be tied up in order to get closure."

Susan appeared to be satisfied with Henry's innocuous explanation for the purpose of his visit.

"I see," she murmured. "Although, frankly, I'm surprised that Freddie's dad would care enough to hire someone about it."

Henry's interest was instantly piqued. "About what?" he inquired as detachedly as possible.

"Freddie's murder. Freddie gave me the impression that he and his dad didn't get along very well. To be perfectly blunt, Freddie was always bad-mouthing his dad."

"You knew Freddie pretty well?"

"Quite well. We'd go for drinks sometimes after work and talk."

Henry frowned. "It was my understanding that Freddie was LDS and didn't drink alcohol."

"Oh, he didn't take Mormonism very seriously," Susan scoffed. "I think that was mainly his dad's thing."

Henry nodded thoughtfully. "How did Freddie get along with his co-workers? As far as you know, did he have any enemies?"

"Everyone loved Freddie." She smiled almost wistfully. "He always went out of his way to help everybody."

"Although Freddie apparently drank, do you know whether he smoked pot or used any other controlled substances?"

Susan shook her head vigorously. "Freddie actually didn't drink very much...only a couple of glasses of wine, at most. I *know* he didn't use drugs. In fact, Freddie was very *anti*-drug. He was a straight arrow, a good guy."

"The cops theorize that Freddie was killed in a marijuana deal that went bad. Based on what you know about Freddie, do you think that's likely?"

"Not at all. Freddie didn't use drugs, period."

"The guy who killed Freddie is named 'Danny Lightfoot.' Did Freddie ever mention that name to you?

"Not that I remember."

"Before Freddie came to work at Best Buy, he worked at one of his dad's businesses. In fact, all his siblings still do. Do you have any idea why Freddie left his dad's employ and took a job here?"

"Like I said, Freddie and his dad didn't get along. Freddie never told me what caused them to fall out."

Henry decided to take a chance. "Do you have any idea why Freddie was killed? Do have any theories?"

"Off the record?"

"Off the record. Nothing we talk about leaves this room."

Susan lowered her voice. "Well, the way Freddie talked about his dad, it wouldn't surprise me if he had something to do with it."

Henry managed to veil his surprise. "You think Freddie's father may have killed him?"

"Maybe not killed him but knows something about it. Freddie didn't like his dad *at all* and made no bones that the feeling was mutual."

"Did you ever go to the police with your suspicion?"

"And say what? It was just a feeling I had, nothing concrete. Besides, Freddie's dad is a 'pillar of the community' as they say. At least that's what Freddie said. The cops would think *I* was on drugs."

"Did you ever meet Williams Smoot?" Henry asked.

"That's his name, 'Williams'? Freddie just called him 'dad.' No, I never met him but I think he must be pretty smarmy from what Freddie said." Susan paused, "But I know he's your client and all..."

"I just work for Mr. Smoot," Henry assured her. "He doesn't own me. Besides, I asked."

"Well, now you have my two cents. I just hope the guy they caught really did kill Freddie." She paused and smiled sheepishly. "That didn't come out right, did it? What I meant is that I hope they have the right guy and that he spends the rest of his life in prison."

The detective glanced at his watch.

"I've taken enough of your time this morning, Ms. Miller," he said, standing. "You've been a tremendous help and I can't thank you enough. Thank you for seeing me." He extended his hand again.

Susan rose from her chair and shook Henry's hand, warmly this time. "It's 'Sue' and it was my pleasure, Mr. Henry. We all miss Freddie."

"Please keep my card, Sue. If you think of anything else, *anything*, about Freddie that you think I should know about, please call me right away, day or night. If I don't pick up leave a message and I'll call you back, I promise. And rest assured that no ears but mine will ever hear anything that passes between us."

"I appreciate that, Mr. Henry. If I think of anything else I'll call you. Have a good day." She led him to the door and held it for him as he stepped into the hallway.

Henry returned to his car, fired up the engine, flicked the air conditioning on full blast, and lit a Kool. Deeply inhaling the reassuring smoke, he pondered his conversation with Susan Miller. Williams Smoot appeared to be playing somebody for a fool, and it was with a growing sense of unease that Henry feared the 'somebody' might be him.

He pulled his cell phone from his pocket and scrolled through his messages. Gwen Harp had finally deigned to return his call ten minutes ago. Henry rapidly called her back; she picked up immediately.

"Hello, this is Lyman Henry. I was away from my phone when you called a few minutes ago. Thank you for returning my call, Ms. Harp."

"How can I help you, Mr. Henry? Your telephone message suggested that you may have some information about Danny Lightfoot."

"That's true," Henry acknowledged. "I'm a private investigator and, if you have a few minutes today, I'd like to meet with you about your client."

"I'm not sure that will be possible, Mr. Henry. What sort of information do you have concerning Mr. Lightfoot?"

"That's what I want to talk to you about. I'd feel more comfortable meeting face-to-face about it and promise that it won't take much of your time."

There was a pause at the other end. "Who hired you, Mr. Henry? What interest do you have in Mr. Lightfoot?"

"I'll explain when I see you. If it weren't important, I wouldn't have called."

Another protracted pause. "I don't have any hearings today and can see you in an hour. Where would you like to meet?"

Henry knew, from his days on the police force, where the public defender's office was located. "You know that sandwich shop around the corner from you? I'll meet you there if that's convenient."

The PD laughed softly. "Are you a stalker, Mr. Henry? How do you know of that sandwich place?"

"No, not a stalker. Just a former cop turned PI. I was with Phoenix Police for twenty-five years."

Henry thought he could discern a genuine sense of relief in Gwen Harp's voice. "Ok, I understand. I'll see you at the sandwich shop in one hour. By the way, I'm 34 and black."

"I'm 49, white, and the best-looking guy in the restaurant," Henry said. "You won't have any trouble spotting me."

She laughed again. "No, I'm sure I won't. See you in an hour."

Henry terminated the call and looked at his watch. It would take at least forty-five minutes to make the drive downtown and find an unoccupied parking meter. He shoved the Hyundai's transmission lever into "D" and pulled from the parking lot.

***

He spotted her immediately: tall, willowy, striking. Gwendolyn Harp looked like a model from a perfume ad in some woman's magazine, rather than a public defender. Henry rapidly concluded that all her male clients must inevitably fall in love, or lust, with her. Too bad they were all criminals. She must've seen him gawking at her because she walked directly to his table.

"Mr. Henry? I'm Gwen Harp." She had a pasteboard file tucked beneath one arm and extended her other hand. The detective stood and shook her slender hand.

"Thank you for taking time out of your day to meet me, Ms. Harp," he said, resuming his seat.

The PD placed the file she was carrying on top of the table, slid the opposite chair out, and sat directly across from him.

"I could hardly say no, in view of the message you left on my office phone. If you have information that may be helpful to Daniel Lightfoot's defense, I need to hear it."

Henry smiled wryly. "Well, given that your client has already entered a guilty plea, I submit the 'defense train' has already left the station."

"I filed a Motion to Suppress to have Danny's confession tossed. That much is public record, so I'm not betraying any client confidences. Of course, the prosecution has opposed my motion and it's currently pending before the court. If the court denies my Motion to Suppress I'll file an expedited interlocutory appeal. If *that* fails, I'll need whatever exculpatory information I can get on Danny for purposes of his sentencing hearing. I presume that's why you wanted to see me today."

"What grounds did you argue for the suppression of Lightfoot's confession?"

"Two, actually. Either Danny is mentally incompetent and his confession was the product of a deranged mind, or his confession was coerced."

"Do you think it was? Coerced, I mean."

She smiled enigmatically. "It doesn't matter what I think, Mr. Henry. The prosecution has the burden of proving that it wasn't."

"I've never met the man, so can't comment on his mental state," Henry remarked.

"Nor will I, Mr. Henry," she replied with a tiny smile.

"Fair enough. And by the way, it's 'Lyman,' not 'Mr. Henry'."

"Okay, Lyman. You can call me 'Gwen.' But, before we engage in further pleasantries, I'd like to see some ID, if you don't mind."

Henry extracted his wallet from his pocket. He flipped it open and removed a laminated card, which he handed to Gwen. It was his state-issued PI license and bore a small photograph of him. Gwen examined it with interest before handing it back.

"If it's *your* license, why did they put your father's picture on it?" she asked, innocently.

The detective replaced his license then slid his wallet back into his pocket. "Very funny." He began to add something he hoped sounded witty but was interrupted by the arrival of their server.

"What are we having today?" the latter chirped.

Henry looked expectantly at Gwen.

"I'll have an iced tea, no lemon, and your hummus plate, please," she informed the girl.

"And I'll have a Diet Coke and a chicken salad sandwich," said Henry.

"Very good." The waitress vaporized as quickly as she'd arrived.

Gwen turned her attention back to the detective. "Now, what did you want to tell me about Danny Lightfoot, Lyman? And a related question: where did you acquire your information?"

Henry hesitated before speaking, mentally framing his response. "I was recently hired to look into Freddie Smoot's murder," he began. "My client can provide an alibi for Lightfoot for the night Freddie was killed." He stopped talking and searched Gwen's face, seeking to gauge her response to what he considered a bombshell revelation. She remained stoical.

"That's very interesting, Lyman. Can you tell me who your client is and where Danny was that night?"

"I'm afraid I can't identify my client, at least not now, nor tell you where they were the night Freddie was killed."

Gwen looked at him dubiously. "Then your information isn't much good, is it? At least not to Danny."

"I'd like to talk to Lightfoot to confirm my information. If he corroborates it, I'll tell you everything I know."

"Why not just tell me now?"

"Frankly, because I don't trust my client. I don't want to give you information that turns out to be false or send you on some wild-goose chase based on faulty intelligence.   Lives   and   careers   could   be ruined...there'd be no way of putting the genie back into the bottle."

Gwen could not conceal her skepticism. "You think your own client may be lying to you? With another man's life at stake?"

Henry raised a cynical eyebrow. "Yeah, kinda like being a public defender. Or are all your clients paragons of honesty and candor?"

She couldn't help but grin. "Touché, Lyman."

Their   drinks   and   lunches   arrived simultaneously. Gwen dipped a celery spear into a plate of hummus and happily crunched on it.

"So, what, exactly, are you proposing?" she asked.

"Let me interview Lightfoot. You'd be there, of course. I'll even submit my proposed questions to you in advance for your approval. I don't have any skin in the game either way. I just want to see whether Lightfoot can confirm what my client told me. If he can, I just gave your guy a get-out-of-jail-free card and can move on."

"What if he can't?"

"Then you're no worse off than you were because you've still got your Motion to Suppress to fall back on. Aside from his confession, there's no evidence linking Lightfoot to Freddie Smoot's murder. And if Lightfoot's confession is thrown out or turns out to be bogus because he was somewhere else that night, Lightfoot walks. It's that simple. As far as I can tell, there's no downside to your letting me talk to him." Henry took a sip of Diet Coke as he awaited Gwen's reaction.

"Why don't you just give me your information and *I'll* ask Danny about it? Won't that accomplish the same thing?"

Henry shook his head. "My source won't talk to you *or* the cops. He has a lot to lose if his info becomes public and he'll clam up. If that happens, there will be no way to pry anything out of him...he'll deny ever talking to me."

"Even if I agree to let you talk to Danny, what if he refuses?"

"Why would he? You'll be there to insure his legal interests are protected. Why would a guy facing a possible death sentence not jump at the chance to save his hide by talking to someone who can throw him a lifeline?"

"Maybe, but Danny has resolutely stuck to his confession. Why, all of a sudden, would he now confirm that he has an alibi? If Danny experienced a change of heart, he'd have already recanted his confession."

Henry shrugged. "Don't ask me. I'm a cop turned private investigator, not a psychiatrist. Besides, *you're* the one who filed the motion arguing that Lightfoot isn't right in the head and you can't have it both ways. Either Lightfoot killed Freddie Smoot or he didn't, irrespective of what Lightfoot *says* he did. And you obviously don't believe that Lightfoot's confession is credible; otherwise, you wouldn't have filed your Motion to Suppress. So, where's the downside to letting me talk to him? If Lightfoot confirms what my guy told me, you'll have concrete evidence that he couldn't have killed Smoot because he wasn't even there that night. You might be able to pull Lightfoot's rump out of the fire in spite of himself. What have you got to lose?" He took a bite of sandwich.

Gwen quietly munched on a carrot stick. "Even if Danny is able to establish his whereabouts that night, what assurance do I have that your client will back him up? You just said that, for whatever reason, he won't talk to either me or the police. You're now telling me that he'll have a spontaneous Road to Damascus experience just because you talked to Danny?"

"That's a fair question, and you're right," Henry conceded. "All I can tell you is that he gave me his word that he'd fully cooperate with me."

"That's it? His 'word'?"

"What else do you have?" Henry softly countered. "If you do nothing, chances are that Lightfoot will be convicted of a murder he may not have committed. You want that on your conscience?"

SEVEN

Williams Smoot picked up the telephone that rested on his office desk and casually punched in the number of the Phoenix Police Department—not 911, just the regular non-emergency number.

A male answered after two rings. "Phoenix Police Department."

"Hello, this is Williams Smoot. I'd like to report a theft. Would it be possible to send an officer to my office immediately? Smoot Funeral Chapel."

"Hold, please." Silence while his call was apparently being transferred.

"This is Detective Wicks. How can I help you?" Smoot repeated what he'd just said.

"What was stolen?"

"Cash. A great deal of it, I'm afraid."

"Where was the money at the time it was stolen?"

"Here, at my office."

"When did you discover the theft?"

"Just a few minutes ago. The money was in a bag in my desk. I was preparing to take it to the bank, for deposit, when I discovered it was gone."

"A bag?"

"Yes, a regular canvas bank bag. You know the type."

"Approximately how much was taken?"

"$10,000, give or take."

"A detective will come by your office later today to take a formal report. I'm sorry I can't give you an exact time. What is the address, please?" Smoot dictated the mortuary's location. "OK, thank you. Try not to touch anything in the room where the theft occurred."

"Of course," Smoot purred. "I'll wait here until your detective arrives. Thank you for your time."

"You're welcome. Have a good day." The call disconnected and Smoot gently replaced the receiver on its cradle. It wouldn't be long before it was once again business as usual, he thought with satisfaction.

***

People who pontificate that "jails are just like country clubs" have manifestly never been inside either a jail or a country club. Jails are dark, noisy, cold, crowded, squalid, and dangerous places.

Although Freddie Smoot's murder occurred in Phoenix, the City of Phoenix doesn't operate its own jail. Instead, Danny Lightfoot was warehoused in the seven-story county jail, the only facility with sufficient capacity to accommodate prisoners for crimes committed throughout the county.

Henry and Gwen approached the walk-through metal detector immediately inside the ground-floor entrance to the jail, where she placed her purse in a plastic bin for scanning by an adjacent X-ray machine. Henry removed his belt, wallet, cell phone, and watch and did the same.

"Hey, counselor!"   One of the massive deputy sheriffs manning the equipment cheerfully greeted her as she stepped through the detector.   "Who's this rough-looking *hombre*?" he grinned, looking at Henry.

"An investigator helping me on a case. How's tricks, Willie?"

"Same old seven and six. Just countin' the days 'till retirement," he laughed. "Who ya here for today?"

"Daniel Lightfoot," she said, retrieving her purse from the bin on the conveyor belt. Henry grabbed his belongings and began to restore them to their proper places.

"You know where to find him," said the deputy. "I'll buzz 'em that you're on your way up."

"Thanks, Willie," Gwen breezily responded. "Talk to you later."

They stepped into the elevator, where Gwen punched the button for the fourth floor.

"We'll have to check-in with the guard then they'll shackle Danny and take him down to an attorney conference room on the second floor. He has no idea we're coming and, frankly, may be a little resistant to your presence."

"I   guess   we'll   find   out,"   the   detective philosophically responded. "But if he's smart, he won't bite the hand that feeds him."

The elevator doors slid open onto what could only be described as a small nook containing a metal desk with a computer and telephone on it, manned by a uniformed corrections officer. On either side of him were floor-to-ceiling screens of thick wire mesh, painted beige, with a narrow electronic door in the center. On the other side of the screens stretched long hallways lined with cells. The wholesale cacophony that reverberated up and down the halls was nearly deafening: scores of prisoners howling, cursing, braying, laughing. The guard appeared oblivious to the chaos.

"Daniel Lightfoot!" Gwen shouted over the din. She removed her driver's license and Bar card from her purse and handed them to the seated turnkey.

The guard scrutinized Gwen's ID's and handed them back to her before typing Lightfoot's name into his computer. He silently gazed at the monitor. Having satisfied himself that Lightfoot was, in fact, currently incarcerated and that Gwen was his attorney, he turned his attention to the detective.

"Who's he?" he gruffly demanded, tipping his crew-cut head toward Henry. Gwen had to bend low in order to hear him because of the unrelenting bedlam.

"My investigator," she told him.

"See some ID." The guard extended his hand and flicked his fingers imperiously.

Henry removed his PI license from his wallet and surrendered it to the corrections officer. He looked at it, then up at the detective, then down at the card again.

"Okay," he scowled, handing Henry's ID back to him. "We'll bring him down."

"Thank you," Gwen shouted.

The two of them hastened back to the elevator and leapt inside as soon as its door slid open. Despite the fact that Gwen pushed the 'close door' button repeatedly, the elevator door didn't budge and noise continued to flood into the stationary car.

Henry leaned toward Gwen. "Somebody told me that 'close door' buttons on elevators are non-functioning...they're just dummy buttons that elevator companies install to make people feel better."

Gwen pushed the button for the second floor and the elevator door finally glided shut.

"I wouldn't be surprised," she said, wearily.

"I don't remember the jail being so damned noisy," Henry idly remarked as the elevator car descended.

"I don't know how long ago you were a cop, but the jails have gotten exponentially worse in just the last four or five years. When I first started with the PD's office ten years ago, they weren't exactly sedate, but they were nothing like they are now. For one thing, there are a lot more prisoners packed into the same amount of space, so everything is magnified."

Henry silently nodded as the elevator door opened onto the second floor. They stepped across the threshold into a hallway harshly lit by overhead neon tubes running its entire length. In contrast to the fourth floor, the second floor was quiet.

"We'll have to check in to find out which conference room we've been assigned to," Gwen explained. Henry followed her into an austere waiting area where, at one end, was a reception window protected by bullet proof glass. She once again removed her Bar card and driver's license from her purse preparatory to showing both to the heavyset female sitting behind the window. The detective followed suit by removing his PI license from his wallet and wordlessly handing it to Gwen.

"Prisoner Daniel Lightfoot," she told the guard as she slipped their respective ID's through a slot in the glass. "He's my investigator," she said, indicating Henry.

She examined their ID's before sliding them back through the slot to Gwen. She then consulted the computer monitor on the counter before her.

"Room two. Out the door and to your right," she mumbled. "The prisoner is en route."

"Thank you, officer," Gwen responded, sweetly.

She returned to Henry his ID, replaced hers in her purse, and headed for their sit-down with Danny Lightfoot.

***

The conference room was little more than a cubicle devoid of furnishings except a small rectangular table with two straight-backed chairs along each of its long sides. The four chairs weren't even padded. Wire mesh covered the small window in the room's steel door. Gwen and Henry sat on one side of the table as they awaited Lightfoot's arrival; she hung her purse over the back of her chair.

"How many times have you met with Lightfoot previously?" the detective inquired.

"Two. Once when his case was originally assigned to me and again when I told him that I intended to file a Motion to Suppress. That was about three weeks ago."

"What was his reaction when you told him that you were trying to get his confession tossed?"

"Honestly, he was basically apathetic. Most of the prisoners I represent are chomping at the bit to get out, but Danny didn't seem to care, one way or the other. He said that he expected to be released with or without my help."

"I'll bet you never heard *that* before," Henry said with a wry smile.

"I wish I had a dollar for every time."

"Did Lightfoot say *why* he thought he'd be released?"

"No, he just seemed confident that he would. But that's not particularly unusual."

The door abruptly opened, interrupting their conversation. A burly corrections officer pushed a shackled Danny Lightfoot into the conference room.

Lightfoot was clad in a jail-issued orange jumpsuit and wore blue plastic shower shoes. His hands were manacled in front of his body and secured to a thick leather belt that encircled his waist. Fetters also encircled his ankles, resulting in the characteristic "prison shuffle" when he walked. Heavily tatted with brown straggly hair hanging to his shoulders, his face acne-cratered, Lightfoot appeared to be appreciably older than 28. He didn't seem to have missed many meals while incarcerated, which Henry attributed to the starchy, carbohydrate-laden food typically served in jails. The prisoner glanced contemptuously at his two visitors as he awkwardly slid one of the chairs from beneath the opposite side of the table and plopped down.

"I'll be right outside," the guard stated. "Lemme know when you're done."

"Thank you, officer," Gwen smiled.

"Who's this asshole?" Lightfoot nonchalantly asked once the guard exited.

"He's an investigator, Danny. He wants to ask you a few questions," Gwen informed him.

"Fuck that. I ain't talkin' to nobody but you."

"His name is Lyman Henry and he thinks he may have information that may help your case."

"I don't need his fuckin' help," Lightfoot retorted. Although he'd been casually eyeing the detective up until then, Lightfoot turned to look directly at Gwen. "I don't want him in here. If it's just you and me talkin', there's attorney-client privilege. That goes to hell if there's somebody else here."

Henry wasn't surprised that Lightfoot was familiar with basic principles of attorney-client privilege. Such knowledge was considered *de rigueur* among cons.

Gwen sighed and turned to the detective. "You're now a Deputy Public Defender, effective immediately." She looked back at Lightfoot. "Satisfied?"

"Whatever," Lightfoot responded, as though he simply couldn't be bothered.

Henry decided it was time to cut to the chase. "I'm here to help you, Danny."

"I don't need your help, asshole. I got plenty of help."

"Gwen? Are you talking about her?" Henry asked, glancing at the public defender.

"Yeah, I guess she's all right," Lightfoot blandly replied.

"Well, 'plenty of help' sounds like you must have a lot of help, Danny. Is somebody besides Gwen helping you?" The detective was grateful that Gwen didn't object to his impromptu interrogation. Not yet, anyway. Henry paused.   "Williams Smoot?   Is he helping you?"

"Who's   he?"   Lightfoot   breezily   asked.   He continued to look at Gwen, refusing to establish eye contact with the detective.

"Somebody I just thought you might know."

"I don't know nobody named 'William,'" Lightfoot said.

"No, not 'William—*Williams*.'"   Henry drew the terminal "s" out so that it sounded like a "z."

"Well, whatever his name is, I don't know him. "Besides,   what   kinda   first   name   is   'Williams'? 'Williams' is a *last* name," Lightfoot smirked.

"You sure you don't know him, Danny? He says he knows you and even has your picture on his cell phone."

Lightfoot's attention was immediately arrested. His gaze slid back to the detective.

"Just because somebody says they know me don't mean I know them," he said.

"True enough.   But why's your picture on his cell phone?"

"That's   bullshit,"   Lightfoot   retorted.   "I   never heard of anybody named 'Williams Smoot.'"

"Maybe, but he told me that you were with him the night Freddie Smoot was killed. Why would a guy you don't know tell me that? But if it's true, you can walk out of here, Danny." The detective leaned back in his chair and folded his arms as his words sank in.

Lightfoot's eyes flitted between Henry and Gwen, who remained impassive.

"My mouthpiece filed some kinda paper to get me outta here," he said.   "So, it don't matter what

William-What's-His-Name told you. I'm gonna walk, no matter what."

"Maybe, but at the end of the day it's all up to the judge. What if he doesn't grant your lawyer's motion?" the detective countered. "If that happens, you're gonna be in here a while...well, until they transfer you to death row, anyway."

Lightfoot reflexively frowned.

"See, Danny," the detective continued, "I really don't think you killed Freddie. I don't know *who* killed him, but I don't think it was you. Although one of your buddies out at 'Shangri La' told me that you're not exactly a choir boy, I don't think you're a murderer."

Lightfoot's curiosity was piqued. "What the fuck are you talkin' about?"

"You know, 'Shangri La'—that big homeless camp out by Tempe Town Lake. I talked to somebody there that knows you. He said that you've got a thing for little girls but are otherwise a swell guy." Henry glanced at Gwen to see whether she would object to his disclosure about Lightfoot's sexual predilections, but she merely continued to listen intently. "Another thing, though," Henry continued, "the guy also told me that you're a body snatcher."

The detective's abrupt disclosure startled Lightfoot. The prisoner's eyes registered surprise for an instant.

"What the fuck's that?" he spat.

"You know, a body snatcher...a guy who peddles corpses."

Lightfoot shifted in his chair. "I don't know what you're talkin' about. I got nuthin' to do with that."

"With what?" Henry probed.

"Peddlin' corpses and shit."

"That's good to know, Danny, because trafficking in dead bodies is serious stuff. The feds take a pretty dim view of it. And I'm not even talkin' about all the diseases you're exposed to from messing with dead bodies...God only knows. But I guess Smoot told you all about that, huh?" The detective adopted a deadpan expression.

"He didn't tell me shit," declared Lightfoot.

"Oh, so you *do* know him," Henry said with mock surprise.

"Yeah, I guess I forgot," Lightfoot shrugged.

Gwen finally spoke. "How do you know Mr. Smoot, Danny?"

Lightfoot switch his gaze to the attorney. "I just know him."

"What I don't understand," Henry interjected, "is that, although your friend Smoot knows you're in here, he hasn't bothered to go to the cops and tell them that you didn't kill his kid. What's with that? You don't think Smoot's settin' you up to take a fall do you, Danny? You've done a lot for him...I mean with the bodies and whatnot."

"I don't know what you're talkin' about," Lightfoot protested. "But between me, you, and the gate post, you're right about one thing, though: I didn't kill nobody. Hell, I didn't even *know* Smoot's kid."

"Then why did you tell the cops that you killed Freddie? And why did you just lie about knowing Smoot?"

It was clear that Lightfoot felt himself boxed in. He tipped his head to one side and wiped onto his orange jump suit the perspiration that had begun to collect on his upper lip.

"Smoot told me that, if I confessed, he'd pay me," he finally said. "He said that nuthin' would happen to me and that he'd get me out of here with no problem."

"Yeah? That's funny because Freddie Smoot was murdered three months ago and yet here you sit, on your rump, in jail. When do you suppose the 'no problem' part kicks in? Williams Smoot even told *me* that you didn't kill Freddie, but he still hasn't gone to the cops with that information, three months later? What's with that? Why's Smoot screwing with you? It looks to me like Smoot's playin' you for a chump, Danny." Lightfoot listened sullenly but didn't reply.

Henry continued to probe. "Why did Williams Smoot want you to confess, Danny? Did he tell you why?"

Lightfoot sighed deeply. "He said he was havin' problems with his kid that had to be taken care of. He said that he had a plan to deal with it but that it would take some time to pull off. If I helped him, he'd pay me. That's all I know."

"'By 'his kid' he meant Freddie?"

"I guess."

"What kind of problems?"

Lightfoot shrugged. "I never asked. He never said."

"Did Smoot tell you how he planned to take care of his problems with Freddie?"

Lightfoot shook his head. "I didn't know and didn't *wanna* know. It just sounded like easy money."

"So how come you're still sitting in jail? I thought Smoot promised to spring you with 'no problem'."

"Yeah, I thought so, too," Lightfoot muttered. He brightened momentarily. "Maybe his plan's takin' longer than he thought."

Henry changed tack. "You've known Williams Smoot for a while?"

"Yeah, I guess," Lightfoot warily replied.

"In what capacity?"

"Huh?"

The detective rephrased his question. "*How* do you know Williams Smoot, Danny? Under what circumstances did you meet him?"

Lightfoot shifted in his chair. "I do stuff for him."

"What kinda 'stuff'?"

"This and that," Lightfoot equivocated.

"Like what, specifically?"

Lightfoot looked helplessly at Gwen, who remained expressionless. "I sometimes sell stuff for him," he finally said.

"What kinda 'stuff'?" Henry pressured.

"For Christ's sake!" Lightfoot erupted. "Back off, man!"

Gwen finally spoke. "Danny, do you want to get out of here?" she gently asked. "We're trying to *help* you."

Lightfoot glowered at Henry for a few moments. "Jewelry, mostly. Odds and ends."

"Jewelry? Is Smoot in the jewelry biz?"

Lightfoot shook his head again. "Like I said, I don't ask...ain't my business."

"Why didn't Smoot sell it himself?"

Lightfoot shifted again. "I know a guy...and there was a lot of it."

"How much is 'a lot'?"

"I don't know...a lot."

"Where'd you sell it, Danny? One place or different places?"

Lightfoot realized he was well past the point of no return. "One place, mostly. A mini-market down on South Central run by some Paki."

"What's the name of it?"

"I don't think it has a name. Just a place that buys gold and stuff."

"What's the cross streets?"

Lightfoot provided them.

"So Williams Smoot gives you jewelry and you sell it to the Paki, right? What do you do with the money?"

"Give it to Smoot. He peels off a few bills and gives 'em to me for my trouble."

Henry pondered Lightfoot's admission. "'A few bills'? The Paki must've bought a lot of stuff from you, huh? How long's this been going on?"

"I dunno," Lightfoot guardedly responded. "A while, I guess."

"Months? Years?"

"Yeah."

Henry glanced at Gwen in frustration but she remained inscrutable. He turned back to Lightfoot.

"Danny, were you with Williams Smoot the night Freddie was murdered?"

Lightfoot looked defiantly at the detective. "I don't even know *when* Smoot's kid was murdered, so I don't know where I was. But the only time I ever had anything to do with the old man is when we was doin' business with the Paki."

"We know you sold jewelry for Smoot. What about the bodies?"

"What fuckin' bodies?"

"The bodies at Smoot's funeral home."

"What about 'em?"

"Did you have anything to do with those?"

"I may have helped on some burials," he circuitously acknowledged.

Henry glanced at Gwen, who continued to listen intently. "'Helped' how?" he pressed.

"Helped get 'em into coffins and stuff."

"How'd you do that, Danny?" Gwen interposed.

"Get 'em in their coffins?" She nodded. The prisoner shrugged. "Sometimes their legs and stuff didn't fit and we'd have to remove 'em."

"Their legs?"

"Yeah. Other stuff sometimes, too."

"What 'other stuff'?" prompted Henry.

Lightfoot shifted uncomfortably. "Their guts sometimes."

"Sometimes you removed their organs, Danny?"

He nodded.

Henry leaned forward intently. "What happened to the parts you removed from the bodies, Danny? What did you do with them?"

"Ask Smoot," Lightfoot muttered.

EIGHT

City of Phoenix Police Detective James Wilfort wheeled into the deserted parking lot of the Smoot Funeral Chapel at exactly 5:37 p.m. He'd telephoned earlier that afternoon to confirm that Williams Smoot would still be on the premises. He parked his nondescript LTD along the curb immediately in front of the mortuary's business office and entered the building. Eileen was still reading a magazine behind her desk in the carpeted waiting area.

"Detective Wilfort," he perfunctorily introduced himself. He removed a white business card from his shirt pocket and mechanically handed it to her.

"Yes, Mr. Smoot is expecting you," she said, taking the detective's card. "Please sit down."

Wilfort plopped into one of the upholstered chairs to impatiently await Smoot's arrival. Less than a minute passed before a door in the far wall door opened, admitting into the waiting room a short, pudgy man with a comb-over and wire-rimmed glasses.

"Mr. Smoot?" Wilfort inquired without getting up.

"Detective Wilfort!" Smooth exclaimed. He hastened across the room with his hand extended. "Thank you for coming. I realize you must have a million other, more important, cases to attend to."

Wilfort stood and automatically shook Smoot's outstretched hand. It felt like a dishrag. "It's not a problem. I understand you've had a robbery. Do you want to talk here?"

"No, in my office, please. I'll show you exactly where it happened," Smoot deferred. He turned toward the door through which he'd just entered.

Wilfort followed Smoot down a plain hallway to the latter's office, where Smoot unlocked the door and bade him sit on the settee. The detective complied and produced a small yellow, spiral-bound notebook and pen. Smoot sat in the massive leather arm chair behind his desk.

"Tell me what happened, Mr. Smoot."

Smoot wrinkled his forehead as if in thought. "You may recall that my son, Freddie, was brutally gunned-down three months ago ... Freddie was shot in the parking lot of his apartment after getting off work."

Wilfort jotted rapid notes as Smoot talked.

"Police apprehended the man who killed Freddie, who promptly confessed. It is my understanding that the man is currently in jail awaiting sentencing and his public defender recently filed an appeal, or some such thing. Anyway, because of the rapidity with which the man was caught, I assumed that Freddie's murder had been solved. However, a man unexpectedly came to see me yesterday about Freddie."

"Here?" Wilfort interjected without looking up.

"He originally accosted me while I was eating lunch. I tried to give him the brush-off, but he was very persistent and even followed me here to the funeral home afterward."

"Where did you eat lunch?"

"'Los Cielos Grill,' downtown."

"So, the first time you saw this man was around lunch time yesterday. Is that right?"

"It was around 11:00 or so," Smoot acknowledged. "I usually eat relatively early, before the regular lunch crowed arrives."

"How did he identify himself?"

"He said his name was Lyman Henry and that he was a private investigator." Smoot paused. "Have you heard of him?"

Wilfort shook his head as he continued to write. "L-Y-M-A-N, H-E-N-R-Y?"

"Yes, I think that's right," said Smoot.

"Did you ask to see his credentials?"

"No, it never occurred to me," Smoot sheepishly confessed.

"Had you ever seen him before yesterday? How did he know where you ate lunch?" Wilfort suspended writing and looked directly at Smoot.

Smoot shook his head vigorously. "No, never. I can only surmise that he knew I was at the Grill because, as I said, he identified himself as a private investigator."

Wilfort looked puzzled but continued the examination.

"You said this man wanted to see you about your late son...what, specifically, did he want?"

"He said that he had some information regarding Freddie's death." Smoot hesitated. "Unless you've lost a child, detective, you have no idea how painful it is to relive that experience. I simply told Henry that the man who did it was in custody and that, if he had any information regarding Freddie's murder, he should immediately convey it to the police."

"What was Henry's reaction after you rebuffed him?"

"He wouldn't take 'no' for an answer. He kept badgering me until I finally left the restaurant and drove directly here, to my office."

"What time was that?"

"Probably 12:30ish."

Wilfort flipped to a fresh page in his notebook and looked at Smoot again. "Even though you were in the middle of lunch, you let a complete stranger button-hole you and talk to you about an extremely painful subject for 90 minutes despite the fact that you'd already told him to buzz off? That's what you're saying?"

The detective's unexpected query flustered Smoot.

"Well," he stammered, "you understand the times I gave were just estimates. I never actually looked at my watch."

"Okay," replied the impassive detective as he resumed writing. "What happened after you left the restaurant?"

"Shortly after I returned here, Eileen frantically buzzed me. She whispered that Mr. Henry was in the waiting area and insisted on speaking with me. She tried to induce him to leave, but he was adamant."

"That's 'Eileen'?" the detective asked, absently pointing over his shoulder with his pen.

"Yes, Eileen Eggleston, my assistant."

"So Henry followed you from the restaurant here?"

Smoot nodded. "Apparently."

"Why didn't you call the police?"

"Well," Smoot faltered, "neither Eileen nor I actually felt threatened at that time. Henry was, at that point, merely an annoyance and I didn't want to trouble the police over such a trivial matter."

"So, even though Henry interrupted your lunch, pestered you for over an hour, and followed you to your office afterward, at no point did you feel threatened by him?" Wilfort skeptically inquired.

"Henry's manner was never overtly hostile, nor even threatening," Smoot defensively responded. "On the contrary, he seemed quite sincere. It was for that reason that I finally relented and agreed to listen to what he had to say about Freddie."

"But you just said that your assistant was 'frantic' when she told you that Henry showed up in your waiting room. That didn't set off any alarm bells?"

Smoot looked at him indulgently. "Like most women, Eileen can be somewhat exciteable, detective."

Wilfort couldn't help but shake his head, even as he continued taking notes.

"So what did Henry want?"

"I finally invited Henry into my office and he sat where you are currently sitting. When I asked him what, specifically, he wanted, Henry said that he was in possession of information about Freddie's murder that he would convey to me for $10,000."

"Henry tried to extort money from you? My information is that you reported a theft. Which is it?" Wilfort looked at him dubiously.

Smoot ignored Wilfort's question. "Like I told you earlier, I told Henry that if he had information about Freddie, he should contact the police. I had no intention of giving him any money."

"Did Henry intimate the nature of the information he supposedly had?"

Smoot leaned forward in his chair. "Only that he'd been a personal friend of Freddie's and that, before he died, Freddie had confided some very important information to him that he thought I should know."

"But he provided no specific details regarding the nature of this 'important information'?"

"Correct." Smoot leaned back in his chair and laced his fingers together over his ample paunch. "But I could tell straightaway that Henry was attempting to con me. In the funeral trade I've encountered the phenomenon many, many times. You certainly know the type, detective: scam artists who prey on vulnerable, grieving people in an attempt to swindle them out of money. Henry obviously knew of Freddie's murder and, as a private investigator, researched my background and determined that I was a man of some affluence. He then concocted his story about knowing Freddie, hoping that, in my grief, I could be induced to pay for the sham information he claimed to possess."

"If you were convinced that Henry was trying to hustle you, why didn't you call the police at that point?" Wilfort asked, pointedly.

"That was my intention. Having seen through Henry's ruse, I immediately resolved to call the police. Indeed, I hoped they'd arrive while he was still in my office. But I, personally, couldn't call the police while Henry was sitting right in front of me. Accordingly, I told Henry that I had to get the company checkbook from another room and excused myself. I went into Ms. Eggleston's office with the intention of having her call the police. Unfortunately, she was apparently in another part of the building. I knew Henry would become suspicious if I didn't return forthwith so I went back to my office, intending to explain that I couldn't find Eileen, who is in charge of the checkbook, and would have to page her. Unfortunately, Henry's suspicions must have been aroused during my absence because he was gone by the time I got back to my office."

"How long were you gone?"

Smoot gazed pensively into the distance. "Probably less than five minutes."

"What did you do then? Did anyone see Henry leave?"

"I eventually located Ms. Eggleston and told her what had occurred. I was still determined to contact the police, notwithstanding that Henry had already decamped, but Eileen urged restraint. She feared that Henry may be an unstable, desperate man who might physically harm me or my family if the police became involved. Eileen urged me to 'hasten slowly,' as the Buddhists say, to wait at least overnight before calling the police. I reluctantly agreed to do so. Eileen said that she didn't see Henry leave, but she wasn't at her desk for part of the time he was here. I don't know if anyone else saw him leave."

"But you *did* end up calling the police. About a theft."

"That's correct," Smoot resumed. "Having slept on it overnight, I came to my office this morning resolved to inform the police about my encounter with Henry. It was only then that I became aware of the theft."

Now we're finally getting somewhere, the detective thought as he continued writing.

Henry slid open a desk drawer at this right hand.

"A number of clients, or their families, pay for funeral services in cash, detective. Our clients are, of course, typically elderly and many of them simply don't trust banks. They're conservative Mid-Westerners who were raised in a different era, when banks and other financial institutions were viewed with suspicion. They often keep money hidden at home and, when they pre-pay for their funerals, it is sometimes in cash. I keep those monies here in this drawer and deposit them in the bank on a weekly basis."

"How much do you generally keep in the drawer?" Wilfort inquired.

"It depends, of course," Smoot replied, "depending on the week's receipts. But I've often had twenty to forty thousand dollars in my drawer at one time." Noting the surprised look that crossed the detective's face, Smoot explained. "You have to bear in mind, detective, that even a modest funeral costs anywhere from eight to ten thousand dollars. Thirty thousand dollars, for example, only reflects the cost of three average funerals. We regularly have two funerals per day, every day of the week!"

"I'm guessing whatever was in the drawer when you left Henry alone in your office *wasn't* in the drawer the next time you checked," Wilfort surmised.

"Precisely," Smoot emphatically confirmed.

"How do you know Henry took it? In fact, how would Henry even have known about the cash in the drawer? Doesn't it seem more probable that your assistant, or another one of your employees, could have taken the money?"

Smoot shook his head. "It's possible, but not likely. My office is always locked when I'm not here and neither Ms. Eggleston, nor any of my other employees, has a key. Furthermore, virtually all of my employees have been part of the Smoot Funeral Chapel family for many years...Eileen for over twenty. And I even lock my office when I step out to use the men's room. The *only* time that my office wasn't either locked, or I wasn't physically present in it, was when I left Henry alone for the few minutes I was searching for Eileen. And don't forget that Henry's entire purpose for being here was to attempt to swindle me, and that he'd fled by the time I got back from my abortive errand to locate Eileen." He paused. "There is simply no other person who could have taken the money under the circumstances, detective."

Wilfort laid his notebook aside and looked at Smoot. "How smart do you think it was to leave a hostile stranger alone in your office when you had thousands of dollars in your desk drawer? Especially someone you'd already had a confrontation with and were convinced was trying to extort money from you?"

"Hindsight is always 20-20," Smoot replied with an exaggerated sigh. "I didn't give any thought to the money in my desk at the time."

"How could Henry have possibly known there was cash in your drawer?"

"I'm sure I don't know, but he claims to be a private investigator, detective. I suggest that you ask him," Smoot advised with a tiny smirk.

Wilfort picked up his notebook, flipped it closed, and returned it to his pocket. "I'll need to talk to all of your employees, starting with your assistant. How soon will they be available?"

NINE

"So the victim's father is your mystery client, huh?" That's a real stunner, all right," Gwen chuckled as she took a sip of iced tea. They'd just departed the county jail and were sitting at a table on the patio of a small eatery located down the block, in the shade of a large colorful parasol.

"I didn't want to tell you until I was able to talk to Lightfoot," Henry responded. "I wanted to gauge his reaction."

"Assuming my guy is telling the truth, your client appears to have left him holding the bag," she observed.

"Seems that way. Like you said, though—if he's telling the truth."

"Assuming he is, why on earth would the victim's dad conspire with Danny to get him to confess to a murder he didn't commit? It was your client's own son, for God's sake! What's in it for either of them?"

Henry drained his Diet Coke before responding. "Three things. As far as Lightfoot goes, he said that Smoot *paid* him to confess, so that's a no-brainer. Secondly, Lightfoot had the old man's assurances that his confession would go nowhere and that he'd only be in the clink a little while.   Third, according to Lightfoot, he and my client have a longstanding, and profitable, business relationship because Lightfoot fences stuff for old man Smoot.   Lightfoot had no reason not to trust what my client told him.   Like Lightfoot, himself, said, 'easy money.'"

Gwen looked thoughtful as she considered Henry's explanation.   "Okay, I suppose all of that is plausible, but how does any of it help your client? Wouldn't your client *want* to find the guy who actually murdered his kid?"

Henry smiled enigmatically.   "Not necessarily.   It all depends on who the murderer is."

"You're beginning to exasperate me, Henry.   Stop mincing words and get to the point," she sternly directed.   "I've got an innocent client sitting in jail."

"According to Freddie Smoot's old boss at Best Buy, Freddie and his dad didn't get along.   On top of that, unique among his siblings, Freddie didn't work at any of the businesses controlled by his dad or live in a house owned by him.   But," Henry continued, "until about a year ago, Freddie *did* both: he was employed at a Smoot company and lived in a Smoot house."

"Gee, you're right, Henry.   Something happened between Freddie and his dad that caused a falling out. It's all very sinister.   But, since you were obviously raised by wolves in a cave, that happens all the time in human relationships."

Henry ignored her sarcastic rejoinder.   "Making matters worse, my client is a bigwig in the Mormon church but Freddie apparently didn't take the whole

Mormon thing too seriously. That couldn't have made the old man very happy, either."

"Okay, I get it now! Williams Smoot was so angry that his son was a halfhearted Mormon that he killed him. Having done so, he then persuaded somebody else to admit to it. It all makes perfect sense now. Thank you, Henry. I'm really disappointed that I didn't figure all that out on my own." Gwen looked at Henry with disdain. "Get serious."

Henry laughed out loud at Gwen's scornful expression. "No, listen to me," he urged.

"I'm listening, but you'd better start doing better than you've done so far. Otherwise, I'm leaving right now for the prosecutor's office, to fill him in on what Danny said."

"I don't have a problem with that," Henry replied, "but I don't think you'll have to."

Gwen took the bait. "Oh? Why's that?"

"You know what kind of work Williams Smoot is in, right?"

"He owns a funeral home. So what?"

"What did Lightfoot tell us that he primarily fenced for Smoot?"

"Mostly jewelry..." Gwen's voice trailed off. "Whoa! Are you telling me that Smoot, your own client, is taking jewelry from corpses and *selling* it? No, no, no...that's crazy."

"You think so?" Henry challenged. "You and I both know that people are routinely buried wearing expensive jewelry: gold wedding bands, an emerald necklace and earrings, a favorite pin their husband gave 'em, whatever. Smoot drives a new Lexus and his office is opulent, so he's obviously pulling in some serious coin. But it gets better. I think Smoot's also running an illicit organ-harvesting operation out of his funeral home. The cash he gets from selling jewelry that he lifts from corpses is just walkin' around money.   The *real* loot is in human body parts and Smoot pays Lightfoot to dismember the bodies."

"You need to switch to beer, Lyman," Gwen advised. "That, and stay out of the sun. Even if what you say is true and, mind you, there's not an ounce of evidence that it is, so what? How is any of it relevant to Freddie Smoot?" Despite her reservations, she was intrigued by Henry's disquisition.

"Here's how I think it came down," the detective resumed. He paused long enough to fish a crushed pack of Kools from his pants pocket. "Okay if I smoke?"

"Man! You smoke Kools?" Gwen laughed. "You actually like those things?"

"Not particularly," Henry shrugged. "But neither does anybody else and it discourages people from bumming cigarettes off me."

She made a droll face.   "I guess that makes sense in a perverse sort of way...Henry-sense, anyway. Did you ever think about quitting?"

"Nobody likes a quitter," Henry noted as patted his pockets, searching for matches.

"Yes, it's okay if you smoke; knock yourself out," she quietly chuckled.

He finally located a book of matches and lit his cigarette. "At a minimum," he resumed, turning his head to exhale a stream of smoke, "old man Smoot has been using Lightfoot to sell stolen jewelry; Lightfoot said so himself. Even though he's obviously not a licensed embalmer or funeral director, Lightfoot's also ass-deep in Smoot's illegal organ-harvesting operation. Anyway, about a year ago Freddie Smoot somehow got wind of what his dad was up to and threatened to blow the whistle on the old man's entire operation. That's when Freddie abruptly quit working for his dad and moved out of the house that his dad owned."

"You're telling me that Smoot hired Danny to eliminate Freddie before Freddie could rat him out?"

"No, not Danny. Smoot has too much invested in Lightfoot. He needs to keep him around so Lightfoot will keep fencing jewelry and cutting up stiffs for him. He just wanted Lightfoot to *confess* to killing Freddie in order to buy enough time for him to shop around for somebody else to pin Freddie's murder on. Smoot knew that with Lightfoot, the ostensible murderer, in jail, the police would automatically stop looking for suspects and the investigation of Freddie's murder would effectively end. While Lightfoot patiently waited to be sprung from the jug, Smoot had the leisure to orchestrate a scheme to pin Freddie's murder on some other chump. Having thereby made good his promise to Lightfoot to secure his release, they would simply resume ordinary business operations and live happily ever after. That's my theory in a nutshell, anyway." Henry took a drag of Kool and grinned triumphantly.

"What's Smoot do with all the body parts he supposedly steals?" Gwen challenged. "And why hasn't he been exposed by now? The families, for instance, would certainly notice that grandpa was missing an arm or whatever."

"Smoot's   obviously   working   through intermediaries to unload the organs and other body parts he pilfers. There's a world-wide demand for that stuff, Gwen. And the buyers don't give a horse's patoot where it came from. In fact, they work directly *with* morticians to get as many body parts as they can get their hands on. Who's gonna complain, the dead guy?"

She scowled at him. "No, obviously not 'the dead guy.' Like I said, family members would immediately notice that something was amiss."

Henry shook his head. "No, they wouldn't. When you go to a funeral, do you have any idea whether the dead guy has all of his organs inside him? Of course not; how could you? You just assume they're all there. So do the family members."

"Maybe, but what about removing the guy's limbs? Kinda hard to miss something like that."

"If they're buried wearing a dress, you're right. But if they're buried in pants, Smoot would just substitute PVC pipe for legs...who's gonna know? And if the body is cremated, the entire problem goes up in smoke. Literally." Henry smiled waggishly.

Gwen leaned back in her chair, folded her arms, and looked disparagingly at the detective.

"You know, Lyman, I've gotta give you a tip of the old hat. I didn't realize until just this moment that private detectives actually *read* detective novels." Eliciting no response, she continued. "You realize, of course, that you sound like a crazy person, don't you? All you're missing is a grassy knoll and three hobos." Gwen paused momentarily as she searched Henry's face for some sort of reaction, but he simply continued to smoke his Kool as though completely uninterested. "At the threshold, there's nothing, I repeat, *nothing*, to support anything you just said. Ever heard of 'Occam's Razor'? It basically says that the simplest explanation of something is correct. Your 'explanation' of Freddie Smoot's murder, such as it is, is about as far from simple as can be imagined. Second, who do you think actually killed Freddie Smoot?"

Henry smiled broadly as he ground his cigarette out in the ceramic ashtray next to him. "I can't tell you his name, but his initials are 'Williams Smoot'."

"The hits just keep on coming, don't they," Gwen dryly responded. "So now you're telling me that your own client murdered his son?"

"That's the one thing I'm still unsure about. I don't know whether Smoot actually killed Freddie or whether he hired somebody else to do it. Either way, Smoot knows *who* killed Freddie...even Lightfoot intimated that."

"But you don't think it was Danny?"

"Nope. Like I said, Smoot needs Danny and it wouldn't make sense for him to shit in his own well. Danny's just playing a role until Smoot can find a permanent replacement."

"And who is that?"

Henry sighed. "I have no idea. But I don't think it'll be long until we find out and I've got a bad feeling that I'm not gonna like who it is."

Gwen reflected a moment. "You realize that I have an obligation to contact the prosecutor about what Danny told us today. That he didn't kill Freddie Smoot, I mean."

"Of course, for all the good it'll do Lightfoot. All the prosecutor will say is, 'What else is new?' and start gearing up for trial because perps change their pleas all the time. As a PD you already know that. Nothing will change as far as Lightfoot's concerned; he'll remain in the clink until Smoot gets around to serving up another suspect. So, go right ahead."

"What are you gonna do in the meantime?"

Henry gazed distractedly into the distance. "I'm gonna drive down and have a chat with the guy Lightfoot sells jewelry to. I don't know what else *to* do at this point." He looked at Gwen. "Thank you for allowing me to speak with Lightfoot today. You didn't have to do it and I appreciate it."

"I didn't do it for you; I did it for my client."

He nodded. "I know."

***

The mini-mart was exactly as Lightfoot described it.

Henry swung open its smudged glass door, plastered with posters of smiling models with abundant cleavage, wearing tank tops, cowboy hats, and abbreviated denim shorts, extolling the virtues of a popular Mexican beer, and was immediately assailed by the odor of rotting potatoes, incense, curry, and human perspiration. Immediately to his left was a scarred counter bearing an electronic cash register and gallon jars containing greenish hard-boiled eggs and pickled sausages. Occupying an entire wall directly in front of him was a cooler with multiple glass doors, completely filled with various brands of beer. An emaciated human with a thin mustache, appearing either Indian or Pakistani, sat on a stool at the far end of the counter watching a Bollywood movie on a blaring TV. He didn't look up when the Henry entered. The detective appeared to be the only customer in the place.

Henry stepped to the counter.

"Hey, Babu!" he shouted at the clerk, who appeared transfixed by his television program. "Let's have some service!" The detective slapped the top of the counter with the palm of his hand. The man looked up, reached forward and reluctantly turned the volume down on his TV, and leisurely rose to his feet.

"My name is not 'Babu'," he sullenly grumbled, annoyed by Henry's intrusion. "It is 'Paganyee.' What do you want?" He shuffled behind the counter toward the detective.

Henry extended his cell phone with Lightfoot's photo as the man approached. "Ever seen this guy before?"

Paganyee didn't look at the photo. "I do not know him," he woodenly responded.

"Hmmmm...that's funny, Paganyee, 'cause he told me, not two hours ago, that you regularly buy old jewelry from him. I guess he musta been lying, huh? Why do you suppose he would lie to me like that?"

"I do not know. You should ask your friend. Are you a policeman?"

Henry pointed to himself and shook his head. "Me? Do I look like a policeman, Paganyee? I'm just a guy with some jewelry to sell, tryin' to make a little scratch. My buddy told me that you sometimes help him out."

"I own a market, not a pawn shop," Paganyee stated in a lilting voice. "I do not buy things. I sell them."

"Yeah, I know you're not a pawnshop. Know how I know? Because pawn shops hafta keep records of all the stuff they buy or lend money on, which the cops regularly check because half the stuff is stolen. You don't keep records like that do you, Paganyee?"

The clerk finally looked at Henry's outstretched phone. "What is your friend's name?"

"Danny Lightfoot."

"I think he maybe come here once...not sure."

"Once? That's not what Danny told me. He told me that he's a regular. Take another look." Henry waggled his cell phone in the man's face.

Paganyee's eyes flicked between the phone and Henry.

"Why are you here?" he asked, suspiciously.

"I told you. Danny told me that you buy jewelry from him and don't ask questions."

"Where is your friend?"

"On vacation. But do you buy jewelry, or not? If not, I'll take my business elsewhere. Just say the word, Paganyee. I'm cool whichever."

The other man hesitated. "Show me."

"I didn't bring it with me," Henry deferred. "I didn't want to haul it around unless I knew you were interested."

"What is? Gold?"

"Yeah, mostly gold and a few stones."

"I look. Bring tomorrow." He paused. "In my country, people do not trust banks. They trust gold."

"India?"

Paganyee nodded.

"Well, at least they're able to trust *something*," Henry remarked.

***

It was after 7:00 before Henry finally returned to his apartment. The hours between three and six in the afternoon were typically the hottest part of the day, when the city's vast network of asphalt roadways, having absorbed wilting heat all day, began to radiate it outward with the approach of sunset. As a consequence, the ambient temperature remained in the triple digits well into the night. Darkness provided no respite from the unrelenting heat.

Henry pulled the Hyundai into his assigned parking place and steeled himself for the wave of scorching air that would batter him once he turned the air conditioning off and opened the car door. He flicked the air off and killed the engine. The vehicle's interior began to get hot the instant the cold air ceased to wash over him.

Henry heaved his door open and stepped from the Hyundai. Although he disliked smoking in his apartment, it was just too damned hot to smoke outside. The detective kept his apartment's thermostat set at 70 degrees and, although his monthly electricity bill was through the roof, he was afforded at least a temporary respite from the relentless heat. He looked forward to getting inside his air-conditioned apartment, where the first thing he intended to do was savor a Kool.

***

Gwen wasn't quite sure what to make of Lyman Henry. In her capacity as a public defender she necessarily engaged in professional and, rarely, personal relationships with law enforcement personnel. But she couldn't recall ever encountering an actual private detective. And, although Gwen had never really given the subject much thought, she basically assumed that private detectives were an anachronism that existed only in novels, movies, or on television.

In addition to her regular contacts in law enforcement, Gwen also had to deal with other attorneys on a regular basis. Some of them she'd known since law school; virtually all of them came from substantial families boasting generations of lawyers. By contrast, Gwen's mother was a waitress and her father worked on a loading dock. Neither of them graduated from high school.

Gwen rapidly ascertained that cops and attorneys tend to fall into one of two overlapping categories: vacuous chatterboxes with virtually no interests outside their job, or arrogant buffoons. But the *primary* disincentive to dating either cops or lawyers was their utter predictability. Almost without exception, both groups exhibited an unfailing compulsion to "talk shop" all evening. Interminable discussions about crime; prognostications regarding pending court cases; observations on the intelligence or competence of judges; recitations on the upcoming, or previous, bar convention; personal opinions about legislation potentially affecting a litany of individual rights, depending on the personal leanings of her dinner companion: prisoners, victims, the accused, the homeless, bankrupts, transgendered people, the unborn, students, undocumented aliens, children, the handicapped. It finally became too much. Gwen vowed to herself that, in the future, she would shun all romantic entanglements involving anyone associated to the slightest degree with law enforcement or the law generally. Unfortunately, an unintended consequence of her resolution was that, because virtually everyone she came into contact with had *some* connection to the law, Gwen hadn't had a date in over eight months.

Lyman Henry, though, appeared to be different. While nominally a detective, his association with formal law enforcement was, at best, tangential. Henry was also an iconoclast, as evidenced by the fact that he was an unapologetic smoker. And it certainly didn't hurt that he was easy on the eyes. Most importantly, though, Henry didn't come across as a pompous bore, which largely described most of her previous suitors. In a word, Gwen found Henry to be *interesting*.

Though not optimistic, Gwen secretly hoped she would hear from Lyman Henry again.

TEN

Henry had scarcely finished dressing when his doorbell rang.

Like finding a windowed envelope in your mailbox, someone ringing your doorbell unexpectedly, day or night, bodes ill. The unanticipated caller is *always* someone with bad news, someone selling something, someone wanting a favor, or the cops. There are no other possibilities.

"Shit," Henry muttered as he headed toward the door. He squinted through the peephole; standing on his front stoop was a short, middle-aged man with cropped hair wearing a dated suit and sun glasses. Henry recognized the type instantly: a cop. He unhurriedly released the deadbolt and opened the front door.

"Lyman Henry?"

"That's me."

"I'm Detective Wilfort from the Phoenix Police Department. Mind if I come in?"

Notwithstanding that he'd spent a quarter-century as a Phoenix cop and had retired as a sergeant, Henry didn't recognize the man standing on his doorstep. That was hardly surprising, however, because law enforcement agencies are like musical chairs: cops often start at one agency then transfer to another, before transferring back to the original agency, throughout their careers. Wilfort probably transferred to Phoenix PD from God knows where after Henry retired.

"Let's see some ID, please," Henry requested.

Wilfort wordlessly reached into the pocket of his suit and removed a black leather wallet that held his identification and badge. He flipped it open for Henry to inspect. Henry glanced at them before gesturing Wilfort to step inside the apartment.

"Thank you." Wilfort stepped across the threshold and waited for Henry to shut and deadbolt the door.

"Old habit," the latter explained as he led Wilfort into his living room.

"Yeah, I understand you retired from Phoenix PD," Wilfort casually remarked once he was seated.

Henry sat in a rocker opposite Wilfort. He ignored the detective's calculated chattiness.

"How can I help you, detective?"

"I had a conversation yesterday with Mr. Williams Smoot, Mr. Henry. Do you know him?"

Henry nodded. "I do. Mr. Smoot hired me on a matter."

"Hired you? That isn't exactly how Mr. Smoot characterized your relationship."

"Oh? How did he characterize it?"

"Mr. Henry, rather than play he-said/she-said, why don't you just tell me about your relationship with Mr. Smoot."

"Very well," Henry guardedly responded. "I'm a private investigator and Smoot telephoned me day before yesterday to ask for an appointment. I suggested that we meet for lunch, which we did."

"That same day?"

"Yeah."

"Where did you meet him?"

"Los Cielos Grill, downtown."

"Why did Mr. Smoot want to see you?"

"He said that his kid was killed recently and he wanted to hire me to find out who killed him."

Wilfort frowned. "You didn't know that a suspect in Freddie Smoot's murder was already in custody?"

"Until talking to Smoot I'd never heard of Freddie Smoot, much less that he'd been killed. It was Smoot who told me that a perp had already confessed to the murder."

"Given that, didn't you find it peculiar that Mr. Smoot purportedly wanted to talk to you about finding his son's murderer? Help me out here."

"*Purportedly*?" Henry raised an eyebrow and carefully parsed his words. "For reasons of his own, Smoot believes that Danny Lightfoot, the suspect in his son's murder, didn't kill Freddie. He asked me to find out who did." He paused. "Why, exactly, are you here, detective? What did Smoot tell you?"

Wilfort focused a penetrating gaze on Henry. "Let's call it 'professional courtesy' because you used to be a cop. Smoot claims that you interrupted his lunch day before yesterday and began to harangue him about his son's murder. He said that even after he left the restaurant you followed him to his office, where you continued to harass him. Smoot's assistant, Eileen, confirms his account of what happened."

"That's bullshit," Henry interjected. "Smoot telephoned *me* and specifically asked if he could meet with me. I suggested that we meet for lunch and he agreed."

"Who arrived at the restaurant first, you or Smoot?"

"Smoot. He was already sitting at a table when I got there. After we talked, Smoot told me that he wanted to hire me and asked me to come to his office so he could pay me. I drove to Smoot's funeral home at his specific request...I didn't 'follow' him there."

Wilfort remained stoical. "Eileen said that you arrived unannounced in an agitated state and demanded to see Smoot."

"If that's what she said, she's lying. I just told you that Smoot specifically asked me to come to the funeral home in order to give me my retainer."

"Did he? Give you your retainer, I mean."

"Yes, he did."

"Did Smoot pay you with a check?"

"No, in cash. He had the money concealed in the wall of his office, behind a refrigerator. Smoot asked me to help him move the refrigerator away from the wall, so he could access the money."

"And you complied?"

"Of course I complied. I wanted paid."

"How much did Smoot pay you?"

"$10, 000," Henry evenly replied. "That's the fee I quoted him over lunch."

Wilfort clucked his tongue and smiled icily. "Pretty good jing for locating somebody who was already in jail. I'll have to tell my wife that I'm in the wrong business. Did you write Smoot a receipt?"

"Of course I did. I wrote the receipt on a pad of paper he provided and left it on his desk. I don't suppose you asked to see it?"

"Smoot says that you lifted the $10,000 from his desk drawer while he was out of the room...why would he have a receipt for money you stole?"

"I shouldn't have to tell you that's a lie. I didn't steal money, or anything else, from Smoot. How could I possibly have known that Smoot had $10,000 in his desk? On top of that, he never left the room. Smoot paid me $10,000 for my fee and I wrote a receipt right in front of him."

"Where's your copy of the receipt?"

"The money Smoot paid me *was* my receipt."

"So Smoot had a stash of money hidden in the wall of his office, behind a refrigerator? That's what you're telling me?"

"That's what I'm telling you."

"What color was the refrigerator?"

"What?"

"It's a simple question. What color was the refrigerator in Smoot's office? You said you helped him move it away from the wall, so you'd certainly remember what color it was."

Henry looked suspiciously at Wilfort. "It was white. One of those little refrigerators like they have in dorm rooms, about four feet tall and a couple of feet deep. What difference does it make what color it was?"

"Because, when I was in Smoot's office yesterday, I didn't see any refrigerator," Wilfort informed him. "No holes in any wall, either."

"So what? Smoot obviously took you into a different office. Big deal."

Wilfort's expression hardened. "I was in every room of that building yesterday, including the embalming room. The only refrigerator in the entire place is in the employees' break room and it's full-sized stainless steel, not a little white one."

"It never occurred to you that Smoot may have moved the refrigerator after I left?"

"Sure," Wilfort responded in a patronizing tone, "that's when he must've repaired the hole in his wall too, huh?"

Henry rose from his chair. "I think this conversation is about over. Unless you intend to arrest me for something."

"Wait," Wilfort deferred without moving. "Aren't PIs obligated by their professional canons, or whatever rules you guys supposedly operate under, to give retainer agreements to clients? Did you have Smoot sign a retainer agreement while you were in his office? You must have a copy of *that*. I mean, would you give a wad of cash to somebody with no formal retainer agreement? Does that make common sense to you?"

"I might, depending on the circumstances. What *you,* or anybody else, would do in my place is irrelevant. But, to answer your question, because of the time constraints involved, I told Smoot that I'd mail him a retainer agreement and he agreed." Henry eyed Wilfort cynically.

"So, Smoot just handed you $10,000 in cash and said, 'Here ya go. Have a nice day.'? You seriously expect me to believe that? You were a cop. Would *you* believe it if a suspect told you that?"

"I told you: Smoot hired me for an investigative matter and paid me $10,000, for which I wrote him a receipt on the spot."

"And which, conveniently, you didn't keep a copy of," Wilfort added. He smiled humorlessly. "It looks like the only thing we can agree on is that Smoot was $10,000 lighter when you left his office a couple of days ago than when you got there. I just have to figure out how he got that way."

Henry looked coldly at Wilfort. "Do you intend to arrest me, detective?"

The other man audibly sighed. "Look, I take no pleasure in this, believe me. You're a former cop but look at the situation from my perspective. A guy you say is your own client claims that you stole money from him. You tell me that he voluntarily *gave* you the money, though you don't have a copy of the receipt or a retainer agreement. And, mind you, we're not talkin' chump change—we're talkin' ten large. You also say that Smoot took the money from a hole behind a refrigerator. Yet, when I was there yesterday, there was no refrigerator or hole. And on top of everything else, Smoot's own assistant told me that you were so wound up at Smoot's office yesterday that you scared the shit out of her. Smoot, himself, said that he was so freaked out that he intended to call the cops."

"And you believe them?"

"I believe them more than I believe the shit you're peddling. Where's the $10,000 you claim Smoot paid you?"

"We're done talking," Henry said.

"Have it your way," Wilfort shrugged. He rose to his feet. Reaching beneath his suit coat to the small of his back, he retrieved a pair of chrome handcuffs.

"Mr. Henry, I'm placing you under arrest for the theft of $10,000 from the office of Williams Smoot. Place your hands behind your back."

"You've fucking gotta be kidding me!" Henry snarled.

"Do I look like I'm kidding?" Wilfort asked, rhetorically. "Put your hands behind your back. Now."

Henry knew better than to resist.

"You have the right to remain silent. Anything you say can, and will, be used against you. You have the right to an attorney. If you cannot afford an attorney, one will appointed to you. Do you understand these rights?"

"Yeah," Henry growled.

ELEVEN

Because he could think of no one else to call, Henry telephoned Gwen Harp from the county jail's pay phone immediately after he was booked for felony theft.

"Are you gonna be able to bond out?" she asked over the clamor in the background.

"Yeah. My bail hearing's scheduled for tomorrow morning, so I should only have to spend tonight in this dump."

Gwen sighed into the telephone. "You want me to come down there?"

"No. There's really nothing you can do, but I appreciate the offer. By the way, I found the guy Lightfoot's been fencing jewelry through, so that much of his story checks out."

"It sounds like you may have been right about Smoot."

"Yep, he played me. But I have only myself to blame because I trusted the bastard. I was a chump and should've seen it coming. But the worst part is that I think it's just a matter of time before the other shoe drops."

"What are you talking about?"

"Remember how I speculated that Lightfoot's nothing more than a warm body, a place-holder, until

Smoot can figure out a way to pin Freddie's murder on somebody else? Once he accomplishes the ole' switch-o change-o, Lightfoot will saunter out the front door of the jail and resume fencing dead peoples' jewelry and hacking up corpses for Smoot."

"Well, that was certainly your theory."

"I'm that guy, Gwen."

"You? Gimme a break, Lyman!"

"No, hear me out. Why do you think Smoot claimed that I stole money in the first place? He's gotta know that I'll make bail and, more than that, once the prosecutor starts analyzing the case all the holes in Smoot's story will emerge. From Smoot's perspective, what would be the point of the entire charade?"

"I'm listening," Gwen dubiously responded.

"Within the next few hours, if it hasn't already happened, the cops are gonna receive an anonymous tip that they should execute a search warrant on my apartment, where they'll find evidence that I killed Freddie Smoot. I absolutely guarantee it, Gwen. And when that happens, I'll be right back in here, except this time for murder. Remember, the *only* thing connecting Lightfoot with Freddie Smoot's murder is Lightfoot's confession. Once I'm substituted as the prime suspect in the case, Lightfoot will either recant his confession or the court will grant your Motion to Suppress. Either way, Smoot will have upheld his end of the bargain and Lightfoot will be released. But, before any of that can happen, Smoot needed to have me arrested in order to provide a court with the legal grounds to issue a search warrant."

"What evidence linking you to Freddie's murder could they possibly find in your apartment?" she scoffed.

"I don't know, but I've gotta get the hell out of here before they search my apartment. There's no telling what Smoot planted there."

"You didn't hear it from me, but you'd better not go home after you're released," Gwen softly cautioned. "If you really think the police will show up at your door with a search warrant, you don't want to be there when that happens. If they actually find something, *anything*, that implicates you in Freddie's murder, you'll be immediately arrested again. Only this time it'll be for murder and you won't be able to bond out."

"Yeah, I know," Henry ruefully acknowledged.

"Do you have someplace you can go?"

"I think so."

"Ditch your phone as soon as you get out and get a burner. Then call my cell with the number; don't call my office because all incoming calls are automatically logged. In the meantime, I'll nose around to see what I can find out, Lyman."

A prisoner waiting in line to use the phone jostled Henry. "Hey man, get off the horn. You talkin' to your fuckin' priest?"

"I gotta go, Gwen," he hurriedly concluded. "You'll hear from me."

"Okay, Lyman. Keep your chin up and your head down." She terminated the call.

Lyman hung up and returned to the jail's general population to await his bail hearing the next morning.

***

Undoubtedly because of his former career as a police officer, a fact the prosecutor gleefully brought to the court's attention, the judge set Henry's bail at the maximum. He put it on his credit card, retrieved his personal belongings from the property room then used Uber for a ride back to his apartment. He had the driver drop him off two blocks away just in case the cops were already there, ransacking his place pursuant to the search warrant Henry was convinced had either already been issued or was forthcoming.

Henry took a meandering route home after the Uber driver dropped him off. From diagonally across the street, he cautiously surveyed the area around his apartment for five full minutes before actually daring to approach. Finally satisfied that the coast was clear, Henry stole across the street, rapidly unlocked his front door, and darted inside.

A quick survey quickly established that the apartment's interior hadn't been disturbed since his arrest the previous day. Because he didn't have the luxury of searching for evidence that may have been planted by Smoot, Henry gathered fresh clothing, essential toiletries, the balance of the $10,000 still in his freezer, and stuffed everything into a large canvas bug-out bag. He grabbed his car keys and headed to his car before the anticipated arrival of a phalanx of search warrant-bearing cops. His immediate plan was to drive to his bank and completely withdraw from his checking account the modest amount of money on deposit. From there, he'd drive somewhere and pay cash for a cheap cell phone and phone card, then rent a motel room in order to shower, get some sleep, and change clothes. Henry knew that it was only a matter of time before the cops would be on the lookout for his Hyundai, so he had to keep off the streets and lay low.

Henry left a dollar in his bank account, just to keep it open, and pocketed the rest of the money. He figured that he'd be able to pay cash for a room at some independent, mom-and-pop flophouse on the south side of town and headed in that direction, confident that he'd pass a supermarket on the way where he could buy a burner phone.

On Nineteenth Avenue, Henry spotted a Safeway and pulled into its parking lot. Sitting in his idling car, he removed the battery and sim card from his cell phone. Having done so, he switched the engine off, exited the vehicle, and locked the Hyundai before entering the Safeway. On his way in, Henry deposited his inoperative phone in a trash receptacle situated near the supermarket's sliding glass door; he'd dump the battery and sim card in different garbage cans located somewhere else.

Henry made a beeline to the store's display of generic cell phones. He swiftly chose a cheap flip-phone and grabbed a pre-paid phone card. He walked to the hardware isle, where he selected a padlock and a box of heavy-duty plastic trash bags. Returning to the front of the store, he paid for his purchases in cash. Once back at his car, Henry tossed the padlock and trash bags onto the passenger's seat before dialing Gwen's cell number. Because she didn't pick up, he was forced to leave a terse message.

"Hi," he said. Henry recited his new cell number then terminated the call.

He popped the Hyundai's trunk and carried the box of trash bags to the rear of the car. Unzipping the bug-out bag, Henry rapidly transferred his clothing and personal effects into one of the plastic bags, leaving the cash in the former. He slammed the truck shut, tossed the trash bag full of clothing onto the back seat of his car, and cranked the engine.

Henry had to find a fast food joint, a storage locker place, and a motel, pretty much in that order. He lit a Kool, exited the Safeway parking lot, and headed south.

***

Gwen returned his call as he sat in his idling car in front of the decrepit office of the "Paradise Motor Lodge." He chose it because it had a number of individual, dumpy "casitas" with attached, roofed, parking stalls, figuring they would make it harder to spot the Hyundai. He'd already stashed his cash-filled bug-out bag at a storage place, securing its steel door with the padlock he'd purchased at Safeway, and ate a couple of tacos in his car while searching for a motel.

"Hi," she greeted him. "Where are you?"

"It's probably better that you don't know," Henry deferred. "Although I doubt your phone is tapped, I'm starting to get paranoid. But I'm out of jail, at least."

"Well, I have to admit that you were prescient, Lyman. One of my contacts down at superior court confirmed that about 90 minutes ago a judge signed a search warrant for your apartment. Phoenix PD is either already there or en route."

"Gwen, is there any way to find out what they find at my place, if anything? Smoot had to have planted *something* there. Otherwise, none of this would make any sense."

"I have a friend who works in the property room downtown," she said, referring to the headquarters of the Phoenix Police Department. "I'll check with her this afternoon. If they find anything in your apartment, she'll find out and tell me on the QT."

"Thanks, Gwen. I appreciate everything you're doing for me."

She paused before responding. "Lyman, I have to tell you that I'm really conflicted about all of this. I mean, Danny Lightfoot is my client and, arguably, I'm aiding and abetting a fugitive from justice by even talking to you. I could lose my law license, or worse."

"Gwen, you're not 'aiding and abetting' anything," Henry assured her. "I'm legally out on bail, so I'm not a 'fugitive from justice.' Nor have I been charged with Freddie Smoot's murder, at least not yet. Hell, it's even possible that I overestimated Smoot...maybe he *didn't* manage to plant anything in my apartment that would link me to Freddie's murder. In fact, by helping me you're actually helping to *exonerate* your client. They should promote, not disbar, you, Gwen."

She couldn't help but smile. "I guess, if you put it that way, I see your point, Lyman. I didn't look at it like that."

"Gwen, I promise that I'll never put you in a compromising position, nor ask you to do anything that you find personally or professionally questionable. If Phoenix PD finds any incriminating evidence in my apartment today, this will be the last you'll hear from me. You have my word."

"What if I'm assigned as your PD?" she chuckled.

"If that happens, that'll be on *you*," Henry retorted. "We'll cross that bridge when we come to it. Hopefully, it won't get that far."

"Well, like I said, Lyman, I'll check with my friend later today to see whether Phoenix PD found anything at your apartment. Call me sometime tonight."

"Will do. Right now, I'm gonna take a hot shower and try to get some sleep; I slept like crap last night. Believe it or not, the jail's only slightly less noisy at night than it is during the day."

"Who knew, right?" she laughed. "Did you see Danny?"

"Lightfoot? No, and I'm not sorry. How would it look if the guy who was grilling him the day before was his new cell mate?"

She chuckled again. "Yeah, it would be sorta awkward, wouldn't it? Call me tonight, okay? Hopefully, I'll have good news."

"I sure hope so, Gwen. Thanks again."

Henry terminated the call. Notwithstanding his sanguine conversation with Gwen, he knew the other shoe was about to drop.

Henry took a casita toward the back of the motel for one night, paying for it with cash. He pulled his car around to the rear and parked in the corresponding stall. Because Arizona does not require a front license plate, Henry slowly backed the Hyundai into place until he felt its rear bumper make contact with the rear wall of the parking stall. All the other casitas were devoid of vehicles.

He gathered the plastic bag containing his personal effects from the back seat and walked the few steps to his room. It was basically what he'd anticipated: dingy with a sagging double bed and an antiquated television atop a battered chest of drawers. Thin curtains shrouded the smudged window. No telephone. Henry heaved the trash bag onto the bed and plopped down next to it. The digital clock on the chipped bedside table showed that it was 11:47 a.m.

He was exhausted. Although he'd originally intended to immediately take a shower, it felt good just to sit there in the quietude. He kicked off his shoes, lay completely down, and closed his eyes. In less than two minutes he was asleep.

***

Henry awoke with a start. The room was silent and dark, marginally illuminated by the glowing red numerals of the bedside clock. He glanced at it. Midnight.

Although he'd promised to call Gwen, he now decided against it because of the lateness of the hour. He checked his burner phone to see whether she'd telephoned him while he slept; she hadn't.

Henry stood, carefully lifted a corner of the curtain, and peered outside. No discernible activity. He let the curtain flop back into place and sat on a corner of the bed. He was hungry but didn't know whether there were any fast food joints within walking distance that were still open. In any case, he first wanted to shave and take a shower.

He rose from the bed and went into the bathroom, where he flicked on the overhead light. Two thin towels and a wash cloth were draped over a wooden dowel affixed to the plaster wall. A miniature, wrapped bar of soap rested on the edge of the sink.

Henry decided to shave in the shower. He pushed aside the mold-spotted shower curtain that enclosed the fiberglass stall and cranked the "H" spigot. Thin streams of hot water began sputtering from the shower head; he moderated the temperature by using the other knob.

Henry stripped, kicked his clothes out the door into the main room, grabbed his razor, tore the wrapping from the bar of soap, and stepped into the blessed shower.

***

"Hey, is there a fast food place around here?" Henry asked the Paradise's night clerk, a homely kid who looked about fifteen sitting behind the counter.

The latter looked up from his porn magazine. "There's a Church's Chicken about two blocks that way." He pointed. "Doubt if it's still open, though."

"What about an all-night convenience store?"

"There's a gas station about a block that way. I imagine it's open." He pointed in the opposite direction. "It sells other stuff, too." He grinned and held up his porn magazine as if to validate his statement.

Henry was confident the gas station would have ready-to-eat food. "Thanks," he told the kid as he exited the office.

The night air was thick and hot as he trudged to the gas station. He'd get something to eat and return to his room with it. In the morning he'd call Gwen to see whether her friend was able to provide any information about what the cops found in his apartment when they searched it. Henry sighed. It was a hell of a way to earn $10,000.

***

He bought two slices of microwaved pepperoni pizza and a Diet Coke at the gas station and ate them in his casita. Afterward, he lay back on the bed and closed his eyes, waiting for dawn.

It was 6:30 when Henry woke. Check-out wasn't until 11:00, so he decided to remain in his room, and off the streets, until then. Meantime, he smoked a cigarette before calling Gwen.

She picked up immediately. "Good God, Lyman, I feared you'd already been arrested!" she blurted.

"I'm so sorry, Gwen. I was so stressed and exhausted yesterday that I just fell asleep and didn't wake up until midnight. I apologize if I caused you any anxiety. It wasn't intentional."

"I didn't call you because I figured, if you'd been arrested, the *last* thing I want is for my number to be on your cell phone log."

"You were right not to call, Gwen," Henry concurred. "If I hadn't fallen asleep I'd have called as I promised I would. Were you able to talk to your friend about what Phoenix PD found at my apartment?"

"Unfortunately, yes. Do you have a gas barbecue on your back patio?"

"Yeah. Why, did they find chunks of Freddie Smoot's body roasting on it?"

Gwen ignored Henry's feeble attempt at levity. "In the little storage place underneath it, where the propane tank goes, they found a 9mm pistol. Do you own a 9mm pistol, Lyman?"

"No."

"I didn't think so. Although forensics has only done preliminary tests so far, it appears to be the pistol that was used to kill Freddie. And it evidently has your fingerprints all over it. How is that possible, Lyman?"

A flurry of thoughts raced through Henry's head as he listened with dismay.

"Remember when I told you that Smoot asked me to help him move a refrigerator in his office so he could pay me? I left my fingerprints all over the refrigerator when I grabbed it. I also handled a smooth padlock in his office. Smoot obviously already had the pistol that was used to kill Freddie, so all he had to do after I left was lift my fingerprints from the refrigerator and lock and transfer them to the pistol."

"How could he possibly transfer your fingerprints?"

"Cellophane tape. It's an old method, Gwen."

"I've never heard of it," she dubiously responded.

"That's because you were never a cop."

She hesitated. "You realize that an arrest warrant for Freddie's murder is inevitable, Lyman. I won't be able to talk to you after today."

"Yeah, I know," he sighed. "I guess the bright spot, if there is one, is that the prosecutor will probably move to dismiss the murder charge against Lightfoot, since they've now got actual, physical evidence linking me to Freddie's murder. That's a good thing, isn't it? I mean, isn't that your job as a public defender?"

"My job is to see that justice is done, and that includes making sure that innocent people aren't convicted of crimes they didn't commit. That means Danny *and* you."

"Well, I sure as hell didn't kill Freddie Smoot, but it's looking like I'm gonna get tagged for it."

"I know you didn't, Lyman, but you need to hire an attorney immediately. There's not much I can do for you at this point."

"I understand," he despondently acknowledged. "I really appreciate everything you *have* done, Gwen."

"What are you going to do, Lyman?"

"I gotta go see a guy," he cryptically said.

"A lawyer?"

"No, not a lawyer. Not yet, anyway."

"Who?"

"Just a guy I know who may be able to help."

"I can give you the names of some good criminal defense lawyers," she volunteered.

Henry scanned the room, looking for a pad and pen. "I don't have anything here to write on, Gwen."

"Then I'll call you later and leave a message on your phone. I can hardly get into trouble for suggesting that somebody seek legal counsel. If I do, there's something terribly wrong with the whole system."

He unconsciously smiled. "Gwen, there's been something wrong with the system since the B.C.'s. Nothing either of us does is gonna change that."

"Well, as an officer of the court, I'm obligated to urge you to turn yourself in, Lyman. But, off the record and as your friend, I sure as heck wouldn't...you didn't hear that from me, though," she chuckled.

"Hear what? I'm sorry, were you talking, Gwen?" He heard her musical laughter over the phone.

"I've gotta go, Lyman. I'll call you with those names later. Be safe, my friend."

"Thanks again, Gwen. This, too, shall pass. And when everything finally shakes out, we'll have a drink together."

"Just one?"

"As many as you want. My treat."

She laughed again. "Bye, Lyman. Take good care of yourself." The call ended.

Henry glanced at the bedside clock; just over three hours until checkout. He stood and headed for the dingy bathroom to brush his teeth and shower.

Henry checked out by leaving his key on the chest of drawers in his room. He figured he'd snag a fast food breakfast somewhere before heading over to Tempe Town Lake.

TWELVE

Henry parked his car in the long-term lot at Sky Harbor International Airport amid hundreds of other homogeneous vehicles. Phoenix's light-rail ran from the airport directly to the sprawling campus of Arizona State University, in neighboring Tempe. It was a relatively short walk from the ASU campus to the rambling Hooverville established on the shores of the Town Lake.

He retrieved the trash bag containing his clothing and toiletries from the back seat before locking the Hyundai. Small courtesy buses shuttled passengers between various airport parking lots, terminals, and the light-rail station and Henry waited only a few minutes before the scheduled arrival of the next bus. He hopped aboard and placed in his lap the plastic trash bag containing his belongings.

The vehicle was crammed with happy, boisterous travelers with piles of luggage. Henry glanced at his watch. He was hopeful Max was still at the homeless camp and that he'd be able to quickly locate him. Henry wished he could smoke a Kool right now.

***

"Max around?"

"Who's 'Max'?" The toothless vagrant frowned at the question.

"I don't know his last name. You know, the 'Nam vet, Max. You seen him around today?"

"Gotta smoke?" the guy abruptly inquired.

"Just Kools," Henry told him.

"That's cool."

Henry feared for an instant that he might become an unintentional participant in a version of the old Abbot and Costello 'Who's on First?' routine. He removed a pack of cigarettes from his pocket and passed it to the man, who tapped a Kool into his free hand. Henry shook his head when the man tried to return the pack.

"Keep 'em. You sure you don't know Max?" Henry asked as the guy fished a tattered book of matches from the pocket of his grimy shorts and lit the cigarette.

"Lotsa 'Nam vets around here," he grunted, inhaling a mouthful of menthol smoke. "What's the guy look like?"

"Older, average lookin', long, braided pony tail. Cabela's cap."

"Yeah, I maybe seen somebody like that," the man somewhat acknowledged. "Don't know his name."

"Today?"

"Hard to say."

Henry withdrew a $20 bill from his pocket. "This make it any easier?"

The guy snatched it from between Henry's fingers. "Yeah, this morning. He was over there, washin'." He pointed generally toward the Town Lake.

"How long ago?"

"I told you. This morning," the man crossly repeated.

"Ok, thanks," said Henry. He turned to leave.

"Hey, dude! How 'bout spottin' me another Andrew?"

Henry disregarded his entreaty and began gingerly picking his way through the trash-strewn encampment toward the muddy lakeshore. He stepped over and around swollen plastic garbage bags, trampled fast food containers, syringes, old tires, and used sanitary napkins.

A handful of people stood ankle-deep in the lake, discarded Styrofoam cups bobbing in the fetid water around them. Max was not among them. They sullenly eyed his approach.

"Hey, I'm a friend of Max's," he greeted the assembly. "Any of you seen him today?"

"Max ain't here," belched a fat woman wearing a dirty muumuu with cats printed on it. Her thinning brown hair was cropped short and she had a large bald spot on one side of her head.

"Know where he is?" Henry smiled.

"His place, I guess," she shrugged.

"Where's that? Around here?"

"Yeah, over there." The woman lifted a ponderous arm and gestured.

"Know if he's there?" Henry hazarded.

"How would I know? Do I look like his keeper?" The fat woman looked smugly at her companions to ensure they heard, and fully appreciated, her riposte. Two of them halfheartedly sniggered.

"Yeah, thanks," said Henry. He began walking in the apparent direction of Max's domicile, hoping to find him there.

"Hey, how about a tip, you faggot!" the fat woman yelled after him.

Henry ignored her.

***

"Hey, Max!" Henry shouted to no one in particular. "Max!"

He was surrounded by more than a dozen castoff refrigerator and washing machine boxes, appropriated by the homeless for use as impromptu shelters, randomly scattered on the ground several yards from the edge of the Town Lake.

"Max!" Henry again yelled. He arbitrarily approached one large carton lying on its side, a naked pair of legs protruding from it, and nudged it with his foot.

"Fuck off," a muffled voice emerged from within the carton.

"Do you know where Max is?" Henry asked.

"Fuck off," growled the voice again.

Henry proceeded to another box, which proved to be untenanted. Four habitations later, he blundered into his objective.

Max was sitting bare chested on a flattened cardboard box, leaning against a warped sheet of plywood that was propped against a dead tree, sunning himself.

Max looked up as Henry stepped around the plywood barricade.

"Howdy," he said.

"Hey, Max. I've been lookin' for you."

"I'm easy to find.   Got a smoke?"   Henry produced an unopened pack of Kools and passed it to him, along with a butane lighter. Max tore open the pack with his teeth, removed a cigarette, and pressed it to his lips. After lighting it, he closed his eyes and reclined against the plywood in sublime pleasure. "What brings you back to my little corner of paradise?" he asked without opening his eyes.

"I need your help, Max."

Max opened one eye and squinted at Henry from beneath the brim of his Cabela's cap. "I'm a homeless bum, an alkie, and a druggie.   I can't even help *myself*."

"Maybe not, but I think you can help me."

Max took a long drag of Kool.   "Didja find Lightfoot?"

"Yeah, I found him," Henry replied. "Mind if I sit down?"

Max opened both eyes and looked around. "Only got one piece of cardboard."

"That's okay." Henry dropped the garbage bag containing his effects to the ground and eased himself onto it. He looked intently at the homeless man. "The cops are lookin' for me, Max."

"That ain't good. What for?" Max nonchalantly asked. Using his thumbnail, he flicked ash from the glowing end of his cigarette.

"They think I killed somebody."

The other man nodded his head thoughtfully. "Did he need killin'?" he asked with genuine interest.

Henry couldn't help but smile. "I didn't kill anybody. But I need time to sort everything out."

Max blew on the stub of his cigarette until it glowed then used it to light a fresh Kool. A Dutch fuck.

"That pretty much sounds like the understatement of the year. What do you want from me?"

"You can help me hide."

"Where?"

Henry gestured to the encircling encampment. "Here."

Max shook his head. "I don't even wanna be here and you sure as fuck don't."

"The cops won't think to look for me here, Max."

"Don't kid yourself. Half the bastards who live here are snitches and every one of 'em would bust a gut to turn you in, sure as I'm lookin' at you. The cops'll tell 'em to be on the lookout for you." He took a luxuriant drag from his cigarette. "Where's your heap?"

"Airport."

"It'll probably take the cops two or three days, tops, to spot it 'cause they'll be lookin' for it and they patrol all the airport parking lots on a regular basis. Once they find your car, this'll probably be one of the places they start lookin' because, if you took the light-rail from the airport, they'll have video of you headin' in this direction. All the light-rail stations are lousy with cameras."

Henry rubbed his forehead in frustration. "Well, you got any ideas on how I can stay outta sight until I figure things out? I'm open to suggestions, Max."

Max looked pensive. "Anything in your heap that you can't live without? If so, too bad because the cops'll have it staked out before they tow it, just like your house."

"No, nothing."

"Got any scratch?"

"Yeah. Money's not a problem," Henry assured him.

"Got it with you?"

"Storage locker. Key's in my pocket."

A mischievous smile briefly illuminated Max's weathered face.

"Yeah, I think I might be able to keep you out of the limelight for a little while. But it'll cost you."

"Name your price, Max. It isn't like I have a ton of options."

The other man vigorously nodded his assent. "You're damned sure right about that! But I guess we can dicker about the price later on. Right now, we better think about getting your ass outta Dodge." He clambered to his feet and grabbed his tee shirt from where it was hanging over the plywood sheet. "C'mon."

Max led Henry to an oblong shipping container, lying horizontally in the weeds, which previously held a refrigerator. It resembled a stout cardboard coffin used to cremate bodies.

"My place," he announced. "Welcome home...*mi casa es su casa*." He gestured for Henry to crawl inside.

Henry balked. "Wait a minute, I thought you said it wasn't smart for me to stay here."

"It ain't," Max agreed, "but you gotta keep outta sight until I talk to somebody." He looked patiently at Henry. "It's up to you. I ain't got a dog in the fight, one way or the other."

Henry stared at the recumbent refrigerator container. "How long do you think you'll be?"

"Pretty quick. The guy I gotta talk to lives here...just gotta find him."

"What are you gonna tell him?"

"Beats the fuck outta me," Max conceded. "But he's just about the only guy around here who ain't a snitch. I trust him."

"I guess that'll have to be good enough," sighed Henry.

"Guess so. Now get in the damned box," Max grinned.

***

Williams Smoot never intended to become a funeral director. His father and grandfather farmed sugar beets in Utah's Wasatch Valley, but Smoot *knew* he didn't want to do that. After graduating from Brigham Young University with a degree in accounting, a dutiful stay-at-home wife, and two toddlers, though, he had to find immediate employment. The first opportunity that presented itself was working third shift at a Provo mortuary, where he performed a variety of tasks: cleaning, answering the telephone, collecting from homes, hospitals, and assisted care facilities the bodies of people who'd died during the night. In that capacity, he came into regular contact with various health care professionals and morticians. Smoot swiftly discovered that he possessed a genuine interest in, to say nothing of an aptitude for, the business of death.

On his own time, Smoot began to study the rudiments of human anatomy and physiology, resolved to obtain the necessary credentials to become a licensed funeral director. It was during that process that he became acquainted with the National Organ and Transplant Act, while his circle of contacts quickly expanded to include a number of ambitious, like-minded people. Soon after securing his funeral director's license, Smoot learned of a mortuary for sale in Phoenix. It was a serendipitous moment. Smoot promptly gathered his growing family and relocated to the Valley of the Sun.

Pursuant to the National Organ and Transplant Act, all organic material intended for transplant, including blood, must be certified as free from diseases such as HIV, cancer, and hepatitis. Although possessing none of the requisite certifications, Smoot began to sell to local plasma banks blood drawn from bodies in his funeral home. Such bodily fluids are ordinarily dumped directly into the city's sewer system during the embalming process, an egregious waste of a valuable commodity.

Indifferent to the significant potential of latent contaminants in blood indiscriminately drained from random corpses, Smoot cheerfully provided all requested documentation attesting to its purity. Chronically short on donations and disinclined to be finicky, blood banks seldom inquired into the source of donated blood and lacked the resources or inclination to perform independent testing, relying instead on the assurances of donors.   In those exceptional cases when someone insisted on additional information regarding the provenance of Smoot's sanguine donations, he arbitrarily changed the donor's age and physical condition to conform to the expectations of the receiving blood bank.

And, for a time, so it went.

But collecting and transporting blood from cadavers proved laborious and time consuming. Worse, it ultimately failed to generate income proportionate to the effort involved.   And there was always the niggling possibility, however remote, of troublesome intervention by the Food and Drug Administration arising out of Smoot's arguable violation of the 1984 Act. It was then he decided to create BioServus LLC.

Peddling blood, Smoot concluded, was a nickel-and-dime trade, scarcely one step removed from digging through dumpsters to retrieve aluminum cans. The only way to achieve significant, consistent profits was by supplying entire human bodies, or pieces of them, to medical schools and research facilities on a worldwide scale.   And, as with blood donations, he would be performing a valuable public service.   More to the point, however, as a non-transplant tissue bank, BioServus would be free to conduct its business affairs unfettered by FDA oversight. Smoot's numerous contacts in the death industry, combined with his business acumen, would serve him well.   Moreover, thanks to his funeral home, he possessed virtually unlimited inventory.   He'd freeze his products and airfreight them to customers in insulated coolers, buried in dry ice. Some of his customers would buy product outright; others would simply rent what they needed for a prescribed period of time.

Beauty schools use thawed, decapitated human heads to demonstrate proper hair and cosmetic techniques. Human hands are utilized to teach the correct application of artificial nails. Following their application as educational props, the remains are boxed up and returned to the tissue bank to be rented-out again to another school. By contrast, medical colleges typically purchase entire corpses outright, because it's often necessary to completely deconstruct them in order to illustrate human physiology or show appropriate surgical methods. The human remains are thereafter disposed of. Frankly, it was a matter of indifference to Smoot if his customers purchased his products for their dogs to gnaw on, provided they paid him for the privilege.

As a non-transplant tissue bank, BioServus LLC would not be compelled to obtain any special certifications, licenses, or permits under provisions of the National Organ and Transplant Act. Smoot intended to register BioServus in either Delaware or Nevada in order to stay below the radar; he feared potential blowback if it were discovered that his organ farm was located next to a daycare or grocer and was shrewd enough to understand the wisdom of keeping his neighbors ignorant and happy. The only significant financial outlay would be the purchase of a large walk-in freezer in which to store human remains. He'd easily be able to buy a used one at a restaurant supply company and keep in a rented storage facility.

A generic pack-and-ship storefront would serve as the LLC's official business address. No fuss, no muss.

Smoot had no doubt that BioServus LLC would be able to unload every scrap of bone and hank of hair it could get its hands on. Because only a handful of non-transplant tissue banks existed, BioServus would be able to charge essentially whatever it wished for its products. But Smoot needed a cutter capable of dismembering bodies on a large scale, a process only slightly more difficult than deboning a ham. And, ideally, the consent of the families would have to be obtained before Smoot could hawk their loved ones' remains to the highest bidder. But who better than a funeral director to counsel the family about the selfless nobility of organ donation? And, if necessary, next-of-kin consent forms could be readily forged.

Actual processing of the bodies could be performed pretty much anywhere. It isn't like anyone would be in a position to complain. Once the families sign the requisite consent forms they're basically out of the loop. And corpses obviously have no opinion about what happens to them. The processing site didn't even have to be indoors, just somewhere inconspicuous with adequate space, electricity, and running water. The loading area at the rear of the funeral home would be ideal. His cutter could do the work at night, after all the other employees had departed for the day. His factotum, Danny, would be perfect for the job; though not especially bright, Lightfoot was compliant, discrete, reasonably reliable, and willing to do just about anything for money. Smoot would simply have to teach him how bodies must be properly dissected.

Money, however, would not be an issue. Smoot's non-transplant tissue bank promised to be an absolute profit machine.

THIRTEEN

Lyman Henry found himself ensconced in a shabby travel trailer, resting obliquely on flattened tires at the rear of a decaying mobile home park on Van Buren Street. Max's friend agreed to rent-out the trailer at the rate of $250 per month, though it was unclear whether the friend actually owned the trailer. In any case, Max promptly agreed to the deal; he and Henry took a city bus to a stop about a block from the mobile home park, where they got off and walked the rest of the way.

"Willy Burns, himself, couldn't find you here," Max declared as they approached the deteriorating travel trailer.

"I think your refrigerator box was probably an improvement," Henry remarked as he lit a Kool and surveyed the trailer's dilapidated exterior.

"You may be right but, that bein' the case, I'd have to charge you more than $250 a month to stay there. Gotta nuther of them smokes?"

The detective handed Max the pack.

"Well, let's take a squint at the inside," Max proposed. He mounted the steps to the trailer's dented metal door, inserted a key into the slot in the exterior handle, twisted it, and wrenched open the door. A wave of hot, musty air surged over them.

"Don't look like anybody's been here for a while," Max observed. He stepped into the cramped trailer. Even though he wasn't exceptionally tall, its low ceiling prevented him from standing completely upright.

The trailer's diminutive windows were grimy louvers of glass that opened and closed with mechanical cranks. All of them were plastered, at least partially, with sheets of torn aluminum foil, intended to thwart the blistering afternoon sun.

"It's hotter than a two-dollar whore in here," Max laconically noted. He stepped forward and punched a button on the plastic faceplate of a small air conditioning unit installed in one window. It squawked to life and began blowing a rush of superheated dusty air into the trailer. Max patiently held his hand in front of the flow. "Hopefully, it'll cool down in a minute," he shouted over the noise of the air conditioner.

Henry flicked his cigarette butt away, stooped to enter the trailer, and surveyed the interior: at one end a sofa that presumably turned into a bed; some cupboards; a tiny propane stove, sink and refrigerator attached to the wall opposite the door; and a rudimentary toilet and shower at the other end. A hinged table hung from the wall immediately adjacent to the door, a wobbly chair propped against it. The good news is that no one would obviously give a damn if he smoked inside.

"Works like a champ!" Max grinned when the compressor finally kicked in and cold air began flowing from the air conditioner. "Close the door." Henry complied as Max dropped onto the sofa.

"It ain't the Taj Mahal," Max said, "and it ain't even got a TV, but it'll keep you outta sight for a while. I'll bring ya some smokes, food, magazines, and whatnot...whatever you want. Maybe a radio, since there's no TV."

Henry pulled the chair away from the wall and sat. "Does your buddy know who's staying here?"

"You, you mean?" Max asked. "Nope. He didn't ask and I didn't say. Not that he'd give a crap, as long as your money's green." He looked quizzically at Henry. "But what, exactly, do ya plan on doin' to pull your tit out of the wringer?"

Henry leaned his head back and wearily closed his eyes. "I have no idea, Max." He opened his eyes, lifted his head, and looked at the other man. "But, whatever it is, it'll involve your buddy, Lightfoot."

"Lightfoot ain't no buddy of mine," Max protested. "I hate that fuckin', little-girl-diddlin', prick."

Max's passion prompted Henry to smile. "Look, I already owe you for finding this trailer. If you wanna earn some more money, I could sure use you for my eyes and ears. Interested?"

"'Course I'm interested," Max affirmed. "Whaddya need?"

"Well, like you said, I'll need some food and stuff. Do you have any cash?"

"I still got 'bout half of the hundred you gave me the other night."

"Okay, use that to buy some lunch meat, bread, bottled water, and whatever else you think I'll need in the short run."

Max looked around the interior of the trailer. "You'll need a coffee pot and coffee, too. And, like I said, a radio would be nice. My fifty ain't likely to go very far."

Henry hesitated, then reached into his pocket and withdrew the key to the padlock that secured his storage locker. He looked solemnly at Max.

"Remember the storage locker I mentioned? I put a canvas bag with money in it because I didn't want to haul the bag around with me and wasn't sure what else to do with it. But since it looks like I may be here a while, I can retrieve the bag and keep it here. I'll need a lift, though."

"How much we talkin'?"

"Ten large, give or take."

Max whistled. "That's a lotta cheese. I got no wheels but a guy I know, Leon, does."

"Think he'd give me a lift?"

"Leon'll carry you on his back if the price is right."

Henry smiled without humor. "I kinda figured that. How soon can you talk to him?"

"Tonight, if he's around. Leon's pretty popular 'cause he's the only dude with a car. Other than you, I mean. But your car's probably already been towed," Max quickly clarified.

"Do you trust him?"

"Trust Leon to give you a ride?" Max laughed. "The only trust you gotta have in Leon is that he can follow drivin' directions! Leon don't know you from the backside of the moon and don't give a damn."

"Okay, then do me a favor and talk to Leon as quick as you can, Max. I'd like to get my money sooner, rather than later."

"I'll try to track him down tonight."

***

At the Phoenix Police Department, Henry's case was transferred from theft to homicide and reassigned to Detective Roberto Ortiz.

Ortiz vaguely remembered when Henry was on the force, though he didn't personally know him. Accordingly, he began his review of the file with uncharacteristic interest. Although he'd received it a couple of days earlier, Ortiz was just now getting to it.

Ortiz noted at the threshold that the case originally arose out of a straightforward theft complaint. Although sufficient probable cause existed to justify Henry's arrest in that matter as Wilfort had, in fact, done, Ortiz would probably have been somewhat more circumspect. Henry was a former cop; it seemed inconsistent with his background that he would have acted so rashly. As Ortiz learned long ago, however, it's impossible to predict human behavior. But there's an obvious motive for stealing money: personal enrichment. What motive did Henry have for killing Freddie Smoot?

Ortiz found Henry's apparent murder of Freddie Smoot to be perplexing. Why would Henry kill Freddie and then brazenly confront the kid's old man three months later, out of the blue, to demand money? It obviously couldn't have been ransom, since the kid had been dead for three months and his confessed murderer already arrested.   What additional "information" about the kid's murder, according to Smoot's statement, could Henry possibly have possessed?   And if Henry was the actual killer, as established by the pistol found in Henry's apartment with his prints all over it, why did that other numb-nuts, Lightfoot, confess to Freddie's murder in the first place?

Phoenix Police would have immediately informed the offices of both the country prosecutor and public defender that a new suspect in the Freddie Smoot murder had been identified. At that point, Lightfoot's PD would have initiated an immediate drumbeat to have Lightfoot released from jail. Whether that had yet occurred depended entirely on the diligence of the public defender.

In order to begin sorting things out, though, Ortiz wanted to talk to Lightfoot, as well as to the prosecutor originally assigned to the Freddie Smoot murder. Unfortunately, the latter had resigned shortly after Danny Lightfoot's confession and relocated to Wyoming, where he took a job as a pharmaceutical salesman. He'd be difficult to track down. Even if he could be located, he'd devoted little time to the case due to Lightfoot's immediate confession.

Ortiz punched the number for prosecutor's office into his desk phone and put the call on speaker. When the receptionist answered, the detective identified himself and asked to speak with a prosecutor he knew.

"Hey, Frank, how's it hangin'?" Ortiz greeted when the attorney came on the line.

"Livin' the dream," snorted the man at the other end. "To what do I owe the pleasure of hearing your mellifluous voice?"

"Daniel Lightfoot. He still in custody?"

"Hang on and I'll check. Be right back." The phone went momentarily silent. "Nope. Cut him loose coupla' hours ago. Aside from the fact that his PD is a cunt, we figured that the pussy judge would probably grant her Motion to Suppress. Without Lightfoot's confession we had nuthin' because there was no physical evidence linking him to the crime, so we let him walk. Why?"

Ortiz sighed. "I wanted to talk to him about the new suspect in the Smoot murder, Lyman Henry. Know anything about him?"

"Nope, though I heard he used to be a cop."

"That's what the file says. His name is familiar."

"Not to me," the prosecutor said. "I never heard of him. He still on the lam?"

"Last I heard, but I'm just now getting to the file. You got Lightfoot's current address?"

"Such as it is, yeah. He's basically homeless but we got contact info on him."

"Think he'd talk to me if I asked real nice?" Ortiz probed.

"For what? Why do you want to waste time talkin' to that dirtbag?"

"I'd like to know why he confessed to killing a guy he apparently didn't kill."

"'Cause Lightfoot's a fuckin' nutjob," Frank replied. "There, I just saved you a lot of trouble. Besides, he'll be back in the clink soon enough and you can talk to him then. You can thank me later."

"Yeah, I'll do that," Ortiz laughed. He grabbed a pad and pen. "Gimme Lightfoot's contact info."

"Hang on." Ortiz heard rustling noises at the other end. "Looks like he works part-time at a mortuary." Frank recited the telephone number.

"What's the name of the place?" Ortiz asked as he wrote.

"'Smoot Funeral Chapel.'"

"Whoa!" Ortiz exclaimed. "Lightfoot works at the mortuary owned by the victim's father?"

"Yeah, I guess. So what? That's obviously where he met the victim. Since you evidently just started bein' a cop, lemme give you a crash course in murderin'. Most murders are committed by people who knew the victim. There will be a quiz at the end of the hour."

"Bite me," Ortiz retorted. "Besides, *Lightfoot* may have known the victim, but Lightfoot didn't kill him. Lyman Henry did, and there's no evidence that *Henry* knew the victim."

"Well, he obviously only had to know him long enough to kill him."

"Yeah, I guess..." Ortiz's voice trailed off. "I guess I'll try to track Lightfoot down. Thanks, Frank."

"Anytime. Lemme know when you need more lessons in basic criminal investigation...I'm always here for the beleaguered men and women of the Phoenix Police Department."

"Like I said, bite me," Ortiz chuckled. "Talk to you later."

***

Lyman debated calling Gwen, just to let her know he was safe. He ultimately decided against it because doing so would put her in an impossible position, both morally and professionally. He glanced at his watch and lit another Kool.

Notwithstanding its location in a blighted area of town adjacent to bustling Van Buren Street, the mobile home park, itself, appeared serene. To the extent Henry was able to see anything through the tiny windows of his travel trailer, the park was compact, containing less than two dozen small trailers inhabited by frail old people. Though neat, the decayed condition of their habitations suggested that most of the tenants had probably resided in the park for decades. Nobody seemed to notice, or care about, the decomposing travel trailer sitting on flattened tires in the back.

Earlier that morning a Phoenix Police cruiser had pulled into the trailer park and slowly driven through it. Henry's initial, panicked thought was that he'd been discovered but, after watching the cruiser's leisurely transit through the park, he concluded that it must simply have been a routine patrol.

Henry looked at his watch again. The window air conditioning unit worked almost too well, so he flicked it down a notch. He went to a grimy window and anxiously squinted out.

***

"Didn't I tell you that everything would work out?" Smoot chortled. "You're just too impatient, Danny." They were sitting in a fast food restaurant not far from the funeral home.

"Impatient my ass," Lightfoot snarled. "I didn't see you sitting on your ass in jail."

"Now, now," Smoot tut-tutted. "We both knew that it would take some time. Rome wasn't built in a day, you know. The only thing that matters is that you're free," he beamed.

"After three months I was startin' to wonder. And I'm gonna need some dough."

"Yes, of course. That won't be a problem." Smoot looked at him slyly. "Some exciting things have been happening while you've been away."

"'Been away' makes it sound like I was on some kind of vacation," Lightfoot scowled.

Smoot ignored him. "All that unpleasantness is now behind us and we're ready to move on to bigger things. I have some ideas about expanding the business and want you to be a part of it."

Lightfoot cocked a distrustful eyebrow. "What kind of 'ideas'? Your last idea got me thrown in jail for three months."

Smoot looked tiredly at Lightfoot. "Danny, what exactly seems to be the problem? We discussed what would happen after you confessed to Freddie's death and things went exactly as planned. Frankly, I don't understand your hostility."

"I didn't think I'd be in jail for three fucking months."

"We weren't sure how long it would take to get all the pieces into place. You knew that at the front end, Danny. And, if I may say so, you were well compensated for your inconvenience." Smoot smiled expansively. "But, like I said, all that's behind us."

"Yeah, you're as happy as a fuckin' Mexican with a leaf blower. But what about your dead kid? How do I know that's put to bed and my ass won't be hauled back to jail again a week from now?"

The smile on Smoot's pudgy face never faltered. "That's all been taken care of. The police have arrested Freddie's *real* killer, so put yourself at your ease."

"What's the poor, dumb sumbitch's name?" Lightfoot idly asked.

"It doesn't matter. You don't know him."

"I know a lot of people and wanna make sure you didn't accidentally finger one of my buds." Lightfoot stared coldly at Smoot. "What's the guy's fuckin' name?"

Smoot sighed. "Lyman Henry."

Lightfoot burst out laughing. "Are you fucking kidding me? Lyman Henry? That guy visited me in jail!"

Smoot was visibly taken aback.

"You talked to Lyman Henry?"

"Yeah, him and my PD came to see me together."

"When?" Smoot was nonplused by Lightfoot's insouciance.

"I dunno. Right before I got released, I think. That's funny as shit!" Lightfoot giggled.

"What did he want?" asked the flustered mortician. "Did you tell him you knew me?"

Lightfoot shrugged. "He said that *you* already told him that you knew me. I didn't have to tell him."

Smoot leaned forward. "What did Henry want, Danny? What did you talk about?"

"He just wondered how I knew you." Lightfoot began to fidget in his seat.

"And what did you tell him?"

"I told him that I do stuff around the funeral home sometimes. That's all."

"Nothing more?"

"Nope, that's all I said."

"Did Henry seem satisfied?"

"About what?"

"About the things you do for me at the funeral home," Smoot responded in exasperation. "Did he ask what kind of things you do there?"

Lightfoot shook his head. "Nope."

Smoot leaned back in his chair and looked into space, thinking. Although unexpected, Henry's jail visit should not have been surprising. Indeed, under the circumstances, it made perfect sense that the detective would have wanted to interview the man wrongly jailed for Freddie's murder, if only to confirm his alibi. Henry was simply doing the job Smoot had ostensibly hired him to perform: identify the person actually responsible for Freddie's murder. No cause for alarm...Smoot was merely being paranoid.

"Well, I guess there's no harm done," Smoot finally said. "Henry's in jail and you're out. That's all that matters." He attempted a feeble smile.

Lightfoot abruptly changed the subject. "What's this new business you're talkin' about?"

Smoot emerged from his reverie. "I want you to do some recruiting for me."

"Recruiting? Like the army?" Lightfoot sniggered.

"In a sense. Demand for product is exceeding supply. I need to address the situation."

"Like how?"

Smoot leaned across the table and lowered his voice. "Stated plainly, we need more product."

"From where? Don't you already have a ton of stiffs down at the funeral parlor?"

Smoot shook his head. "BioServus is proving to be appreciably more successful than I anticipated. I simply can't keep up with demand for product and need more donors."

"I don't know why you keep callin' it 'product,'" Lightfoot guffawed. "It's fuckin' body parts!"

Smoot looked at him sourly. "BioServus strives to maintain an air of professionalism and decorum, Danny."

"Yeah, whatever," Lightfoot scoffed. "Parts is parts. So what about the 'recruitment' you're talkin' about? What's it got to do with me?"

"As I said, BioServus needs more donors."

"So?"

"I believe you may be able to provide them."

Lightfoot snorted. "You want me to button-hole people and tell 'em, 'Hey, why the hell do you need two eyes? Why don't you march down to my buddy at the chop-shop and donate your extra one? Some rich bastard could use your cornea.' Maybe I'll get a sandwich board and stand on a street corner."

"No, I simply want you to direct people to BioServus," Smoot responded with equanimity. "I'll take care of the rest."

"What 'people'?"

"Anyone who'd like to make a little extra money. I suspect that's essentially everyone you come into contact with."

"True dat," Lightfoot acknowledged, bobbing his head. "How much 'extra money' am I supposed to tell 'em?"

"You're not. BioServus will make that decision on a case-by-case basis."

"So how am I supposed to get 'em to sign up if they don't know how much money they're gonna get? They won't bother because it's a fuckin' a crap shoot."

"I anticipated that," Smoot replied. "Simply spread the word that a new government program forgives all child support obligations, tax debts, and student loans. Even criminal restitution payments. "

"Wow! When did *that* happen?" Lightfoot excitedly blurted.

"It doesn't matter," Smoot replied. "Just get the word out, Danny. I'll give you a phone number for everyone to call."

"Fuck-a-duck, yeah!" Lightfoot exclaimed. "Pretty much everybody I know owes that shit! If they can bag it, they'll cum in their pants!"

Smoot's rotund face glowed. "Once applicants call the number, they'll be directed to an address where they'll receive more information about the new debt-forgiveness program."

"How much?"

"You'll be compensated $25 per applicant. All they have to do is tell us that you referred them."

Lightfoot furrowed his brow. "How am I supposed to do that? Once I put the word out, I got no idea who'll call. They're sure as hell not gonna remember where they heard it from and I'll get boned out of $25!"

"You're resourceful, Danny. I'm sure you'll be able to figure out a way to ensure that doesn't happen. You could tell them, for example, that if they fail to identify the person who referred them, they'll automatically be turned away and won't be able to sign up for the debt-forgiveness program or receive any money."

"So, it's just the honor system? I'm supposed to trust you that you'll keep a head-count and pay me $25 for everybody that mentions my name? How do I know you won't screw me?"

Smoot looked genuinely hurt. "Haven't I always been square with you, Danny? Why would I do something like that? Besides, if I cheated you I'd only be hurting myself because you'll stop referring people to me." He smiled amiably. "I'll tell you what...why don't we do it this way? As a token of good faith, I'll pay you a flat $500 per month, whether you refer anyone or not. In addition, you'll still get $25 for each candidate who mentions your name. Does that sound fair?"

Lightfoot grinned. "Now you're talkin!" That way I'll know you're not fuckin' with me."

"I would never do that, Danny. In fact, I'm sure there will soon be lots more work around the funeral home for you, too."

"But you don't want nobody who don't owe child support and stuff?"

"Not at all," Smoot suavely assured him. "Those that don't need to avail themselves of the government's debt forgiveness program will automatically receive a trip to Las Vegas. All they have to do is mention your name...they'll go to Las Vegas for free and you get $25." He spread his plump fingers. "Everyone wins, Danny."

Lightfoot reflected a moment. "Yeah, I s'pose I could probably get the word out for you. I just don't wanna get fucked outta my referral fees."

"Put yourself at your ease. I assure you that won't happen. As I said, I'd only be hurting myself."

"You're sure I'm completely outta the woods with the cops? I don't gotta worry about bein' hassled in the future?"

"Absolutely. You have my word, Danny. Mr. Henry has generously agreed to pinch hit for you in that matter. You will hear nothing more about it. All you need concern yourself with is how much money you're going to make just by making your friends aware of the government program I just told you about that wipes out all of their bothersome debts, so they can stop living in the shadows. Even if they don't want or need the program, they still get a free trip to Las Vegas."

"When ya gonna pay me my $500?" Lightfoot challenged.

"This very moment. I have it with me." Smoot reached into his inside pocket and produced a white envelope, which he extended to the other man. "Five, crisp one-hundred dollars bills, Danny.   And that's just the beginning...the sky's the limit."

Lightfoot grabbed the envelope from Smoot's hand. "Drive me over to the Town Lake," he ordered. "Most of the dickheads out there owe child support and alimony through the ass. I'll start with them."

Smoot smiled and stood.   "I was confident I could count on you, Danny."

FOURTEEN

In February 1933, vivacious 30-year-old Jessie Costello ostensibly discovered the lifeless body of her stodgy, dyspeptic husband, William, crumpled on the bathroom floor of the couple's Salem, Massachusetts, home when she went to retrieve her purse in order to buy some fudge. The subsequent autopsy revealed that the unfortunate Mr. Costello died from cyanide poisoning, which led to the prompt arrest of the curvaceous Mrs. Costello. The grieving widow's trial, which one British wag characterized as, "the most astonishing crime-farce in living memory," took place in the summer of that year.

The evidence against Mrs. Costello was damning and overwhelming: she collected her late husband's life insurance before his body had even grown cold; testimony from friends that Mr. Costello had been the veritable picture of health immediately prior to his death; a local pharmacist's testimony that he'd sold Jessie cyanide capsules identical to those found in her late husband's stomach after specifically warning her of its toxicity; a married lover's breathless recitation of the prurient details of his affair with the faithless Mrs. Costello. Despite the accumulation of evidence against her and a death sentence staring her in the face, the beautiful defendant projected an air of utter serenity throughout the proceedings. And not without reason.

Crowds cheered when Mrs. Costello arrived at court every day in a limousine. The all-male jury was mesmerized by the "glamorous siren," who freely conversed with jurors during breaks, one of whom asked if he could send her a box of chocolates as a token of his esteem. Four jurors organized an impromptu barbershop quartet and serenaded Mrs. Costello with renditions of "My Wild Irish Rose" and "Sweet Adelaide" during breaks in the proceedings, during which time she read through the stack of 500 love letters she received each day. Even the court bailiff was not immune to her charms and regularly sent the defendant flowers. In the words of a journalist who covered the sensational trial, the jurors were "as helpless as twelve rabbits under the influence of those glittering ophidian eyes."

To the surprise of no one, the "buxom prima donna" was acquitted.

There is no new thing under the sun.

Alas, Jessie Costello's day in the sun was fleeting. She quickly disappeared from the headlines and she and her four children were eventually evicted from their home. After an additional series of reversals, the family relocated to New Hampshire, where they survived on welfare and a small pension provided to widows of war veterans. The Cyanide Widow died in 1971.

Although William Costello's death is among the most celebrated examples, sodium cyanide has long been utilized as a reliable poison. In Britain in 1781,

John Donellan was hanged for the murder of his brother-in-law, Sir Theodosius Boughton, through the ironic expedient of cyanide-laced medicine. More recently, in 2012 disgraced financier Michael Marin committed suicide in open court by ingesting a lethal dose of cyanide immediately after a verdict of arson was entered against him.

There is no new thing under the sun.

Sodium cyanide is among the most rapidly acting of all known poisons. Its appeal is further enhanced because of its absolute lethality and the convenient fact that it readily dissolves in liquid and is colorless. Tasteless and odorless when dry, cyanide sometimes emits a faint almond-like odor when mixed with water, though many people cannot detect it.

An ounce of cyanide is sufficient to cause instantaneous death in a healthy adult. Even in much smaller doses, symptoms of cyanide poisoning typically manifest themselves within thirty seconds of ingestion, with death occurring within one minute to two hours. Classic symptoms include headache, nausea, vomiting, difficulty breathing, and confusion, followed by gasping respiration, seizures and, ultimately, coma. Total cardiovascular collapse is inevitable. Cyanide targets critical enzymes in the body to prevent respiration at the cellular level, resulting in metabolic asphyxiation. Organs like the brain and heart, which are acutely sensitive to oxygen deprivation, are subject to immediate collapse. Not for nothing was cyanide the poison-of-choice for suicide pills utilized by the Nazi regime, several of whose luminaries availed themselves of its astonishing toxicity.

Notwithstanding its appalling deadliness, sodium cyanide is currently utilized in the mining, jewelry, and computer industries. Available for purchase over the Internet, it is routinely shipped directly to consumers as pellets or briquettes, though cyanide sold in bulk ordinarily comes in the form of large nuggets or "cyanide eggs."

***

It was in the sweltering late afternoon, when the shadows were already starting to lengthen, that a rusted-out Dodge Coronet of indeterminate color pulled up to Henry's trailer. Max swung open a massive passenger door and began to climb out even before the vehicle came to a complete stop. Notwithstanding that it had been switched off, the Coronet's engine continued to rattle and shudder until, with a final belch of blue smoke, it grudgingly stopped running.

"Howdy," Max greeted Henry, who stood in the trailer's open doorway.

"Hey," Henry reciprocated.

The fat driver strolled around the rear of the Coronet. Appreciably younger than the other two men, he was clad in swimming trunks and mismatched rubber flip-flops; his hairy stomach sagged beneath a Che Guevara tee shirt that was at least two sizes too small. A scuffed derby perched incongruously atop his massive head and he sported a pair of women's cat's-eye sunglasses.

"You the guy that needs a ride?" he abruptly demanded.

"You Leon?" Henry asked.

Leon gallantly tipped his derby. "In the flesh."

"My friend needs to pick something up," Max volunteered.

Leon redirected his attention from Henry to Max. "Where'bouts? I charge by the mile, plus gas."

"About five miles," Henry interjected from the doorway.

Leon turned back to Henry. "That'll be $50, plus gas," he said.

"How much extra is gas?"

$50," Leon responded, as if it were the most obvious thing in the world.

"$100, total?"

"I don't know where you went to school but, where I went, fifty plus fifty equals one hundred. Payment in advance, no refunds."

Henry pointed to the Coronet. "$100 is pretty rich and your ride doesn't seem to be very dependable. How do I know it'll get me there and back?"

"You don't," Leon sneered. "You pays your money and you takes your chances. If you're too cheap to pay the freight, it's all the same to me."

"I think I'll pass," Henry said. "Thanks, anyway."

"Don't matter to me," Leon shrugged. "There's plenty of other flakes willin' to pay to get where they wanna go." He slopped back to the open driver's door and fell heavily onto the Coronet's stained bench seat. He slammed the door shut, causing dust to cascade from the fabric headliner. "You comin'?" he called to Max through the open passenger's window.

"Naw, I'll hang here for a while."

Leon wordlessly inserted the key into the vehicle's ignition switch and rotated it. The Coronet's solenoid clicked, then silence.

"Mother fuck!" Leon spat. He turned the key again. Unmitigated silence. "Mother fuck!"

Leon flung open the driver's door and heaved himself out of the car.

"Hey, either of you gotta cell phone?"

The other two men shook their heads simultaneously.

"Sounds like you may just have a lose connection," Henry suggested.

"What-the-fuck-ever," Leon sourly retorted as he glared at the inert Coronet.

"If that's all it is, there's some tools in the trailer I can use to fix it," Henry offered.

Leon brightened. "No kiddin'? That would be bitchin'! Thanks, Dude!"

"No problem. You'll just have to pay for my time, plus the use of the tools," Henry said.

"You gotta fuckin' be kiddin' me!" Leon yawped.

Max started laughing.

"How much you gonna gouge me?" Leon bemoaned.

"$50 for my time, plus $50 for the use of the tools."

"Fuck that. I'll just fix it myself," Leon spat.

"Be kinda hard without tools," Max noted. "But suit yourself. A man's gotta do what a man's gotta do." He began to climb the steps to Henry's trailer.

"Hang on!" Leon yelped. "If you can get it goin', I'll drive you to pick up your shit for free."

Max halted mid-way. "I reckon that's fair. What do you think?"

Henry adopted an exaggeratedly thoughtful expression. "Yeah, I suppose I could do that. Hang on and I'll get the tools." He ducked inside the trailer.

Max returned to the Coronet.

"You bastards got me by the balls," Leon grumbled.

"What goes around, comes around," Max observed.

Henry emerged from inside the trailer holding a canvas tool bag and descended to the ground.

"Pop the hood," he ordered Leon.

"There's nuthin' to pop," Leon responded. "Just stick your fingers through the damned grille and jack around with that little fuckin' lever."

Henry placed the canvas tool bag on the ground and began groping for the release lever. The metal grille burned his hands so he moved rapidly. Finally locating the lever, he pushed it downward, releasing the latch that secured the Coronet's hood. He swung the hood upward, locking it into place. Leon and Max both crowded around him and peered into the engine compartment. Wrapping a rag around his hand to protect it from the hot engine, Henry wiggled the terminals on the vehicle's battery. The clamp attached to the positive terminal twisted in his hand.

"There's your problem...loose cable."

Henry bent and lifted the canvas tool bag onto the car's protuberant bumper. Rummaging through it, he removed an open-end wrench and tightened the loose clamp.

"Now try it," he directed Leon.

Leon slid into the Coronet and twisted the key. The engine roared to life. Henry slammed the hood and stepped away.

"That's it?" Leon groused from the driver's seat as he raced the engine. "I coulda done that fuckin' much."

"Yeah, but you didn't and a deal's a deal," Max reminded him. He turned to Henry. "Let's blow!"

With Henry occupying the front seat next to Leon and Max in the back, they rolled from the trailer park onto Van Buren Street.

"Where the fuck are we goin'?" Leon muttered.

"Storage place on Seventh Street and Thomas," Henry told him.

"I gotta put the kids in the pool," Leon announced as they drove. "Keep an eye out for a gas station or something."

"There's a chicken place," Max slid to the edge of the back seat and pointed through the windshield to a fast food restaurant up the block. "I can get a soda, too."

Leon slowed as they approached the building. He cranked the Coronet into the restaurant's parking lot.

"You may want to keep it running, just in case," Henry cautioned as Leon shoved the transmission lever into 'P'.

"Fuck you, Mr. Mechanic," Leon retorted. "I'm gonna get my $100 worth, so if it takes another shit you're gonna fix it." He defiantly switched the engine off and exited the car. Max piled out the back door.

"You want anything?" he called to Henry as he trailed Leon to the entrance.

"I'm coming in," Henry responded as he swung open the passenger door. "Too damned hot to wait out here."

***

Admittedly, Smoot wasn't entirely optimistic about the ultimate efficacy of his agent's recruitment campaign. But he had to start somewhere if he entertained any hope of satisfying the insatiable global demand for product. There were simply not enough bodies coming into the funeral home. Smoot was frustrated by increasing competition from India, China, the Philippines, and Malaysia. He'd even heard through the grapevine that the Chinese had recently established actual "organ farms," where donors were raised from infancy for the specific purpose of harvesting their tissue.

Other enterprising governments around the world would undoubtedly follow the Chinese model. Smoot had to do *something* to avoid being entirely swept away by the tide of human remains flooding the marketplace.

His first step toward combatting his competitors' ruthless aggression was to purchase a used motor home from a dealer located not far from the funeral home. Smoot instructed Danny to remove most of the vehicle's interior accoutrements, which he subsequently sold on eBay. Lightfoot also installed a makeshift wall with a communicating door, dividing the RV's main cabin into two separate compartments. The larger compartment contained a cheap couch along each exterior bulkhead, a small table, a cramped desk and chair, some cabinets, a sink, and a compact refrigerator-freezer. The other compartment was bare to the walls.

Once the calls started coming in as a result of Lightfoot's recruiting efforts, Smoot planned to drive the RV out somewhere into the surrounding desert in order to rendezvous with potential donors. Afterward, they could conveniently be transported back to the funeral home.

Smoot parked the RV behind the mortuary, next to his Lexus. All he could do now is wait for the phone to start ringing.

***

"Hey, man," Lightfoot called to the stranger with a peculiar melon-shaped head.

The shirtless man's greying beard was stiff with dirt and food detritus.

"Huh? Do I know you?"

"Don't think so, but you're gonna want to."

"That so? You look like a douche who likes takin' it up the ass," the guy opined.

"Well, this douche knows somebody who's givin' money away, if you're interested."

"Fuck you," the other man scoffed. "You don't know shit."

Lightfoot shrugged. "Okay, if you say so. No skin off me. I just figured you might could use a little juice."

"Ever'body can use bread," the guy responded, his interest slightly piqued. "Got any weed?" He tentatively drew nearer.

"This must be your lucky day, my man, because I just happen to have a joint with your name on it," Lightfoot said.   He produced a squashed marijuana cigarette, only marginally thicker than a broom straw, and offered to the other man.   He examined it with suspicion.

"What the fuck is this?" the guy finally asked.

"I thought you wanted some pot."

"Yeah, I did," the man grumbled.   "Be lucky to get one hit off this fuckin' twig."   He carefully stuck the attenuated joint between his scabby lips.   "Light me."

"Well, you get what you pay for," Lightfoot remarked as he held the flame of his lighter to the joint, close to the man's grimy face.   "Speakin' of which, if ya wanna quit bummin' shit and buy as much as ya want, I know a guy."

"Big deal," the guy responded.   "Ever'body 'knows a guy.'   You can buy weed anywhere 'cause it's legal now."

"Not without juice you can't," Lightfoot corrected him.   "The guy I'm talkin' about's givin' it away."

The thin marijuana reed disintegrated after three puffs.

"Fuck!" the man groused as he scrutinized with dismay the crumbling fragments clinging to his fingertips.   He looked at Lightfoot.   "What's his deal?"

Lightfoot smiled reassuringly.   "All ya gotta do is talk to him.   If you like what he says, he'll pay you. Even if you don't, he'll still give you a free trip to Vegas."

"Bullshit.   Nobody's givin' free money away, dumbass."

"Got any kids?"

The other man shrugged. "I guess. Who the hell knows. What's it to you?"

"My buddy's with the government and there's a new program where you don't have to pay child support anymore. Interested?"

"Fuck that. I don't pay child support, anyway," the man said with apathy.

"Maybe not," Lightfoot replied. "But if the cops get a hair up their ass and arrest you for non-payment, they'll throw your butt in jail 'til doomsday."

"Fuck 'em. At least in jail I'll get a decent meal and a shower."

"Okay, dude. Sorry I wasted your time. I didn't realize that you got plenty of bread. I guess I'll go talk to somebody who'd like some free money." Lightfoot turned to leave.

The other man extended a scaly hand to stay his departure. "Hang on, man. Why's this guy givin' shit away?"

"I dunno, you have to ask him," Lightfoot responded. "All I know is that it ain't his money. It's the government's, and if they don't give it to you they'll end up givin' it to some illegal Mexican. Why do you care? I'm just tryin' to do to you a solid. Either way, you'll either get some free government dough or a trip to Vegas."

The homeless man brooded a few moments before continuing to probe.

"So, what do I have to do?" he asked.

"Call him." Lightfoot shoved a scrap of paper at the guy. A telephone number was scrawled on it. "He'll tell ya where you can pick up your money."

The other man took the paper and glanced at it before cramming it into the pocket of his ragged shorts. "That's it? All I gotta do is call the dude?"

"Well you gotta actually *meet* him so you can pick up your dough. And you gotta tell him that 'Danny' sent you. If you don't tell him that Danny sent you he can't give you any money; it's the law because the government keeps track. Otherwise, that's all ya gotta do...easy as breathin'. Like I told you, it ain't his money so he couldn't care less who he gives it to, one way or the other. The government just makes him give it away. If you know somebody else that needs some cash you might wanna tell them, too. Just give 'em that number and make sure that they tell him that Danny told 'em about it. They can get rid of student loans and shit, too."

"Who the fuck's 'Danny'?"

"Beats the shit outta me," Lightfoot said. "I think it's a government abbreviation, or code, or something. All I know is that you gotta use it before he'll pay you, so it must be pretty important."

The other man narrowed his eyes. "What's in it for you? How come *you* didn't get any free money?"

"I did!" Lightfoot exclaimed. "How do you think I know about it? I just figured I'd pass it along before all the dough runs out."

"How much money the guy give you?" the man pressed.

"$500," Lightfoot informed him.

"And you didn't have to do shit?"

"Nope. Just showed up and got paid. Like I said, easier than breathin'."

"How'd you find out about this guy?"

"Somebody told me, just like I'm tellin' you. Like I said, if you don't want the money, he'll be happy to give it to a Mexican...he don't give a damn who gets it. I just figured it might as well be you."

"Got that fuckin' right," the man declared. "'Bout time the fuckin' government started treatin' us like white people. If you ain't a scratchback who don't speak English, they treat you like shit!"

"That's what I'm sayin'," Lightfoot empathized. He pointed to the guy's pocket. "Just call that number and talk to the guy before all the money's gone. If you don't want it, that's cool, too. I'm just tryin' to do you a favor and maybe you know somebody who'd like some extra dough. Like I told you, I already got my share."

"Fuck, yeah!" the guy exclaimed. "I know lotsa people who could use some coin. You think there's enough for them, too?"

"Couldn't say. Probably a good idea to round up ever'body you know and tell 'em to get while the gettin's good," Lightfoot urged.   "I'm just glad somebody told me and I got my dough before all the Mexes. Just don't forget that all your buddies gotta say that 'Danny' told 'em about the free money. Otherwise, they won't get squat."

"No, man, don't worry about it. I'll make sure that everybody says the magic word," said the man excitedly. "Thanks for the heads up. I'm sorry for bein' such a dick at first...ever'body's always tryin' to fuck ever'body over around here." He extended his hand.

"That's cool, my brother," Lightfoot responded as the two men shook hands. "One hand washes the other."

"Got that right," the other man concurred with a toothless smile.

***

From research on the Internet, he knew that a mere ounce of cyanide would prove lethal to an adult. Still, Smoot had to experiment in order to get the mixture precisely right; he could afford no miscalculations. He started incrementally, using dogs of various sizes adopted from local shelters.

Wearing a respirator and gloves, he carefully placed one of the cyanide eggs in a heavy sack and, using a hammer, crushed it into a coarse powder. Smoot kept painstaking record of the dosages he administered to the dogs, including the animal's breed, approximate age and weight, and the exact duration of time between ingestion, the onset of symptoms, and death. It was a simple matter to mix the powder into the animals' food and, because it is flavorless, the famished dogs bolted it down without hesitation. Smoot also dissolved the powdered cyanide into the animals' water in order to ascertain whether drinking, rather than eating, the toxin culminated in more rapid death.

Smoot's meticulous logs revealed that dissolving sodium cyanide in drinking water proved appreciably more efficacious than mixing it into food. Large dogs often exhibited no evidence whatsoever for as long as three-quarters of an hour after eating cyanide-laced food. Only then would the characteristic symptoms rapidly begin to manifest themselves: labored breathing, unsteadiness, extreme salivation, coma. By contrast, it was not uncommon for even large breeds to collapse mid-drink when the toxin was dissolved into their drinking water. Irrespective of the method of administration, however, Smoot noted that smaller breeds succumbed with gratifying rapidity.

The challenge was to create a dosage sufficiently potent to produce rapid expiration, though not so robust as to be capable of being tasted or detected. In addition, it was absolutely essential that the entire amount remain inside the body until death actually occurred and not be inconveniently expelled, for example, through vomiting. It was a ticklish business, particularly since Smoot was necessarily forced to extrapolate his results with dogs to the hypothetical ingestion of cyanide by exponentially larger human beings.

Because he had no choice, Smoot persevered.

***

Gwen Harp returned Detective Ortiz's call two days after listening to his banal message on her office telephone. She'd heard nothing from, or about, Henry for several days and was forced to conclude that he was lying low somewhere.

Lyman Henry had still not turned up, having seemingly vanished from the face of the earth. But Ortiz knew that, as a former cop, Henry undoubtedly knew how to disappear for a while. He'd turn up, sooner or later. Until that happened, Ortiz wanted a sit-down with Danny Lightfoot's former PD in the hope of figuring out what relationship, if any, existed between Henry and her former client. Besides, Ortiz was meticulous. Freddie Smoot was dead and buried, so the detective had plenty of time to conduct an unhurried investigation of his murder.

Because the weapon used to kill Freddie Smoot, bearing Henry's fingerprints, was found at Henry's apartment, it was evident that Lightfoot wasn't the murderer. Even if Lightfoot was ignorant of the serendipitous discovery of the pistol, he obviously knew he didn't kill Freddie. So why did he steadfastly maintain the charade that he'd done so? And why was Henry careless, or stupid, enough to hang onto the murder weapon before placing it where it could readily be found? *No* cop would be that sloppy. And the presence of the pistol notwithstanding, why would Henry kill Freddie then, months later, approach Williams Smoot with some asinine story completely out of the blue, and demand money? There were clearly aspects of Freddie Smoot's death that failed to make sense. Ortiz hoped that Gwen Harp might be able to provide some insight, given that she presumably knew Lightfoot about as well as anyone. The detective recalled meeting Harp tangentially on a couple of cases over the years but had formed no opinion of her. Just another law hustler, he thought, when her call came in.

"Hi. This is Detective Bob Ortiz," he announced into the receiver.

"Detective Ortiz? This is Gwen Harp from the Public Defender's Office."

"Thank you for returning my call, Ms. Harp. I'm calling about your former client, Daniel Lightfoot."

"I see. What about him, Detective? You must know that Danny was released from custody and is no longer my client."

"I'm aware of that. I wanted to talk to you, among other things, about the new suspect in the Freddie Smoot case, Lyman Henry."

There was a delay at the other end.

"I don't represent Mr. Henry," Gwen finally responded.

"I realize that. I was simply hoping that you might be able to provide some information."

"I doubt it," she replied, too abruptly. "Is Mr. Henry in custody yet?"

"No, not yet, but we're confident he soon will be." Ortiz paused. "Do you know whether Mr. Lightfoot knew Mr. Henry?"

She reflected before answering.

"Mr. Henry interviewed my client while he was incarcerated," she finally said, carefully parsing her words.

"Oh? How do you know that?" he probed.

"Because I was present."

"Wait. You were there when Lyman Henry talked to Danny Lightfoot in jail?"

"Yes, detective, I was. I authorized the interview."

"Without asking you to betray any client confidences, Ms. Harp, why did Henry want to talk to your client?"

Gwen chuckled. "Don't worry, detective. I have no intention of betraying any client confidences. But isn't that information already in your file?"

"Honestly, the case file has almost nothing in it," Ortiz ruefully admitted.   "Because your client immediately confessed to Freddie Smoot's murder, wrongly as it turns out, it wasn't necessary to devote much time to investigating the case. And the detective originally assigned to it has since transferred. So, I'm kinda starting with a blank slate here.   Any information you could provide would be much appreciated." The detective paused. "It's unfortunate that your guy got caught up in everything but, of course, it was basically his doing...Mr. Lightfoot confessed to a murder that he didn't commit."

"So it would seem," Gwen concurred. "What, specifically, would you like to know, detective?"

"Like I said, do you know why Lyman Henry wanted to talk to your client?"

"The victim's father, Williams Smoot, was convinced, for his own reasons, that Danny Lightfoot didn't kill Freddie. He hired Mr. Henry to find out who did. I agreed to allow Mr. Henry to interview my client because I felt his efforts on behalf of Williams Smoot might ultimately redound to the benefit of my client."

Unconsciously, Ortiz grasped the telephone receiver more tightly. "Wait, wait...you're telling me that Freddie Smoot's dad *hired* Lyman Henry?"

"Yes, that's what I'm telling you, detective. You're aware that Mr. Henry is retired police officer and private detective, yes?"

Ortiz flipped through the slender file while he listened. He finally found the information he was looking for, which he skimmed.

"According to Williams Smoot, Lyman Henry attempted to extort money from him. When that failed, Henry just *stole* the money from Smoot's office," he summarized for her. "It was that theft that led to the discovery of the murder weapon at Henry's apartment."

"Yeah, so I heard. But that's complete nonsense. Smoot, himself, hired Lyman Henry to exonerate Danny Lightfoot."

Ortiz was puzzled. "So, Williams Smoot hired the guy who killed his kid to find the guy who killed his kid...the guy was lookin' for himself. That's what you're saying? It sounds like the plot from an old film noir."

The detective knew that it was relatively common for child-abductors, for example, to be among the first to volunteer in neighborhood searches for a missing child. In so doing, the perps hope to deflect suspicion away from themselves, though their disproportionate enthusiasm inevitably betrays them. If what the public defender was saying about Lyman Henry was true, though, Henry *didn't* volunteer to find Freddie Smoot's killer. Rather, Freddie's own father specifically hired Henry for that purpose.

"Call it what you like," Gwen said. "But I don't believe that Lyman Henry killed Freddie Smoot."

"I thought you didn't represent Henry," the detective countered.

"I don't. I'm just expressing my opinion based on my knowledge of the case."

"Okay, I'll play along," said Ortiz. "If Danny Lightfoot didn't kill Freddie and, despite the fact that the murder weapon was found at Henry's apartment with his fingerprints all over it, you don't think that

Henry did, either, who did? Mind you, counselor, this is just you and me kickin' ideas around off the record."

"Can't help you there, detective. That's above my pay grade."

"Your job is just to get the perps off the hook after I arrest 'em, huh?" he glibly retorted.

"No, detective, my job, to the extent humanly possible, is to ensure that justice is done in the cases assigned to me. By the way, what's *your* job?"

"Ouch!," Ortiz winced. "I guess that sorta came out wrong, huh?"

"Yeah, I think it did," Gwen laughed. "Call me naïve, but I like to think that we're both on the same side."

"No, we are. I didn't mean to come across as a hard-ass."

She laughed again. "You're fine, detective. I didn't take it personally. Is there anything else I can help you with today?"

"Your former client works, or at least worked, for the funeral home owed by the victim's father. Do you know where he actually lives? On site?"

"No, I don't know where Danny Lightfoot lives. Besides, how is that relevant? He's no longer a suspect."

"Agreed. But, honestly, I'm finding this case to be something of a head-scratcher...too many things don't add up. I'd just like to talk to Lightfoot to see whether he might be able to shed some light on it."

Gwen clucked her tongue. "Even if I knew where to find Danny, I don't think you'd find him very cooperative when it comes to talking to the police, detective."

"Maybe, but I've gotta start somewhere."

Gwen smiled to herself. "Let me give you some advice that Danny recently gave me."

"What's that?"

"Ask Williams Smoot."

FIFTEEN

Max continued to ferry both provisions and intelligence to the trailer park. As he'd predicted, it took little time for the cops to descend on the Town Lake in search of Lyman Henry. Aside from the customary, perfunctory reward offered by the police department for information relating to Henry, Max learned that a significantly larger reward had also been floated by an unidentified private individual.

"Do you think anybody knows where I am?" Henry inquired. He was having a difficult time adjusting to Marlboros and asked Max to return next time with a carton of Kools.

"Nobody besides me," Max replied. "If they did, you'd already be in jail. But it don't look to me like nobody's exactly bustin' the door down lookin' for you, neither."

"What about Leon?"

Max scoffed. "Leon ain't got the brains God gave a pissant, and what brains he has is so fried from dope that he can't remember from one day to the next."

"What if they increase the reward?" Henry uneasily asked.

Max took a drag of Marlboro. "Who? The cops or the other one?"

"Either. Both. Speakin' of the 'other one', any idea who offered it?"

"Nope," Max said. "But *somebody* must wanna to know where you are pretty bad."

"How bad is 'pretty bad'?"

"$5,000 bad," Max grinned. "I'd be tempted to turn you in myself if you wasn't already into me so deep!" He ground his cigarette out in an old tuna can. "But it gets better. There's also shit goin' around that the government's handin' out cash and paying ever'bodys' bills and such...you know, like an Obama phone. Between the government handout and the two rewards on your head, I could make off with a pretty good chunka change!"

Henry frowned. "What are you talking about, 'the government handout'? Welfare?"

"No, it ain't welfare. Hell, everybody's already either on welfare or disability. It's supposed to be somethin' new that just started."

"You heard about it down at the Town Lake?"

Max shrugged. "Not just there. Somebody named 'Danny' has been puttin' the word out ever'where. Hell, I even heard some people already got their free money. Like I said, I'm even thinking' about gettin' *me* some. Danny must work for the government or somethin'...there's always a bunch bureaucrats and Bible thumpers out tryin' to save all the bums."

Henry was genuinely startled. "'Danny'? You mean Danny *Lightfoot*? Is that who you're talking about?"

"Lightfoot? Never thought of that asshole," Max noted as he stuck another Marlboro between his lips without lighting it, "but it couldn't be him. Lightfoot don't work for the government and I *know* he ain't a Bible thumper. Besides, I ain't seen Lightfoot for a while."

Henry smiled wryly. "The guy you heard about doesn't work for the government, either. The whole thing's a scam and, whoever he is, 'Danny' is hustling for somebody."

"What are you sayin'? The government ain't really givin' money away?"

"Sorry to break it to you, Max."

The other man looked completely disgusted. "Son of a bitch! I s'pose the next thing you're gonna tell me is that there's no Easter Bunny, neither." He leaned his head back and appeared to doze. "Well, if the government ain't givin' money away, who's Danny and what's his angle? Who's he workin' for?" he asked without opening his eyes.

"He's gotta be lining his pockets," Henry speculated. "Somebody's obviously paying him."

Max slowly bobbed his head up and down without lifting it from the back of the couch, the unlit cigarette still protruding from his lips.

"For what? For telling people that the government is givin' shit away when it ain't? Who'd pay him to do that?"

"That, my friend, is the $64,000 question. Do you think you could do something for me?"

Max raised his head and looked aslant at Henry. "Like what? Whatever it is, it's gonna cost you."

"Yeah," I kinda figured that," Henry chuckled. "Try to find out who 'Danny' is without his knowing that you're asking around about him. Also, get as much information as you can about the free-money thing: how you go about applying, who's behind it, whatever."

"I can do that," Max said. "But how's any of that gonna help you? You can't stay hunkered down in this trailer forever, you know. Sooner or later, the cops are gonna sniff you out and, when that happens, there's not a damned thing me, or anybody else, can do about it."

Henry nodded at the truth of Max's statement. "Well, I'm thinking that 'Danny' is Danny Lightfoot and that the guy who put the reward out on me is the same guy who's paying Lightfoot to tell people about the free government money, Williams Smoot. And, as it happens, Smoot's the guy who set me up for his kid's murder." He focused his gaze directly on the other man. "The long and short of it is that I think Williams Smoot is behind everything."

"'Everything' *what*?" Max pointedly responded. "Why's Smoot got a hard-on for you?"

"Smoot and Lightfoot conspired to kill Smoot's kid, Freddie, and they're trying to hang it on me. But the bottom line is what you told me the first time we met: they're trafficking in human body parts. That's what's at the bottom of everything, Max. If I can just get enough information to put all the pieces together, I'll be outta the woods." He looked around. "And this shitty trailer."

The other man finally lit his cigarette and took a long drag before responding. "Okay, I'll see what I can turn up. Just keep on keeping' on until I get back to you." He exhaled a cloud of smoke. "And don't blow through all your damned money, 'cause you're gonna owe me big time before all this is said and done."

Henry spread his hands in a helpless gesture. "Tell me something I *don't* know."

***

He stretched the blue plastic tarps that Smoot purchased from Harbor Freight around the lighted portico at the rear of the funeral home, more-or-less shielding his work area from the gaze of passersby. Within the tenuous walls of this makeshift enclosure Lightfoot wheeled an industrial fan, which he plugged into the gang plug on the end of an extension cord he ran from the main building. His power tools were plugged into the remaining slots on the gang plug. He also placed a large stainless-steel table, purchased from a restaurant supply company, inside before uncoiling a garden hose attached to a spigot on the exterior of the funeral home.

In the mortuary's embalming room, Smoot had demonstrated the manner in which all bodies *had* to be sectioned. Shortcuts or sloppiness would not be tolerated; clients would categorically reject product that was not precisely dissected and attractively displayed, thereby providing BioServus's eager competitors opportunity to capitalize on Smoot's missteps.

Notwithstanding Smoot's incessant carping and hand-wringing, however, Lightfoot quickly determined the process wasn't that difficult. It was basically quartering a chicken. The hardest part was wrestling the bodies from the wheeled gurney onto the stainless-steel dissecting table. Even working at night with the industrial fan blowing on him, he really worked up a sweat. Lugging the dismembered parts around afterward was no walk in the park, either.

After scrutinizing Lightfoot's initial handiwork, Smoot grunted begrudging approval, though he was displeased the former's recruitment efforts had so-far failed to produce any results. Despite increasing demand for product, Smoot remained entirely dependent on bodies that came through the funeral home. Things had to change, quickly, if he entertained any hope of staying competitive.

On the cement patio behind Lightfoot three human ribcages formed a haphazard stack. He'd just finished rinsing them with water from the garden hose. According to Smoot, the ribcages were destined for some medical school in Macedonia.

Lightfoot had to get them on dry ice, ready for shipping, before they began to decompose. That week alone, BioServus had already shipped two dozen feet to Florida, a baker's dozen of hearts to Minnesota, and two pounds of blonde human hair to India. Lightfoot assumed the hair would be used to make wigs. Four human heads reposed in the freezer across town until Lightfoot could find time to box them up for shipment to Brazil. The funeral home's cremation oven rendered it a simple matter to eliminate the valueless offal resulting from his dissections. But he was already busier than a one-armed paper hanger with the crabs...how the hell did Smoot expect him to keep up once his recruitment efforts began to bear fruit?

Smoot was sure-as-hell gonna have to pony up additional simoleons if he expected him to stick around in the future. Lightfoot also intended to talk Smoot out of one of those fancy infant's coffins on display in the funeral home. He wanted to rip the lining out and convert it into a cool ice chest.

"How many people have you spoken to about what we talked about, Danny?" Smoot had demanded earlier.

"Fuck, I don't know," he'd testily responded. "I don't count 'em. I just tell 'em what you told me to say and they go on their merry way. What am I supposed to do? Hogtie 'em and drag 'em in here? Besides, like you said, Rome wasn't built in a day. Stop actin' like somebody shoved a dick up your ass and broke it off."

"I'm not sure you understand the gravity of the situation," Smoot snorted.

"You don't pay me to 'understand the gravity of the situation,' whatever the fuck that means," Lightfoot derided him. "You pay me to cut bodies into pieces. If that ain't good enough, I'll hit the bricks and you can do it yourself."

Smoot immediately became more conciliatory. "Now, now, Danny," he prattled, "there's no need to become defensive. I only meant that it's important to increase volume in order to keep pace with demand." He slid his wallet from an interior pocket of his pink suit jacket and peered at its contents.

"Why don't you take the rest of the day off and have dinner?" He extended his pudgy hand, holding a $100 bill. "If you'd like a little break, I have some jewelry for you to dispose of, too."

Lightfoot snatched the money and stuffed it into the pocket of his shorts.

"Yeah, I think I may do that. I'll come back later for the jewelry." He turned and stalked away from the funeral director.

The day following their squabble, Lightfoot retrieved a modest collection of jewelry from the funeral home and rode the bus south on Central Avenue to Paganyee's convenience store. The clerk was watching another earsplitting Bollywood movie on his portable television behind the counter when Lightfoot flung open the glass entry door.

"Hey, dude!" Lightfoot greeted him with forced gusto. He placed the cache of jewelry on the counter. Paganyee observed his arrival without enthusiasm before reducing the volume on the television and slowly getting to his sandaled feet.

"I have not seen you for a long time," the clerk flatly remarked as he walked parallel to the counter toward Lightfoot.

Lightfoot unceremoniously dumped the contents of his sack onto the countertop, scattering them.

"Yeah, I was outta the loop for a while but I'm back in the saddle now. You still buyin'?" He gestured toward the collection of baubles spread before them.

Paganyee began to pick through them. "One of your friends was here," he said idly.

"What are you talkin' about?"

The clerk looked up. "Your friend was here."

"I didn't send any of my friends here," Lightfoot responded with suspicion. "How do you know he was my friend?"

Paganyee separated a few pieces with a fingertip before pushing the bulk of the merchandise away.

"He said he was your friend. Beyond that, I do not know." He pointed to the small pile of jewelry in front of him. "I will take these. Twenty dollars."

"Twenty!" Lightfoot cried. "That shit's worth at least a hundred!"

"Twenty, no more." Paganyee looked at him through heavy-lidded eyes. He seemed bored.

"Well, fuck-a-duck! But I guess twenty beats a poke in the eye with a sharp stick. You sure you ain't a Jew instead of a Paki?"

"I am from India, not Pakistan," Paganyee patiently informed him, sweeping his purchase into a cardboard box held at counter level. He pulled a folded twenty-dollar bill from the pocket of his crumpled trousers and handed it to Lightfoot, who seized it with alacrity.

"Yeah, well, close enough. Was it a man or a woman?"

The other man looked confused. "Who?"

"Whoever came in and said they were my friend."

"A man."

"Did he tell you his name?"

Paganyee shook his head, clearly anxious to return to Bollywood.

"What'd he look like?"

"I cannot tell you. He looked like everyone and no one," the clerk informed him. "There was nothing special about him. I am sorry I cannot help you."

"When did he come in?"

"A week, perhaps. Maybe more. I have not seen him since. Sorry," he repeated, hoping to jettison the bothersome interloper.

"What did he want?"

"He said he was your friend and that he had some things to sell, but he never returned. Nothing more."

Lightfoot scowled. He scooped the unsold jewelry from the countertop and returned it to his sack.

"You let me know if the guy comes back, yeah?"

"Of course," Paganyee assured him, having no intention of doing so.

***

Detective Ortiz got the distinct impression that Williams Smoot was not exactly overjoyed to see him. His first inkling was that he had to leave repeated telephone messages at the funeral home, none of which Smoot returned.

"Mr. Smoot has been very busy with funerals," Eileen clucked.

"Did you tell him that it's very important that I talk to him?"

"Certainly," she snipped. "Mr. Smoot is fully aware of your calls and I'm confident he will return them as soon as he is able. In the funeral business, one doesn't enjoy the luxury of simply dropping everything to take time off," she lectured, intimating that the purpose of Ortiz's calls were merely to invite Smoot to join him in a round of golf.

"I see. In that case, let me simplify it. I'll be at your funeral home this morning at eleven to see Mr. Smoot. Since he apparently has non-stop funerals, he's certain to be there. If he's *not* there at eleven, a warrant will be issued for his arrest. Is that clear enough?"

"Arrest?" she yelped. "Mr. Smoot is hardly a criminal! Why would you possibly arrest Mr. Smoot?"

"Just make sure you give him the message. I'll see you at eleven." Ortiz terminated the call.

***

"I'm very sorry, detective. Things have been so busy around here that I've simply not had opportunity to return your telephone calls. Thank you for taking time out of your busy day to come here."

They were sitting in Smoot's plush office. The stubby funeral director sat at his polished desk, the tidy surface of which was littered with obligatory, framed photos of his wife, children, and grandchildren. He was wearing a dove-grey suit; a neatly folded handkerchief peeked from his breast pocket. Ortiz sat on the adjacent settee.

The detective cocked an eyebrow. "You were too busy to acknowledge any of my telephone calls?"

"I fully intended to return them today," Smoot smiled. "Happily, your fortuitous visit has rendered that unnecessary. How can I be of service to you today, detective?"

"Yeah, I'll bet," Ortiz mulled. "During one of our many chats your assistant told me that your business has been booming. But I didn't see any funerals going on when I arrived."

Smoot's unctuous expression didn't waver. "As it happens, today has been uncharacteristically tranquil. That's why your visit is so opportune."

"That's interesting because I checked the obits in the paper over the past coupla weeks before driving over and, as far as I could tell, Smoot Funeral Chapel had a grand total of four funerals during that period. That doesn't exactly sound like hellzapoppin' around here."

"You must understand, detective," Smoot explained, unperturbed, "that funeral directors are responsible for much more than just funerals. We counsel grieving families, coordinate with other funeral homes regarding the transport and disposition of remains, discuss end-of-life arrangements with individuals and families, prepare bodies for shipment out of state, contact various florists to make arrangements for floral deliveries, make sure the funeral coach is in perfect running order...a multitude of tasks that demand a great deal of time. Actual funerals represent a relatively modest percentage of what funeral directors do." His small, pig-like eyes sparkled behind his bifocals. "And, though I'm flattered by your interest in my occupation, I'm sure you didn't come here today just to talk shop."

"Speakin' of hearses, I didn't see one outside. Where do you park yours?"

"'Hearse' is an obsolete term, detective. We prefer 'funeral coach,'" Smoot officiously corrected him.

"Where's yours?"

"We keep it parked securely in the back. Unfortunately, our funeral coach has been periodically vandalized in the past, particularly around Halloween."

"Yeah, I can see how that could be a problem," Ortiz commiserated. "Wouldn't want your hearse breakin' down en route to the cemetery. Could be kind of embarrassing."

Smoot looked at him acerbically.

"So, who works on yours? Do you take it to a regular garage, or what?"

"We perform most of the routine maintenance on site." Smoot was clearly becoming irritated by the detective's desultory questions. "Commercial garages are often reluctant to work on funeral coaches and, frankly, charge too much."

"You have somebody onsite who works on your hearse?"

"Yes, that's correct. For routine things, anyway. Is that why you wanted to see me today?"

"What's his name?"

"I'm sorry, who's name?"

"The guy who works on your hearse. What's his name?"

For the first time, Smoot appeared flustered.

"I'm afraid I don't know his name," he stammered.

"Wait a minute," Ortiz said. "You just said that, as a funeral director, you're responsible for insuring that your hearse is always in tip-top shape. Yet, you don't know the name of the guy who keeps it that way?"

Smoot attempted to appear blasé.

"I'm sure Ms. Eggleston knows his name. I just can't recall it off the top of my head."

"Don't know it or can't recall it?"

"Can't recall it."

Ortiz frowned. "When Detective Wilfort recently came here in response to your original theft complaint, you told him that most of your employees had worked for you for several years. You even referred to them as 'family.' Yet you can't remember the name of the employee who works on your hearse?"

The funeral director managed to reestablish his poise.

"We sometimes hire temporary help, independent contractors. The person you're referring to may have been one of those. I simply don't recall."

"Danny Lightfoot?"

"Pardon me?" Smoot's eyes narrowed.

"Danny Lightfoot. Is he your gofer?"

"I'm afraid I don't understand," Smoot pretended.

"Does Danny Lightfoot do any work around your funeral home, Mr. Smoot?"

The funeral director mentally weighed his response. "That may be his name. As I said, I don't exactly remember. You'll have to ask Ms. Eggleston. She does the payroll and keeps track of all our independent contractors."

"*'That may be his name*'? You don't remember the name of the man arrested for killing your own son?" snapped an incredulous Ortiz.

"Oh yes, yes, of course," Smoot faltered, his rotund face turning crimson. "I've simply been under terrible stress since Freddie's death and haven't been able to think clearly. You have no idea, detective, what it's been like." Smoot pulled the handkerchief from his pocket and dabbed his perspiring face before stuffing it back without refolding it.

"Will you call Ms. Eggleston in here, please?"

Smoot affected a bland smile. "I'm afraid Ms. Eggleston isn't available at the moment. She stepped out on a personal errand."

"I see," Ortiz slowly nodded. "Well, that's okay. I didn't stop by to talk about Danny Lightfoot, anyway."

Smoot was visibly relieved. His smile broadened in anticipation of the detective's disclosure of the real purpose for his visit.

"How well do you know Lyman Henry?"

"The man who robbed me and murdered my son?" Smoot smoothly responded. "I don't know him at all and told everything I know about him to the first detective...Wilfort?"

"Yeah, I read Wilfort's report," Ortiz said. "But there's been a suggestion that you actually hired Henry to do some investigative work for you. I thought maybe that, since you forgot all about Danny Lightfoot working here, Lyman Henry may also have slipped your mind."

"Slipped my mind? That's absurd!" Smoot snorted. "Why on earth would I hire the man who murdered my son? Where did you hear such twaddle?"

Ortiz spread his hands, palms outward. "I can't remember where I heard it...I guess my memory must be getting as bad as yours! I didn't think there was anything to it and just wanted to confirm it with you, though. There's always all kinds of unsubstantiated gossip floating around the rumor mill."

"I have no idea where you could have heard such nonsense. Have you arrested Mr. Henry yet?" Smoot was dismayed that his $5,000 reward had failed to generate any information about Henry's whereabouts.

"No, but it's just a matter of time." The detective stood. "But I'm glad I can check the report that Henry worked for you off my list."

"Yes, detective, you may. If that's all you have today, I'm afraid I must get back to work now. Thank you again for coming by. I hope I was of some help."

Smoot stepped from behind his desk to escort Ortiz from his office. He extended his fleshy hand with the pinkie ring, which the detective reflexively shook. Although sweaty, the funeral director's skin was cool in Ortiz's hand and felt like clasping a water balloon.

"Good day, detective. Call me should you need anything further." Smoot held the door open and stepped aside to allow Ortiz to wordlessly depart.

Outside, the detective walked behind the funeral home. The entire rear of the property was surrounded by a chain link fence, twelve feet tall with coils of razor wire strung along the top. Opaque aluminum slats were threaded completely through the fence to discourage inquisitiveness. Access to the other side, where the hearse was presumably parked, was provided via an electronic gate.

Ortiz pressed his face close to the fence and attempted to peer between the aluminum slats. All he could see were large, blue tarps swathing the back of the building, frustrating additional scrutiny. He turned and walked back to his car before it got any hotter.

Smoot buzzed Eileen.

"Call Danny right away. Tell him not to come around until he hears from me again. That cop was asking about him."

SIXTEEN

"Somebody named 'Danny' said I should talk to you about my fuckin' child support."

"That's correct, you've come to the right place," Smoot beamed. The motor home was parked on a dirt lot in the purlieus, only recently cleared for the erection of model homes that heralded the creation of a vast new residential community. Because it was Sunday, the site was abandoned. Notwithstanding the fierce temperature outside, the motor home's thrumming air conditioner insured that its interior remained comfortable.

"What's with this place?" the guy asked, gawking around. "You ain't got a regular office?"

"Of course. But as a courtesy to our clients, we also use the motor home so that we may come to them."

"That's cool," the man asserted. "I ain't got a car, so that's a good idea." He perched uncomfortably on the edge of one of the sofas in the front section of the motor home, as though fearful his threadbare clothing might soil the cheap fabric. "But I don't even know if any of my kids is mine," he continued. "The bitch fucked around on me so much that they could be anybody's. But the fuckin' court said they was mine and ordered me to pay child support! I had a good job but, when they started takin' out child support, I couldn't even afford to pay rent! Threw me out, lost my job, been sleepin' on the fuckin' street ever since."

"Well, you're in luck," Smoot assured him. "Your troubles will soon be over." He poured the man a glass of tea from a plastic pitcher that rested on the small table adjacent to the sofa. Ice cubes bobbed in the pitcher as the amber liquid sloshed into the man's glass. The mortician handed the brimming glass to him and gently replaced the pitcher onto the table before resuming his seat on the opposite sofa. Smoot glanced at his watch, taking particular note of the exact position of the ticking second hand. He watched with satisfaction as the man guzzled the tea.

"You think you can help me?" the guy asked after draining his glass.

"I don't know why not," Smoot assured him. "How's the tea?"

"Yeah, it's good. I haven't had any in a while. Thanks."

"Help yourself," Smoot gestured to the pitcher. "I've got plenty." He looked again at his watch.

Twenty-five seconds.

"Feeling okay?"

"Sure, I guess so," the man responded. He reached for the pitcher and proceeded to fill his glass again. Smoot was sure he detected a slight quiver in his hand as he drank. Once he gulped down a second helping of tea, the man slid his empty glass onto the table, next to the pitcher. "I think maybe I drank too fast," he burped. "I feel kinda sick to my stomach."

Forty seconds.

"Why don't you rest until it passes?" Smoot suggested. "We'll resume our conversation when you feel better."

"Yeah, I think I will," the man slurred. He slumped back onto the couch.

Smoot remained motionless, watching the unconscious man's chest surge as he struggled to breathe. After a few minutes, even that ceased.

Smoot stood and bent over the inert form sprawled on the sofa. Because his earlier trials had been confined to animals, he wasn't sure how large a dose to use, nor how a real person would react to cyanide. It was one thing to experiment on dogs, or read about it on the Internet, but quite another to actually administer poison to a human being.

The guy was as dead as Pompey. Smoot knew he had to get him into the motor home's refrigerated second compartment before the onset of rigor mortis. Once the body stiffened, it would prove far more difficult to maneuver. Moreover, four other indigents had scheduled afternoon appointments and would begin to arrive shortly.

Smoot grabbed the dead man's ankles and dragged him from the couch. His insensate head bounced when it struck the motor home's floor. The funeral director laboriously tugged the body toward the communicating door that led to the second compartment. Although not a long-term solution to BioServus's chronic shortage of product, he should be able to stay one jump ahead of his competitors for the time being. That is, if Lightfoot continued to gin up business and didn't completely flake out on him.

***

"Yeah, Danny Lightfoot's the 'Danny' who's been spreading all the hogwash about 'free money'," Max confirmed.

"How'd you find out?" inquired Henry.

"Asked around. Weren't too hard. A buncha people already knew who he is and I just described what Lightfoot looks like to ever'body else. They all said it was him."

Henry reflected a moment. "How many people do you think you talked to?"

Max looked pensive. "Prob'ly twenty, or thereabouts. I just told 'em that I heard somebody was givin' away money and who did I talk to about gettin' some of it? Turned out the deal's even better than I thought: Lightfoot's promisin' ever'body cash *and* a trip to Vegas! How can you beat that?" he grinned.

"Well, somebody's obviously paying him to do it...but why?" Henry ruminated. "Did anybody happen to know whether Williams Smoot is involved?"

Max shook his head. "If they did they didn't say. They just said that 'Danny' gave 'em a number to call and somebody would tell 'em where to go to pick up their free money."

Henry brightened. "You got the number?"

"'Course I got it. I'd be a pretty sorry detective if I didn't." Max reached into the pocket of his jeans and extracted a crumpled piece of paper. He squinted as he recited a local telephone number before handing the jotting to Henry.

The detective perused the hand-written scrap. "You call it?"

"Nope. I wasn't sure if that would bollix the whole thing up, so I just wrote the number down."

Henry hesitated. "Max, there *is* a number I'd like you to call...a friend of mine. I'd like you to call and tell her that I'm okay. Don't even identify yourself; just tell her that I asked you to call."

"Girlfriend?"

"Just a friend. Frankly, she may not even care, but *I* care."

Max nodded thoughtfully. "I guess I could do that. But the meter's runnin'," he reminded Henry.

"Yeah, I know," the detective sighed. "Use a pay phone when you call her. If you can find one, that is."

"Got no choice since I got no cell phone."

Henry wrote the telephone number of the public defender's office on a slip of paper and extended it to Max, who crammed it into his pocket without looking at it.

"That's her office number. Ask for 'Gwen Harp.'"

"What do ya want me to say?"

"Just tell her that you're a friend and that I asked you to call to tell her that I'm okay. That's all ya gotta say...don't identify yourself and don't volunteer anything else."

"She cute?" Max asked.

Henry beamed. "Actually, yeah...she's very cute."

"Then don't give me that 'just a friend' crap," Max retorted. "I may be a homeless bum but I ain't dumb. Or blind."

The detective burst out laughing.

"When do you want me to call her?"

"Whenever you're able. Sooner, rather than later, preferably."

"Okay," Max said. "I'll call your 'friend' today or tomorrow. What are ya gonna do with that?" He indicated the slip of paper bearing the telephone number that Henry still grasped.

"I'm not sure yet...gotta think about it."

"Want me to call it and see what happens?"

"Negative. I don't want you sticking your neck out any more than you already have. If Lightfoot gets wind that you're helping me it won't be long before Smoot finds out, then things could *really* get dicey."

"If you say so," Max replied. "But I ain't worried about that pin-head, bedwettin' wuss, Lightfoot. He ain't shit compared to the gooks in 'Nam. Or my ex-old lady. Besides, we need to come up with some kinda plan."

"Yeah, well, everybody's got a 'plan' until they get punched in the mouth. And I don't want either of us to get punched in the mouth, either literally or figuratively."

"Whatever," Max idly responded, looking around the interior of the travel trailer. "You need more grub or anything?"

"Naw, I'm good for now," Henry said. "And it's not Lightfoot I'm worried about...it's the guy who Lightfoot works for that worries me."

Max rose to his feet and extinguished his Marlboro in the empty tuna can. "I'll call your friend and be back in a day or two. Write down whatever you need and I'll get it when I come back." He opened the door and pulled it shut quickly behind him as he exited, to minimize the amount of scorching air that rushed into the trailer.

Henry watched through an incrusted window as Max trudged from the trailer park in the blazing heat, toward the bus stop.

***

"Hi," Max hunched into the truncated shelter of the pay phone in an effort to reduce the ambient traffic noise, "I'm a friend of Lyman Henry's. He asked me to call you."

Gwen's first reaction was that the startling call was a prank.

"Who is this?" she demanded.

"I just told you. I'm a friend of Lyman Henry's. He wanted me to call to tell you that he's okay."

"Who are you?"

"Christ, I told you twice already. I'm a friend of Henry's. He asked me to call 'cause he thought you might be worried about him."

"Where is Lyman?"

"It don't matter where he is. He just wanted you to know that he's okay. Don't make this more complicated than it needs to be," Max amiably suggested.

"Lyman's still in town? Wait, I don't want to know where he is," she quickly corrected herself.

"He's in *a* town, if that's what you're askin'," Max informed her. "But I can't talk. He just wanted me to tell you that he's okay. Okay?"

An unexpected sense of relief flooded over Gwen. Words began pouring from her in a torrent.

"Tell Lyman that Danny Lightfoot was released and I talked to the detective assigned to the case. His name is 'Roberto Ortiz'; maybe Lyman knows him. Tell Lyman I told the detective that Lyman didn't kill Freddie, and that the detective needs to talk to Williams Smoot. Give Lyman my cell number again in case he lost it." She began to recite it.

"I don't have a pen. I'll get it later," Max deferred.

"When will you see Lyman again?" Gwen anxiously asked.

"Next day or two."

"Okay, call me again after you talk to him. And tell him to take care of himself, okay?"

Max didn't anticipate that he was apparently expected to record telephone numbers and convey messages, and was beginning to mildly regret calling. "Yeah, okay. And just in case you were wonderin', this call never happened."

"What call?"

Max chuckled. "That's the ticket."

"Okay, please call me again after you talk to him. Don't forget to tell him everything I just told you. And tell Lyman to take care of himself."

Max terminated the call by replacing handset on its hook. He'd already forgotten the name of the detective she said had been assigned to the case. He didn't figure it mattered, though, since he intended to do a little detective work of his own.

***

Ortiz telephoned Eileen Eggleston to inquire about Danny Lightfoot, his bullshit meter firing on all cylinders.

"Yes, we previously hired Mr. Lightfoot as an independent contractor," Eileen revealed. "Mr. Lightfoot did various odd jobs around the funeral home, but my recollection is that it was some time ago."

"How long?"

"I couldn't be sure," she deflected. "I'd have to check the records."

"Five minutes? A month? Six months? Two decades?"

"I really couldn't say," she hedged. "I just know it's been a while."

"That's funny because, when I talked to your boss, he told me that Lightfoot is the mechanic for your hearse."

"If Mr. Smoot said that, he misspoke," Eileen spluttered. "I make most of the personnel decisions, so Mr. Smoot would simply have no idea."

"You're telling me that you don't currently employ Danny Lightfoot as a mechanic?"

"That's correct."

"Do you, and by 'you' I mean you, Smoot, or the funeral home, currently employ Danny Lightfoot in *any* capacity?"

"No."

"So, who *does* work on your hearse?"

"No one at present. Our funeral coach doesn't currently require any mechanical attention."

"Hmmm...how long did Lightfoot work there? When he *did* work there, I mean."

"I'm not sure. It was so long ago..."

"Do you know whether Lightfoot met Freddie Smoot during the time he worked at the funeral home?"

"I suppose it's possible. I really have no idea where they met. I didn't know either of them very well."

"When's the last time you saw, or talked to, Danny Lightfoot?" the detective probed.

"It's been quite a long time," Eileen assured him.

"Five minutes? A month? Six months? Two decades?"

"Oh, my goodness, certainly less than two decades!" she responded with a brittle laugh. "But it's been quite a while."

"And you have no idea where Lightfoot currently lives or how to contact him?"

"No."

"Well, how did you contact him in the first place? I mean, when you originally hired him to work at the mortuary, how did you contact him?"

Ortiz was far from surprised by the protracted silence at the other end of the line.

"I think Mr. Lightfoot may have just come by the funeral home, looking for work. I really don't remember," Eileen stumbled.

"I see," Ortiz dubiously responded. "Did Lyman Henry ever work for Mr. Smoot?"

"Lyman Henry? The man who robbed Mr. Smoot?"

"That's the one," said the detective.

"No, never. The only time I saw him was the day he burst in, demanding to see Mr. Smoot."

"Uh huh," Ortiz intoned. "Well, thank you for your time. You've been a great help. I'll contact you again if I have additional questions."

"Of course."

Eileen hung up. She was unnerved by the detective's unwelcome call, feared she'd never get him off the phone, and realized it was essential to discuss it with Smoot. Unfortunately, the funeral director had departed earlier that morning in the motor home and Eileen had no idea where it was currently parked. Although she could call him on his cell, Smoot left strict instructions that he was not to be disturbed while meeting potential donors.

Smoot had forbidden Danny to come around the funeral home until he was satisfied that Detective Ortiz's investigation had run its course. As a result of his prohibition, there was no one to process the accumulating bodies, creating a backlog of unfilled orders. Eileen urged, under the circumstances, that BioServus suspend efforts to increase its inventory, at least temporarily, but Smoot eschewed her advice. The funeral director insisted that it was essential for

BioServus to accumulate as much product as possible, as he characterized it, "for a rainy day."

"BioServus cannot afford to dawdle. We must secure as much product as we can, as quickly as possible, so we can hit the ground running following Lyman Henry's apprehension," Smoot insisted. "In the meantime, BioServus will continue to pursue its business interests. If we do as you advise and suspend business operations even temporarily, BioServus will fall so far behind its competitors as to become completely marginalized in the global marketplace. I will not allow that to happen, Eileen. I already instructed Danny to spread the word about the increased reward for Henry and, pending his imminent arrest, BioServus will continue to augment inventory."

Eileen waited and fidgeted until Smoot deigned to return to the funeral home with another cargo of product.

SEVENTEEN

Freddie Smoot was squeaky clean, Ortiz determined. No run-ins with the police, no civil law suits, never married or divorced, not even a traffic ticket. It's like the guy never existed. How'd such a nonentity end up dead at the hands of Lyman Henry, an ex-cop with an exemplary record? Although it was conceivable that Freddie got sideways with Henry for God-only-knows-what reason, why did Danny Lightfoot confess to killing Freddie when he knew, absolutely, that he hadn't? If Lightfoot was just bat-shit crazy, like most false confessors, Ortiz suspected he was crazy like a fox. The fact that Smoot and his Doppelganger, Eileen, contradicted one another about Lightfoot further clouded things. Alternatively, if Lightfoot was nothing more than a narcissistic publicity whore, he had a strange way of demonstrating it because, like Henry, he'd completely dropped from sight.

Ortiz figured he'd shake the tree by digging further into the principals' backgrounds, hoping to uncover information that would resolve the niggling questions surrounding Freddie's death. Freddie sure as hell wasn't going anywhere, Smoot and Lightfoot were paradoxes, and Lyman Henry was still nowhere to be found. The detective had the luxury, if not the obligation, to attempt to connect the dots.

The perfunctory research he'd already conducted revealed that, unique among his siblings, Freddie was the only one of Williams Smoot's children who didn't work for a company owned or controlled by Smoot. Even so, Freddie *did* work for a Smoot company, and live in a house owed by Williams Smoot, until a few months before his murder. Maybe there was a connection, maybe not. But Ortiz decided it wouldn't hurt to talk to Freddie's last employer, Best Buy.

***

"Frankly, detective, I'm surprised that Freddie's death is still being investigated. I already talked to somebody from your department about it." Best Buy manager Susan Miller escorted Ortiz into her bland office and closed the door behind them. She motioned him to a chair.

"Excuse me?"

Miller slid the chair away from her steel desk and sat. "A detective was here about a month ago, asking about Freddie. He said the police had already arrested somebody. Don't you guys ever talk?"

"You previously talked to someone from Phoenix Police about Freddie Smoot?" Ortiz asked in surprise.

"Yeah, I think he was a police officer. He said he was a detective, anyway."

"Do you remember his name?"

"He gave me his card."

Miller opened her desk drawer and noisily rummaged through its contents.

"Here it is." She extended a plain white business card toward Ortiz, who rose from his chair to take it:

Lyman Henry Investigations
Nunquam Dormio

Ortiz looked up from the card. "You talked to this guy about Freddie Smoot's murder?"

"About a month ago, I think...I honestly can't remember. My recollection was that he was a police officer but, looking at his card again, I remember he said he was a private investigator."

"Why did Lyman Henry want to talk to you?"

"He told me that Freddie's dad had hired him to investigate Freddie's murder, to wrap up some loose ends or something. He also told me the name of the guy they arrested, but I can't remember it."

Ortiz leaned forward in his chair. "Wait. Are you sure that Lyman Henry told you that Freddie Smoot's father hired him?"

"That's what he said. He said the dad's name was 'Williams'. I remember because it was such an unusual first name. I told him I found it strange that Freddie's dad would hire somebody to investigate Freddie's death."

"How so?"

"Because Freddie and his dad didn't get along."

"How do you know that?"

"Freddie told me," she matter-of-factly stated.

"Did he tell you why they didn't get along?"

She shook her head. "I didn't think it was any of my business and figured that Freddie would tell me if he wanted me to know."

"What else did you talk to Henry about?"

"Nothing, really. I just told him that Freddie got along with everybody and everybody liked him."

"Did Freddie ever mention someone named 'Danny Lightfoot'?"

Miller reflected a moment before responding. "If he did, I don't remember. He actually didn't talk much about anything."

"Danny Lightfoot was the original suspect in Freddie Smoot's murder," Ortiz informed her. "Turns out he didn't do it, though."

"He must've been the guy the other detective mentioned." She appeared puzzled. "But if he didn't kill Freddie, who did?"

Ortiz smiled wryly. "The guy you talked to, Lyman Henry."

"No way!" Miller hooted. "You're telling me that the guy investigating Freddie's murder was actually the guy who murdered him? Am I missing something? Why would he do that?"

"That's a good question," Ortiz acknowledged, "only I'm the one who should be asking it."

***

Smoot eased the lumbering motor home onto the vast parking lot of a derelict warehouse club. He changed locations frequently to avoid arousing the curiosity, or ire, of neighboring property owners when homeless people began to congregate in response to

Lightfoot's recruitment drive. Smoot verbally provided the exact location of the peripatetic vehicle when donors called the telephone number that Lightfoot gave them.

Smoot had done his best to calm Eileen, who was in a state of near-panic over her recent telephone conversation with Ortiz.   He wished she'd simply played dumb and referred the detective to him, but that was water over the dam at this point. He couldn't unring a bell.   Henry's arrest, which would automatically render Ortiz's entire investigation moot, was inevitable. The only thing Smoot had to ensure in the meantime is that Lightfoot remained beyond the grasp of the police.

Smoot had no illusions that, were the cops to start questioning him, Lightfoot would promptly throw the mortician overboard by telling them everything he knew, merely to save his own hide.

Despite   the   funeral   director's   initial ambivalence, however, Lightfoot's recruitment efforts had begun to generate results. An average of three donors per week managed to straggle their way to Smoot's   motor   home   and   he   was   becoming increasingly adept at determining the most efficacious dose of cyanide to administer. As a result, BioServus's freezer was filling with bodies, notwithstanding that Lightfoot's temporary banishment from the funeral home prevented them from being processed quickly. Still, Smoot remained determined to stockpile product.

He drove the motor home behind the building and pulled next to its abandoned loading ramp. Smoot killed the engine before flicking a toggle switch on the dashboard to start the vehicle's onboard gasoline generator. Once it began humming, Smoot swiveled the driver's seat around and switched on the motor home's rooftop air conditioning unit. According to Eileen, only a single applicant had made arrangements to see him today. He glanced at his watch; the donor was scheduled to arrive in less than ten minutes.

Smoot rose and stepped to a cabinet above the vehicle's stainless-steel sink. Taking a plastic pitcher and drinking glass, he placed both on the nearby countertop. He then bent and removed a handful of milky ice cubes from the adjacent freezer and deposited them into the pitcher.

In the adjoining refrigerator, a quart bottle of amber liquid, sealed with a threaded cap, sat on the top shelf. Smoot lifted it out and vigorously shook it before carefully unscrewing the cap. He decanted a sufficient quantity of the tea into the plastic pitcher to cover the ice cubes resting at the bottom, taking care not to splash any of it. Smoot resealed the bottle and returned it to the refrigerator. He consulted his watch again: less than five minutes.

Smoot moved to the motor home's window to survey the area outside. Plodding toward the vehicle in the blistering mid-day heat was a solitary figure.

The visitor, lean as a wolf, was clad in denim jeans, a ratty T-shirt, and an orange baseball cap that said "Cabela's" on it. He abruptly halted to wipe perspiration from his face and study the area immediately around the motor home. Smoot observed a grey, braided pony tail hanging down his back. The leathery skin of the man's face and arms, furrowed with wrinkles, was deeply tanned.

***

"I read your report, of course. Other than fingerprints, did you find anything else on the weapon?"

Ortiz was in his office, interviewing the criminalist who performed the forensic analysis on the pistol found at Henry's apartment.

The lab-coated criminalist looked perplexed. "Like what?"

"Like *anything*," Ortiz responded in exasperation. "Dirt, lint, paint, blood, moon dust...hell, I don't know. Whatever you guys look for."

The other man opened the pasteboard folder in his lap and began to silently review its contents.

"There were four latents and three partials, all on the slide," he muttered, mostly to himself. "Left thumb, right thumb, left ring finger, left and right index, two smeared palm prints." He looked up and blinked.

"Yeah, I already know that," Ortiz said. "It's in the report. Was there anything *else*?"

The criminalist looked down at the folder again.

"Minute traces of some kind of sticky residue."

Ortiz sat up in his chair. "Sticky residue?"

"That's what is says," the man blandly acknowledged.

"Where?"

He consulted his notes. "Also on the pistol's slide, contiguous to the fingerprints."

"Could you tell what it was?"

The criminalist shook his head. "Just that it was sticky. Maybe some kind of adhesive...not a large enough sample to specifically identify. My guess is that it was probably incidental to the crime and has no probative value."

"And, other than the sticky stuff, just the suspect's fingerprints?"

"That's it. Slick as the proverbial hound's tooth, otherwise." He looked expectantly at the detective and blinked again.

"Did it strike you as peculiar that the suspect's prints were on the pistol's slide but nowhere else, not even on the grip? How could he *not* leave his fingerprints on the grip if he held the gun to shoot the victim?"

"I wouldn't know," burped the criminalist. "Maybe he wore gloves."

"If he wore gloves there wouldn't be any fingerprints on it at all."

"Look, I don't even like guns. My job is to identify and collect evidence. I don't speculate about how it got there, or didn't get there. I think that's *your* job."

Ortiz was getting tired of people telling him his job.

"Okay, thanks for your time. You've been a big help," the detective sarcastically concluded their conversation.

***

Smoot swung open the motor home's door and stuck his head out.

"Hello. I think you may be looking for me," he called to the immobile figure.

"Where's Lightfoot?" the man responded without moving.

Smoot was taken aback by the man's abruptness.

"Danny's not here right now. Are you here to pick up your money? Come in, please." He stepped away from the open door, deeper into the motor home.

The figure resumed ambling toward the vehicle. Once there, he grasped the chrome handle bolted to its exterior and climbed the two steps that led inside. Cold air washed over him as he stepped across the threshold. Smoot moved around him to shut the door then extended his hand.

"I'm Mr. Stanley. Thank you for coming today."

Max ignored the gesture. "Where's Lightfoot?" He flopped onto one of the sofas.

Smoot's hand wavered in mid-air. "Danny had to step out for a moment," he smiled. He finally lowered his hand. "You're a friend?"

"I know him," Max said.

Smoot eased onto the couch opposite Max. "I'm sorry, what was your name? In the event he doesn't return in time, I'll tell Danny that you inquired about him."

"I'm Dr. Livingston," Max informed him.

"Yes, of course." Smoot's smile dwindled. "How can I help you today, doctor?"

"You work for the government?"

"Yes, the government," Smoot assuaged him.

"The state or the feds?"

Smoot frowned. "Excuse me?"

"Do you work for the federal government or the state government?" Max reclined on the sofa and watched the other man intently.

"Um, I work for the federal government," Smoot finally bumbled.

"So why the motor home parked behind a building? Don't you have a regular office?"

Having been asked the question repeatedly by previous donors, Smoot had plenty of opportunity to rehearse his response.

"Certainly. I ordinarily meet clients at my office downtown but sometimes use the motor home as a convenience because many of my clients don't have transportation."

Max remained inscrutable. "What department?"

"What?" Smoot blurted. He resented the inquisition by the enigmatic visitor and was beginning to fear that he was being set up.

"You said that you work for the federal government. I asked what department of the government you work for."

"I confess that I find all these questions very curious, doctor. I'm simply here to help you," the funeral director assured him.

"That so? Well, you can start by cuttin' all the bullshit," Max replied. "Seems to me that, if you were on the up-and-up, you wouldn't be in business with Lightfoot."

Whoever he was, the man's visit was prompted, at least in part, by an obvious animus toward Danny Lightfoot. If that's *all* it was, and not some clumsy sting operation orchestrated by Detective Ortiz, Smoot could deal with it.

"We utilize Mr. Lightfoot's services simply because of his contacts within the homeless community," Smoot adroitly explained. "Otherwise, it would prove difficult for us to make clients aware of all the new government programs that are available to them. So, in the end, Danny performs a valuable service to the community we serve." Smoot paused to assess the other man's reaction to his facile explanation, but Max was unreadable.

Smoot quickly resumed. "Let me get you something cold to drink and I'll be happy to answer all your remaining questions."

Without waiting for a response, he rose and stepped to the counter where he filled the drinking glass from the plastic pitcher. A couple of ice cubes gently splashed into the glass as he poured.

"I made this fresh this morning," the funeral director smiled as he handed it to Max.

Max accepted the glass and cupped it in his lap.

"Where'd Lightfoot go?" he asked again, once Smoot resumed his seat.

"He had to run an errand. I expect him to return imminently."

Max lifted the glass to his mouth and took a quaff, never taking his gaze from Smoot.

"Good?" the funeral director solicitously inquired.

"It's all right," Max said. He took another swallow. "You don't want any?"

Smoot invoked his practiced smile. "Unfortunately, I can't drink tea. But as soon as you're finished, I'll answer all your questions."

Max spontaneously gulped as a spasm shuddered through his body. His fingers clutching the glass involuntarily jerked, spilling its remaining contents onto his clothing. Max belched then began retching violently.

"What the fuck?" he gasped before crumpling sideways onto the couch.

EIGHTEEN

Uncharacteristically, Max failed to return to Henry's trailer after three days. Aside from running low on supplies, Henry was becoming alarmed over his friend's welfare. Fully mindful of the risk, Henry decided he had no alternative but to hazard a telephone call. Although he could use his cell phone, he didn't want to run the risk of having its number pop up on an incoming call history. Chafing at the delay, he waited until nightfall before creeping from his trailer.

The harsh sound of televisions emanated from several darkened trailers as Henry cautiously stole through the mobile home park, heading for the pay phone on the corner. No one was about, nor did he encounter anyone one en route. Although traffic on Van Buren Street was still heavy, Henry wore a baseball cap pulled low and, despite the darkness, sun glasses, and was careful to avert his face.

Once at the deserted public telephone, he glanced about to satisfy himself that no one was lurking nearby. He deposited the requisite coins and quickly entered the cell number. She answered on the third ring.

"Gwen, it's Lyman. Don't hang up," he breathed into the handset.

"Lyman!" she cried with unanticipated emotion. "I've been so worried about you!"

"Did my friend call you?" he blurted.

"Somebody who said he was your friend called me a few days ago. He didn't tell me his name, but said you asked him to call to tell me that you were okay."

"Yeah, that was Max and I'm okay. For the time being, anyway. Have you heard from him since then?"

"His name is 'Max'? No, he only called me the one time. Like I said, a few days ago...three, I think. Why?"

"Max been helping me keep out of sight and we usually hook up about every other day, but I haven't seen or heard from him since before he called you. I confided in him my suspicions about Lightfoot and Smoot and I'm worried he may have gone off half-cocked and done something dumb."

"Like what?" Henry could detect concern in Gwen's voice.

"I wish I knew," he confessed with dismay. "All I know is that I've not heard from him and am getting a bad feeling."

"Can I do anything?"

"I was hoping you might have some suggestions, Gwen, because sure as hell I don't know what to do. I debated about even calling you because I don't want to involve you more than I already have."

She thought a moment. "I'm sure your friend is okay, Lyman. But let me nose around a bit. What's his last name?"

"Berkley."

"What's his address?"

"None. He's homeless."

"Do you know how old Max is?"

"I'd guess late '60's, early '70's."

"Okay, Lyman, I don't know where you're calling from and don't want to know. But call me again in a couple of days. I'll try to get some information on your friend."

"Okay, thanks, Gwen. I'm sincerely sorry to suck you into all of this."

"Occupational hazard, I guess," she softly chuckled. "I told Max that I talked with the detective assigned to your case."

"What's his name?"

"Roberto Ortiz."

"Don't know him," Henry affirmed. "Probably hired on after I left the department. What'd he say?"

"Not much...didn't seem to know a whole lot about the case, though."

"Doesn't surprise me. The homicide guys are up to their eyeballs in work and there's a ton of turnover. How long ago did you talk to him?"

"It was before your friend called, so maybe a week. For what it's worth, I told him that I didn't think you killed Freddie and said that he should look at Williams Smoot."

"What'd he say?"

"Nothing, and I haven't heard from him since."

"Well, lemme know if you do, Gwen. I've gotta go now but will call you again in a day or two. Hopefully, Max will show up between now and then."

"Okay, Lyman. Take good care of yourself. And, just to cover my rear end, I have to advise you to turn yourself in immediately."

"Yeah, I know," Henry smiled. "You've done your job, counselor. I've missed you."

"Me, too."

He placed the receiver back on its hook, terminating the call, and headed back to the trailer park.

***

Notwithstanding Detective Ortiz's meddling, Williams Smoot decided he could simply wait no longer. Inventory was accumulating and clients were clamoring for product. He knew his competitors were poised to rush in to fill the vacuum. On top of everything else, he couldn't rely on Lightfoot to stick around. Unless Smoot had sufficient work to keep him busy, Lightfoot was likely to bolt for seemingly greener, and more profitable, pastures. BioServus had no choice but to recommence operations.

The good news was that Smoot had heard nothing from, or about, Ortiz since the latter's intrusive telephone conversation with Eileen. Hopefully, the detective decided to stop pestering them and was out looking for Lyman Henry, which is what he should have been doing from the beginning.

"Eileen, get hold of Danny and tell him that I want him to start cutting again. Also tell him that, if he's still recruiting, to stop until we get caught up."

"How soon do you want him?"

"Immediately. Tonight, if possible."

All Smoot could do now was hope that Lightfoot actually showed up.

***

For the next two days, Henry kept an anxious vigil at the trailer's grimy window, watching for Max's reassuring figure. The tuna can next to his chair was overflowing with cigarette butts as he chained-smoked Kool after Kool. His meals consisted of warm beer, cold Pop Tarts, and a gallon can of roasted, salted peanuts. It seemed like a week since he'd talked to Gwen. He looked away from the window long enough to check his watch: three hours until he could call her again.

***

It was after 1:00 a.m. when Lightfoot pulled up to the 24-hour storage-locker facility. The air in the funeral home's cargo van was cranked full blast because, even at that hour, the outside temperature hovered in the 90's.

Lightfoot pushed the button to lower the driver's side window and leaned out to enter the numerical passcode into an electronic keypad situated on an adjacent pole. After a slight pause, the steel gate in the van's headlights began to slide open with a noisy grind. Lightfoot eased the van through the opening and sat in the idling vehicle while, in the rearview mirror, he watched as the gate reached its maximum transit then slowly began to reverse itself. Once he was satisfied that the gate had returned to its fully closed position, Lightfoot drove slowly to BioServus's unit located in the rear of the property.

In order to accommodate its massive walk-in freezer, BioServus found it necessary to rent the most commodious unit available. Slightly larger than a two-car garage, the interior of the storeroom was accessed through an articulating roll-up door.

Lightfoot drove slightly past the storage unit, then placed the van in reverse and slowly backed until its rear doors faced the storage unit at an angle. He switched the engine off and hopped out. Walking around the back of the van, he squatted and, in the beam of a small flashlight clenched in his teeth, inserted a key into the large padlock securing the locker's roll-up door. It sprang open with an audible click. Standing, he bent to grasp the door's projecting handle and flung it open. Curved tracks on either side of the steel door guided it as it rattled upward.

He reached into void and flicked a switch affixed to an interior wall. An overhead neon tube flickered on, though such marginal illumination as it provided was largely blocked by the bulky freezer that filled the room, reaching nearly to the ceiling. Fortunately, the freezer had its own interior light that automatically came on when its door was opened. Smoot acquired the freezer by bidding on it at a bank auction. A supermarket had originally owed it; when the supermarket collapsed into bankruptcy, all of its assets were summarily liquidated. Smoot scoured published legal notices for such an opportunity and his diligence had paid off.

Lightfoot stepped to the freezer and grabbed the stainless-steel handle on its thick insulated door. He tugged it open.

A wall of freezing air greeted him.

The area directly immediately inside the freezer's open door was bare. Along each side, however, were rough wooden shelves, resembling bunk beds, on which rested clothed human bodies. The harsh interior light glittered off the blanket of frost that covered them. Lightfoot counted eight, all whom appeared to be male. When Smoot originally acquired the freezer it was, essentially, a big empty box. In order to house inventory until it could be adequately processed, he'd instructed Lightfoot to construct interior shelving. Lightfoot completed that task while carrying out the modifications to Smoot's motor home.

He regularly grumbled to Smoot that things would go a lot smoother if the bodies were already stripped when he got them. It already was a massive pain in the ass to flay and dismember them; having to cut their reeking clothing off just slowed everything down.

"But, Danny, that's why you get paid," the funeral director dismissively responded.

Lightfoot retreated to the van, where he opened the rear doors and removed a collapsible gurney. He slipped on a pair of leather gloves before wheeling the gurney to the storage unit. Bumping it over the threshold, he pushed it into the glacial container. He didn't expect to be there long enough to require a jacket. In fact, the freezing air felt good.

Lightfoot failed to recognize any of the individuals he'd hitherto processed for BioServus, attributing the vacuity to the ripple effect of his recruiting campaign. Even so, he avidly scrutinized each frozen visage as he grappled to arrange the unwieldy bodies on the gurney. He'd be lucky to process two donors per night; he chose the two closest to the door.

The first guy looked surprisingly young, probably in his twenties. It was anybody's guess how he ended up in BioServus's freezer...probably just some fucked-up druggie who pissed his life away before it even began. Because of his youth, Smoot would undoubtedly charge a premium for him. But that wasn't Lightfoot's concern.

Lightfoot wheeled the gurney outside and slid the remains into the back of the van, the slippery covering of frost facilitating the process. It would take a half-hour or so to drive back to the funeral home, so he should be able to start processing by 2:30 and, hopefully, finish by dawn. He returned to the storage unit to retrieve another body and be on his way.

He recognized the second guy.

Appearing to be in his 70's, the man was exceedingly thin. Although Lightfoot didn't know his name, his long braided ponytail was unmistakable. Like all of them, he was obviously homeless and wore threadbare, soiled clothing. Smoot hadn't bothered to remove the guy's orange Cabela's cap and it remained frozen to his head, tilted at an angle.

Lightfoot remembered encountering the guy down at the Town Lake, the first time when he was bargaining for some snatch. Lightfoot had approached a destitute mom and her two daughters, the cutest of whom looked to be about ten or twelve, and was in the process of negotiating when the old bastard butted in, threatened to bust his chops, and told him to take a hike. The guy acted like he was the fucking hall monitor or something! Lightfoot didn't feel like getting into an argument over pussy so he bagged it and ended up going somewhere else...there's no shortage of moms with cute daughters, if you know where to look. He also went to the mall, where he chatted-up teen girls and paid them twenty dollars for their used bras and panties.

Even after that initial hostile confrontation, the old man had been an antagonistic prick every time their paths subsequently crossed. It pleased Lightfoot mightily to see him laid out like that, frozen as stiff as a preacher's dick and, for once, he actually looked forward to dismembering a body. He considered it teaching the guy a lesson.

Lightfoot wrestled the unwieldy corpse onto the gurney and trundled it outside to the van, where he quickly placed it alongside the first guy. He tossed the gurney and gloves atop the two bodies then slammed the rear doors shut. Returning to the storage unit, he confirmed that the freezer door was closed and securely latched. Flicking off the interior neon light, Lightfoot grasped the nylon rope dangling from the overhead steel door and gave it a firm yank; the door descended with a roar. He knelt, slipped the padlock through the hasp at the bottom of the door, and snapped it shut.

***

Henry crept back to the pay telephone. Notwithstanding the late hour and pounding heat, he wore a hooded sweatshirt and sun glasses. This time she answered on the second ring.

"I had a feeling you'd call tonight. At least I was hoping you would," Gwen confessed.

"Hi," he responded. "It seems like a month since we talked."

"You felt that way, too, huh? I thought it was just me." Henry thought he could detect a smile in Gwen's voice. "Did you hear from Max?"

"No, nothing," he tersely responded.

"Darn it! I had my fingers crossed! I wasn't able to find out much, other than Max hasn't been arrested and no local emergency room has apparently admitted anyone meeting his description. Because he's homeless there's just not much to go on, Lyman."

"Yeah, I know," he sighed. "Something's happened to him, though. Max wouldn't just disappear." If nothing else, it was unlikely that Max would summarily abandon the accumulated money the detective owed him.

"I'm really sorry I couldn't do more to help," Gwen confessed. "Now what?"

Henry didn't immediately respond. "I'd like to talk to you," he finally said, softly.

"We *are* talking."

"No, I mean face-to-face." He hesitated. "I realize what I'm asking, Gwen."

"What would that accomplish, Lyman?"

"I don't know.   Probably nothing...I just don't know what else to do. More to the point, I just want to see you," he said.

She was glad Henry was unable to see the blush that warmed her face. "Well, I've actually been thinking about some things," she cryptically revealed.

"'Some things'?" What are you talking about?"

"I came up with an idea but don't know whether it's completely off the wall, or what. I wasn't even going to mention it until you brought up seeing me."

Henry quickened. "An 'idea'?   What kind of 'idea'?"

"I don't think we should talk about it over the phone. But neither do I think that meeting is the smartest thing I've ever done, either. Like I told you before, I could lose my law license for aiding and abetting, or assisting, a fugitive," Gwen fretted.

"Meeting me is definitely not the smartest thing you've ever done, Gwen," Henry admitted. "But you can't be guilty of aiding and abetting because that requires that you intentionally assisted me in the commission of a crime. I didn't even *know* you when Freddie Smoot was killed, so you couldn't have aided and abetted me...and that's putting aside the fact that I didn't kill Freddie in the first place. As for assisting a fugitive, the reason for our meeting would be to provide you the opportunity to convince me to turn myself in, not to 'assist' me in my flight from justice. It would be just the opposite." He stopped to await her response.

All rationalizations aside, she wanted to see him.

"When and where were you thinking?" Gwen hoped her voice didn't betray the emotion she was feeling.

"The only place we could risk meeting is at my place."

"Your place?" Gwen exclaimed. "Your apartment?"

"No, no," Henry chuckled. "Where I'm hiding out."

Her laugh was melodious. "A 'hide out' sounds like something from a B-gangster movie. I didn't think they had 'hide outs' in real life."

"Do you want to meet?" If not, I can't blame you, Gwen."

She deliberated before replying. "I guess we could meet like you said, just for the purpose of convincing you to turn yourself in. When?"

"Exactly!" Henry concurred. "As soon as we can."

Gwen sighed. "This is against my better judgment, Lyman, but I really want to see you. Assuming you're still in Phoenix, I can meet you tomorrow after work."

"I never left town." He provided the address of the trailer park, as well as a description of his travel trailer.

"I should be there around 6'ish tomorrow evening," she said.

"If you want anything to eat, you'll have to bring it with you. That, or eat before you get here, 'cause I don't have much here," Henry apologetically confessed.

She laughed again. "I'll bring dinner for both of us...what would you like?"

"As long as it's not Pop Tarts or peanuts, I don't care. I'd just like to see you, whether you bring dinner or not."

"I'm eager to run my idea past you, Lyman. You can tell me if it's totally whacky."

"See you tomorrow, Gwen. Good night."

Henry replaced the telephone's receiver and headed back to the trailer park, his step a little lighter.

NINETEEN

She arrived at 6:20. He was concerned that she'd changed her mind, or that something had come up, and was jubilant when Gwen's Nissan Sentra finally pulled up to his trailer. He threw open the door, heedless of the potential exposure.

"I wasn't sure you were gonna make it," he called to her as she climbed from her car.

Gwen walked around the vehicle and opened the passenger's door, where she bent to retrieve a flat box.

"I stopped to get us something to eat, but it took longer than I expected. The traffic on Van Buren is a bear, too. I hope you like pizza...I brought some sodas, too."

"As long as it's not peanut or Pop Tart flavored."

Henry descended the trailer's two steps to the ground and took the pizza box from Gwen. She removed two large plastic bottles of Diet Coke from the car and followed him into the trailer.

"Nice place," Gwen joked as she deposited the sodas onto the table. She wrinkled her nose. "But either you built a campfire in here or you've been smoking non-stop."

Henry placed the pizza box next to the bottles.

"I tried to air it out before you got here by opening the windows, but it didn't work too well...sorry 'bout that. I've probably been smoking a little too much, worryin' about Max."

"'Probably'? Lyman, *any* smoking is too much, especially if you're still smoking those God-awful Kools." She then smiled. "But I guess I can't blame you. If one of my friends went missing, I'd be so worried that I'd probably *take up* smoking!"

Gwen sat on the sofa and watched Henry remove a stack of paper plates and two drinking glasses from a cupboard.

"I hope the sodas are cold 'cause I don't have any ice," he said, arranging the plates and glasses on the table by the other items. He pulled a drawer out and removed some plastic knives and forks.

"Well, they were coldish when I bought them," she said. "I guess they'll have to do."

Henry unscrewed the cap from one of the hissing sodas and filled their glasses. Gwen stood and placed slices of pizza on two of the paper plates before resuming her place on the sofa.

"Hope you like mushrooms," she said.

"Like I said, I like anything as long as it's not peanuts or Pop Tarts," Henry smiled. He plopped down beside her.

"Before I forget, I'm advising you to immediately surrender yourself to the authorities," Gwen sternly informed him. "Now that I've got that out of the way, let's eat." She took a bite of pizza. Henry followed suit.

"Man, that's good!" he beamed.

"Just be sure not to bite your fingertips while you're cramming it into your mouth," she chuckled.

Henry happily nodded between mouthfuls of pizza. "Max kept me in groceries but, since he hasn't been around, I haven't had much to eat."

"Where'd you meet him?" Gwen inquired.

"I ran into Max while I was investigating Freddie's murder for Smoot...down at the Town Lake."

"Why's he helping you?"

Henry stopped chewing and gazed thoughtfully into the distance.

"Well, ostensibly because I told him I'd pay him," he finally responded, "but he hasn't asked for a dime. Max is a good man, Gwen. *That's* why he's helping me."

She took a sip of tepid Diet Coke. "Max found this place?" Henry nodded as he helped himself to another slice of pizza.

"Tell me about your idea, Gwen," he invited as he resumed eating.

She slid her paper plate onto the table and wiped her mouth. She looked at him gravely.

"Well, I've been thinking," she began. "Things can't just go on indefinitely the way they are. The police are obviously looking for you and it's just a matter of time before you're arrested. Frankly, I'm surprised that hasn't already happened. Something's gotta give, Lyman, and I'm thinking the best defense at this point may be to go on offense."

He listened intently. "Max was trying to help me put the pieces together, but I'm convinced that something's happened to him...Max wouldn't just not show up."

"Smoot?"

"I wish I knew," Henry glumly replied. "It wouldn't surprise me if Smoot's involved, but keep talking, please."

Gwen continued.

"If what you told me before is right, Smoot is the common denominator behind everything that's happened: Freddie's murder, Danny's bogus confession, your arrest, maybe even Max's disappearance. But we've gotta figure out a way to prove that Smoot is the puppet master."

"Agreed, but how do we do that?"

"Like I said, we need to go on offense. What I'm about to propose may sound totally off-the-wall but hear me out."

"That sounds intriguing," Henry smiled.

"You said that Smoot is pilfering jewelry from the bodies in his funeral home, that Freddie found out and threatened to blow the whistle, and Smoot either killed Freddie or had him killed."

"That's my theory," Henry agreed. "But Smoot's also a body broker...that's where the real money is. Remember that Lightfoot already admitted to us that he cuts up bodies for Smoot. *That's* what got Freddie killed: he was gonna blow the whistle on his old man's illegal body farm.

"Okay, if that's true," Gwen resumed, "what if we could catch Smoot in the act? What if we caught him red-handed?"

"How?"

She hesitated.

"Okay, here goes. Somebody would have to pose as a local buyer interested in purchasing body parts from Smoot. He'd deliver them to such-and-such an address, but the police would be there when he arrived. Because Smoot would be in possession of a vehicle full of human remains, and no documentation, standard police protocol dictates that they would arrest him. Once in custody, Smoot would start to sweat. The police would undoubtedly search the mortuary and begin interviewing people, including Danny Lightfoot. They might even exhume bodies that would, presumably, be missing parts. People will inevitably start talking, especially Danny if he thinks that he may end up going down in flames along with Smoot. As a result, everything will ultimately be revealed...'sunlight is the best disinfectant,' as the expression goes. And that, my dear Lyman, is my idea in a nutshell," she concluded.

Henry pondered Gwen's proposal. "I see three immediate problems. First, who would pose as the buyer? Second, the cops aren't gonna just drop everything and stake out some address based on the possibility that a crime *might* be committed there. More problematical, some idiot judge might put the kybosh on the whole thing because he considers it entrapment. Remember, I used to be a cop."

"I'd be the buyer." She smiled enigmatically. "And we'd give the police a very good reason to be at that location, completely independent of Smoot."

He cocked an eyebrow. "Oh? What's that?"

"You'll be there to give yourself up."

Henry was genuinely startled. "Wait! You want me to give myself up...just like that?"

"I told you, Lyman: I came here tonight to convince you to surrender. Besides, I can't see any other way to make it work. Like you, yourself, just said, the cops *have* to be given a reason to be there. Yes, you'll be in jail for a while until the police sort things out, but you'll eventually be cleared. I told you my idea is completely off-the-wall but if you have a better one, I'm all ears. Like I said, something's gotta give, Lyman...you can't stay holed-up in this trailer forever. I mean, don't get me wrong, it's really lovely and all..." she grinned.

"Yeah, right," Henry scoffed. "But lemme make sure I understand what you're saying, Gwen. You, or somebody else, will tip the cops off that I'll be at a specific place, ready to turn myself in. When they swoop in to nab me, and trust me there will be more cops there than you can shake a stick at, Smoot will blithely drive up to deliver an order of human body parts...'did somebody order a dozen stiffs?' At that point, the cops will basically forget about me and snap the ol' bracelets on Smoot. Does that pretty much cover it?"

"I'm not sure I'd put it as glibly as that but, yes, that's essentially what I'm proposing."

"What's the likelihood that Smoot will arrive on site at exactly the right moment? 'Cause if he doesn't, and he out-snookers us, I'm royally screwed."

"I think the likelihood is actually quite high," she confidently replied. "Smoot obviously wants to make money and I'll present myself as a very convincing buyer with deep pockets. Why would he pass up such an opportunity? Smoot is such a narcissist that he'll simply consider me just another customer, ready to be fleeced. *Of course,* he'll show up."

"Even if that's true, there's still no guarantee that Smoot'll show up exactly when you want him to, if he shows up at all."

"You're right," Gwen conceded. "It's a matter of probabilities, Lyman. But right now, at this moment, I submit that your options are quickly dwindling. You're fleeing justice by hiding in this crappy trailer and it's only a matter of time before the police find you. Even if you manage to elude them indefinitely, which is just wishful thinking, Williams Smoot is undoubtedly looking for you, too. In fact, he's hoping to find you before the police do because, if the police find you first, Smoot runs the risk that you'll tell them everything you suspect about Smoot's role in Freddie's murder.   If Smoot can eliminate you before that happens, the police will permanently close the books on the entire case. And, if all that isn't enough, your friend, Max, has disappeared. You have nowhere else to go, Lyman, and have run out of options. The entire roof is poised to collapse on you at any moment. At least my proposal offers the potential of extricating yourself and, maybe, finally getting some justice for Freddie Smoot. But, like I said, if you've got a better idea, let's hear it."

He didn't.

"I don't know what to say, Gwen. But, you're right about one thing: I haven't the slightest idea what do to at this point."

"I'm right about something else, too, Lyman. You don't have any other options, certainly none that I can see and, believe me, I've looked at this thing forwards and backwards."

Henry tiredly rubbed his forehead.

"When do you propose contacting Smoot?" he asked.

"Immediately. I can't see how waiting helps anything...they'll only get worse. I'll call Smoot this week and tell him that I'm in the market for some body parts."

"What if he plays dumb?"

"If that happens we'll drop back and punt. But I don't think he will. If you're right about Smoot, he traffics in corpses. Why would he decline to do business with a cash buyer?"

"He may suspect that it's a set-up which, in fact, it is."

"Yes, that's a possibility. But I'm guessing that given the nature of the entire business, Smoot is no stranger to dealing with marginal types...it kind of comes with the territory, wouldn't you think? I'm not too worried about convincing Smoot that I'm legit."

Henry pondered Gwen's plan. "You realize that, if the whole thing goes south, I'll have fallen on my sword for nothing."

"I'm aware of that," she granted. "But tell me, what other choices do you have, Lyman?"

"Okay, I guess," he said with an utter lack of conviction. "What do you want me to do?"

"There's nothing you can do other than keep out of sight. The first thing *I've* gotta do is contact the Corporation Commission so I can establish my *bona fides*. If Smoot decides to check my credentials after I talk to him, he'd better be able to find something."

"I don't suppose I could induce you to bring me some food in the meantime?" Henry hopefully requested.

She chuckled. "Yeah, I suppose I could do that."

***

It took less than fifteen minutes for Gwen to complete and file online the forms necessary to create an Arizona limited liability company. She chose the name "Arminius Holdings LLC," after the German chieftain whose forces annihilated three Roman legions in 9 CE, and indicated that "Gwendolyn Clarine" would serve as the company's only officer. According to the Arizona Corporation Commission's website, a public records search undertaken less than a week thereafter would conclusively establish that "Arminius Holdings LLC" was an Arizona limited liability company in good standing.

In the interim, she would talk to Detective Ortiz.

***

"Ms. Harp! This is a surprise. I didn't expect to hear from you again," Ortiz greeted her over the telephone, though she was unable to determine whether his seeming cordiality was genuine.

"Hello, detective. I'm actually kind of surprised, myself."

"How can I help you today?"

"Well, at the threshold, I was curious whether you took my advice and talked to Williams Smoot about his son's murder?" she inquired.

"As you know, counselor, I'm not at liberty to discuss an ongoing investigation. That said, I did speak with Mr. Smoot," the detective guardedly replied.

"I surmise, then, that because your investigation remains 'ongoing,' you haven't apprehended Mr. Henry yet."

"Not yet," he grudgingly admitted.

"Well, detective, this may be your lucky day. As it happens I spoke with Mr. Henry."

"What!" the detective blurted. "You saw Lyman Henry?"

Gwen laughed. "I said I *spoke* with him, not that I *saw* him."

"When?"

"Yesterday."

"Where is Henry?" he curtly demanded.

"I didn't ask," she said. Technically true, since Henry had volunteered his location on Van Buren without her having to ask.

Ortiz was skeptical. "Why would Henry call *you*?"

"Probably because I'm the only attorney he knows and didn't know who else *to* call."

"What did he want?"

"As you know, detective, I'm not at liberty to discuss client confidences," she parroted him.

Ortiz laughed out loud. "'Ouch' again, counselor. I can't seem to avoid stepping right in the middle of it every time I talk to you, can I?"

"That's okay, detective. I just couldn't pass up the opportunity to pay you back in the same coin."

"Well, you succeeded. Again."

"But, as it happens, Mr. Henry specifically authorized me to share our conversation."

"Really? Okay, what did he want?"

"Mr. Henry indicated that he's prepared, in principle, to turn himself over to the authorities."

"If he wants to turn himself in, why didn't he just do it instead of calling you?" Ortiz dubiously inquired.

"He wanted to talk to an attorney first because he obviously doesn't trust the police. I remind you that Mr. Henry is, himself, a retired police officer. He's also presumed to be innocent of any crime and wants to make certain that his interests are protected."

"Forgive me for being direct, but that sounds like lawyer double-speak."

"Call it what you like," Gwen said. "I didn't write the Constitution, detective. I simply called you because it's my duty as an officer of the court."

"What did you tell Henry about turning himself in?"

"I urged him to do so immediately, of course."

"And?"

"And he said that he'd come to a decision and call me back."

"What you're basically telling me is that Lyman Henry called you, without warning, and told you that it's metaphysically, theoretically, arguable that he might possibly be thinking about maybe turning himself in. That's what you're saying?"

"In a nutshell, yes."

"Well, thanks, I guess," Ortiz dryly replied. "I assume you'll let me know if and when Henry calls you back, counselor?"

"Certainly. Despite your sarcasm, detective, I'm confident that Mr. Henry's call was made in good faith."

"I guess we'll see. Thanks for the info, counselor. Anything else I can help you with today?"

"No, I just wanted to make you aware of my conversation with Mr. Henry, detective."

"Okay, thank you again, Ms. Harp. Hopefully, Henry will call you back."

"I'm sure he will, detective. Have a good day."

She hung up the phone and smiled to herself.

TWENTY

"Williams Smoot, please."

"Who's calling?" Eileen mechanically inquired.

"I'm calling about biological material."

"I'm sorry, what are you calling about? This is a funeral home."

"I realize that. Is Mr. Smoot available?"

Eileen was conflicted. Calls to BioServus were supposed to be automatically routed directly to Smoot's private cell phone, not the funeral home. But if she played dumb and sent the caller packing, BioServus might lose a potential customer. Worse, if Smoot found out, he'd have an absolute fit.

"Hello?   Are you still there?" the caller interrupted Eileen's reverie.

"Yes, I'm sorry. I'm still here. Who were you calling for?" she stalled.

"I would like to speak with Williams Smoot, please."

"I'll see if Mr. Smoot is available," Eileen finally resolved. "Who may I say is calling?"

"Gwen Clarine."

"Please hold." Eileen punched a button on the phone and beeped Smoot's office.

"Yes, what is it?" he barked. He was irritable: BioServus had fallen far behind on shipments because of the irksome investigation into Freddie's murder. He hadn't anticipated that Henry would disappear underground and Detective Ortiz's consequent snooping had prevented Lightfoot from promptly processing bodies, creating a bottleneck.

"There's a woman on hold asking about 'biological material'."

"Who is she?"

"I don't know. She said her name was Gwen Clarine," Eileen informed him.

"What does she want?"

"Just that she wants to talk to you."

While it wasn't unusual to receive spontaneous communication from potential customers, such inquiries were invariably directed to BioServus, not the funeral home. Several of BioServus's largest orders had, however, emanated from such unsolicited contacts. And, although uneasy about taking cold calls, BioServus's business was tanking because of Smoot's paranoia over the tenacious Detective Ortiz.

"All right, put her through," he sighed. When a red light began silently flashing on his desk phone, he picked up the receiver.

"This is Williams Smoot. How may I help you?"

'Mr. Smoot, my name is Gwen Clarine. I'm calling about acquiring biological material."

"I'm sorry, this is the Smoot Funeral Chapel. I think you must have misdialed."

"Please don't fence with me, Mr. Smoot. You and I both know this is the correct number."

Smoot's mind raced.

"Have we met previously, Ms. Clarine? I'm sorry, but your name isn't familiar."

"No, we've not met. I learned of you though business contacts."

"Oh? What business are you in?"

"I'm president and CEO of Arminius Holdings."

"I see. And what is the nature of Arminius Holdings' business?"

"We supply organic and biological material to clients globally."

"I'm sorry?" Smoot simulated ignorance.

"Arminius Holdings operates as a distributor for certain products and services that I understand you may be able to provide."

"Ms. Clarine, I operate a funeral home. If you or your clients require assistance with respect to funeral services, grief counseling, or the transfer of remains, Smoot Funeral Chapel is at your disposal. Otherwise, I'm not sure how I can help you."

"I'll be blunt, Mr. Smoot. My clients have a continuing need for human tissue, organs, cartilage, and bone. I am informed that you may able to discretely supply such items. If I was misinformed in this regard, please accept my sincere apology."

Smoot briefly pondered Gwen's representations.

"From whom did you learn that I might be able to help you?"

"One of my medical school contacts on Grenada," she replied. "He was highly complementary of your services."

Although BioServus provided product to two Grenadian medical colleges, negotiations and transfers had always been conducted through proxies, as was typical.   Accordingly, Smoot personally knew no one on the island of Grenada.

"I think you may be referring to BioServus, a non-transplant tissue bank with which I'm associated," he guardedly disclosed.   "If so, I'm, frankly, puzzled why you didn't you contact BioServus directly, Ms. Clarine."

Aside from Henry's speculative musings, Gwen possessed no independent corroboration that, in fact, Smoot trafficked in human remains.   His unprompted admission regarding BioServus immediately dispelled all uncertainty.   She hurriedly jotted down the name.

"I make it a point to talk directly to the decision makers, Mr. Smoot, not to functionaries who merely answer telephones," she smoothly responded.   In point of fact, it would have been impossible for her to have contacted BioServus directly because, until seconds ago, Gwen possessed absolutely no knowledge of its existence.

"I understand, but submit that you may find it more expedient to address your inquiries to BioServus," Smoot urged.

She decided to call his bluff.

"Let me be frank, Mr. Smoot.   It was my understanding that you're the principal, which is why I directed my call to you, personally.   My hope was that we might be able to do business, but if you find it preferable to give me the runaround, I'll simply find another supplier."

"No, no," an alarmed Smoot backtracked .   "We are always delighted to accommodate our clients in any way we can.   I apologize if I was unclear, Ms. Clarine.   How may I be of service?"

Gwen couldn't help but smile at the efficacy of her masquerade.

"Very good, thank you. One of my clients in Brussels requires a number of human torsos within the next two weeks. Can you provide them?"

Smoot maintained a meticulous account of BioServus's inventory, but would have to review it, and talk to Lightfoot, before he could provide a definitive answer. He also needed to confirm that the caller was a legitimate buyer.

"I'm sure we can help," he confidently assured her. "I'll simply have to verify our current inventory...how many torsos will your client need? Rest assured we'll do everything in our power to assist you."

"A dozen to begin with. If my clients are satisfied with your service and the quality of your product, additional orders may be forthcoming. No less than six torsos are to be locally delivered within a week, COD. The remaining six must be delivered one week thereafter," she crisply informed him.

"Do you have a preference with respect to gender?"

"No. I will leave that to your discretion."

An order for twelve complete human torsos was a bonanza that Smoot could scarcely believe. Local COD delivery was, however, highly unusual.

"You are located here in Phoenix, Ms. Clarine?"

"Arminius Holdings is headquartered in Phoenix, though we have satellite offices worldwide."

"I see. Well, if you'll give me your number, I'll check our inventory and call you back," he excitedly promised.

"Very good."   Gwen recited the number of her burner phone.

"Got it," Smoot said. "I'll get back to you by the end of the day, Ms. Clarine. You may rely on it."

"I look forward to your call, Mr. Smoot."

"Certainly. Thank you for calling."

As quickly as their conversation terminated, Smoot turned to his desktop computer. He had no inkling whether Arminius Holdings was an authentic company or simply a fictitious entity dreamt up by the caller. He typed the purported name into the Google search box and was gratified to learn that Arminius Holdings was, in fact, an official limited liability company in good standing, organized under the laws of the State of Arizona. As she'd stated over the telephone, Gwendolyn Clarine was its president and CEO.

Smoot was thrilled that Arminius Holdings LLC was unquestionably legitimate. Moreover, because she was local, doing business with Clarine would prove uncomplicated and, furthermore, explained the specified COD arrangement.

He next undertook Google, Facebook, and Linked In searches for "Gwendolyn Clarine."   As expected, a significant number of people shared that name.   However, none of their profiles referenced "Arminius Holdings," Arizona, or corresponded to anything the caller had revealed during their telephone conversation.   Smoot found the lacuna far from surprising.   Given the inherent ghoulishness of commerce in human remains, most participants kept intentionally low profiles.   Indeed, he'd have been surprised, and extremely wary, had he encountered information about the caller on any social media website.

Smoot beeped Eileen.

"Get hold of Danny. Tell him that I have to see him right away. Today."

"Who was that woman?" Eileen indifferently inquired.

"Potential customer. Call Danny," he repeated.

Smoot checked the Hublot on his wrist. He and Lightfoot had a lot work to do.

***

"Where's the fuckin' fire?" Lightfoot grumbled. "I just about popped a nut gettin' here. Eileen made it sound like the whole damned place was about ready to implode."

"We had a large order this morning that you'll have to start processing at once." Smoot imperiously informed him. "How many bodies do we currently have in storage?"

The other man scratched his ragged beard. "Not countin' the two I just cut up, six, I think."

"All male?"

"Yeah. How many we need?"

"All of them. You'll have to start prepping them tonight."

"Tonight?" Lightfoot protested. "It's hotter than two rats fucking in a wool sock! I can't start until after dark and I'll be workin' all damned night!"

"I realize that it's a significant imposition, Danny, but I will compensate you accordingly. I also have an additional surprise waiting for you at the end."

"What kinda 'surprise?'" Lightfoot suspiciously asked.

"You'll see...all I can tell you is that she's very eager to make your acquaintance," Smoot winked. He had no doubt that Lightfoot would greatly resent being pressured to rush the dismemberments but was absolutely determined to secure a permanent client in Arminius Holdings LLC. In order to guarantee Lightfoot's compliance, Smoot had gone online to arrange a rendezvous between Lightfoot and a teen runaway.

Lightfoot grinned wickedly. "When?"

"Just as soon as you've finished prepping the bodies, Danny. As I said, she's extremely eager to meet you.

"Here?"

"Wherever you wish. I've arranged for her for as long as you want."

"How old?"

A sly smile crossed Smoot's chubby face as he rubbed his plump hands together.

"As you may imagine, she was quite circumspect about her age, Danny. However, she confided to me that she just experienced her first period."

Lightfoot smirked. "I'll start ferrying the stiffs over here tonight. How do you want 'em prepped?"

"The buyer specified that she only wants torsos so, at a minimum, you'll have to remove the lower extremities. I'll have to ask whether she wants their arms and heads to remain attached."

"How soon she need 'em?"

"This week." Smoot chose to ignore Lightfoot's pained expression. "Wait until at least 9:00. I want it to be fully dark outside. I'll talk to the buyer in the meantime so you'll know exactly how much cutting you'll have to do."

"I guess I'll just hang around until then," Lightfoot shrugged. "No sense leavin' because it's a pain in the ass to keep takin' the bus back and forth."

"Why don't you take a little siesta in one of the back offices?" Smoot invited. "There's probably some snacks in the break room, too."

The other man nodded. "Cool."

As soon as Lightfoot left the room, Smoot picked up the phone to call Gwen Clarine.

***

Gwen was far from surprised when the burner phone began ringing, its screen identifying the caller as "Smoot Fun." She answered it on the fourth ring.

"Gwen Clarine speaking."

"Ms. Clarine, this is Williams Smoot, calling back as promised."

"I appreciate your diligence, Mr. Smoot."

"My pleasure. I'm delighted to report that we currently have sufficient inventory to accommodate your client's needs and can arrange delivery at your convenience. COD, as discussed."

"Wonderful news!" she gushed. "My client will be extremely pleased."

"The torsos are all male. I hope that won't be a problem."

"Not at all; males will be perfectly satisfactory," Gwen affirmed.

"Excellent! In order to ensure that our product fully meets your client's expectations, please inform me exactly how you wish it prepared."

"I thought I made that clear. My client needs a dozen complete human torsos."

"Yes, I know. My question is whether your client desires the removal of the head and upper limbs. Also, there's the question regarding the disposition of the internal organs...does your client wish to purchase those, as well? Naturally, there will be an additional fee."

"*Of course* we'll want head, limbs, and all organs. But be advised that my client is disinclined to purchase the merchandise on a piecemeal basis, Mr. Smoot.   We   are   only   interested   in   a   flat-fee arrangement and do not intend to haggle over prices like Moroccan rug merchants."

"I see," Smoot muttered. "Well, Ms. Clarine, if those are your terms..."

"They are," she interjected.

"...our fee for a human torso, including all associated organs and appendages, will be $8,000 per unit." Smoot hesitated. "I think you'll find that to be immanently reasonable."

Under normal circumstances, Smoot would have charged a minimum of $8,000 for just a hollowed-out torso, essentially a rib cage with the attached spinal column, sans head and internal organs. However, he was desperate to make a substantial sale after weeks of enforced idleness and even prepared to suffer a financial loss simply to close the deal.

"I will tell you, candidly, that is significantly less than what my client customarily pays, Mr. Smoot," Gwen informed him.   "When will the product be available?"

"The first six units will be ready to ship in three days," he assured her. "Payment will be expected, in certified funds, at time of delivery."

"Of course."

"What is the local address where the product is to be delivered?"

"I will telephone you again with that information," she responded. "Will you personally be delivering it? I would very much like to meet you, as my instinct is that we may be doing additional business in the future."

"Unfortunately, deliveries are handled by an associate. I'm sure we'll have the opportunity to meet in the very near future, Ms. Clarine, and look forward to that occasion."

Gwen was dismayed that Smoot declined to deliver the remains himself, obviously intending to send Lightfoot instead.   That unanticipated development significantly complicated her plan, but she dared not allow her disappointment to betray her.

"As you wish. I'll call you day after tomorrow with the address," she evenly replied.

"Good afternoon, Ms. Clarine. I look forward to speaking with you again."

"Good afternoon, Mr. Smoot."

Gwen ended the call. She had to talk to Henry and Ortiz, in that order, without delay.

Smoot beeped Eileen.   "Find Danny...he's somewhere in the building."

TWENTY ONE

It was dusk by the time Gwen arrived, unannounced, at Henry's trailer. A large container of take-out Mexican food, and a six-pack of cold beer, rested on the seat beside her. Henry was standing on the bottom step of his trailer when she drove up.

"I saw you pull in from Van Buren," he explained as she stepped from the car. They briefly hugged before she handed him the container of Mexican food.

"I hadn't heard from you and was worried..." she began, but he waved her off.

"I've been kinda depressed," he admitted. Gwen grabbed the six-pack and led him inside.

"No word from Max, huh?" she asked. Henry merely shook his head.

She placed the six-pack on a counter top. "Well, maybe one of these will help," she said as she removed a can, popped it open, and handed it to him.

"It sure as hell can't hurt. I haven't had a beer since Max was here." Henry took a deep draught then nodded toward the food container. "Man, that smells good!"

"Hope you like Mexican," Gwen smiled.

He removed paper plates from the cupboard and plastic eating utensils from the drawer and, together, they began to eat.

Henry finally broke the silence. "I'm really happy to see you, Gwen."

"Me, too," she smiled, taking a sip of beer. "You know, I ordinarily don't care much for beer, but this tastes pretty darned good...must be the company."

"Yeah, that must be it," he wryly responded

She placed her can on the floor beside her. "I talked to Smoot, Lyman."

"Today?"

"Yeah."

"And?"

"He agreed to sell me the torsos."

Henry was taken aback. "No kidding? Just like that?"

"Just like that. He must be pretty hungry, 'cause he accepted my story without batting an eye."

"The fact that I'm still on the loose, combined with all the poking and prodding around Freddie's murder, has probably made Smoot pretty damned gun-shy. Did you talk to Ortiz?"

She shook her head. "Not since talking to Smoot. I was gonna call him again tomorrow. But first I wanted to talk to you because I need to know what to tell him."

Henry nodded. Gwen's entire plan hinged on his surrendering to the cops, which had to be precisely choreographed.

"But there's some bad news," she continued. He raised a quizzical eyebrow. "Smoot won't deliver the stuff...he's apparently gonna have Danny, or *somebody*, be his bagman."

"So where does that leave us? What good is the plan if Smoot isn't even gonna be there?"

"I honestly don't know," Gwen confessed. "But whoever shows up with a car full of human body parts will be arrested, no matter *who* it is."

"Yeah, but it's *Smoot* we're after, not one of his hirelings," a disappointed Henry asserted. "And don't forget that I'll be hauled off, too...and for murder, not hauling around a bunch of body parts."

"I know, Lyman. But even if, say, it's Danny who does the delivery, he'll be arrested and I don't think it'll take very much pressure to get him to drop the dime on Smoot...you saw how Danny was when we talked to him in jail."

'What if it *isn't* Lightfoot?"

Gwen placed her hand atop Henry's. "Irrespective of *who* it is, we'll use 'em to get to Smoot. There's nothing else we can do."

Both were momentarily silent.

"When do you want to do it?" he finally asked.

"Smoot told me he'll be ready to deliver the bodies in three days," Gwen said.

"That'll be Friday."

She nodded.

"That's it, then," Henry sighed. "Call Ortiz and tell him that I've decided to turn myself in this coming Friday. Tell him that you'll personally bring me in."

"Okay. I'll call him tomorrow. After I talk to Ortiz, I'll call Smoot to coordinate with him. And once the table's set, I'll let you know."

Henry squeezed Gwen's hand.

"On a one-to-ten scale, what do you think the chances are of pulling this off?"

"Ummm...a five?" she ventured.

"Wrong. About a negative three. At best." He stood. "I need another beer."

***

"Lyman Henry's prepared to turn himself in on Friday? That's what he told you?"

"Yes, detective, that's what he told me," Gwen reiterated. "The only proviso is that Mr. Henry will surrender only to me, and I will personally transport him to the rendezvous point."

"So, it appears that you *do* know where Henry's been," Ortiz smugly observed.

"He told me that he'll call me with his exact location," Gwen said. Literally true, if non-responsive, though the detective appeared not to notice.

"You don't find it a little strange that Henry agreed to surrender just to you, counselor?"

"'I'm a human being, so nothing human is strange to me.' The Roman poet, Terence, said that, detective. I remind you again that Mr. Henry is a former police officer. Right or wrong, he evidently trusts me more than he trusts the constabulary. But the only thing I care about is that he finally came to the right decision...that should be all any of us cares about."

"Don't get me wrong, Ms. Harp. I'm delighted. This entire case has been a puzzler from the get-go, so I guess I really shouldn't be surprised by anything that happens."

You ain't seen nuthin' yet, Gwen thought to herself. Wait 'till Lightfoot drives up with a car full of human torsos.

"But," Ortiz continued, "as long as I have your personal guarantee that Henry will be as docile as a lamb, I don't have a problem with you carting him in. The last thing I want is a bloodbath trying to arrest the guy."

"Agreed," Gwen said.

"So what time, and where, am I supposed to rendezvous with you two scamps on Friday? Or is that a secret, too?" Ortiz dryly inquired.

"Mr. Henry will call me with that information. As soon as he does, I'll contact you."

"How did I know it wasn't gonna be easy," Ortiz mused aloud, "but okay. Lemme know when, and if, you hear from Henry again. I'll be standing by."

"Fair enough. Thank you for your time, detective. I'm confident we'll wrap this matter up with a minimum of risk to everyone."

"Yeah, maybe. Just get back to me as soon as you hear from Henry."

***

"What kind of progress are we making, Danny?" Lightfoot and Smoot were sitting in the latter's luxurious office.

"What's with the 'we'"? Lightfoot asked. "I don't see *you* out there, sawin' up frozen stiffs in the middle of the fucking night, sweatin' like a butcher."

"I realize it's hard work," Smoot empathized. "But the product must be delivered tomorrow."

"Yeah, yeah, I got it," Lightfoot dismissively acknowledged.

"Just make certain that you have plenty of dry ice and enough coolers to hold all the product," Smoot reminded him. "This is a big order and I want it to be perfect."

"I know what I'm doin'. Don't get your bowels in an uproar. Where's it supposed to go, anyway?"

"The buyer will contact me later today with delivery instructions. I just want everything to be ready tomorrow. No foul-ups."

"It'll be ready. Don't worry about it."

"One more thing, Danny. The sale is COD. The buyer will be on site and will give you $48,000 in certified funds upon delivery. $3,000 of that is yours, over and above your regular compensation...plus the favors of the young lady, of course. Just make certain to bring the payment directly here afterward. I'll give you your money at that time."

"When do I get the trim?"

"She'll be here tomorrow. Maybe the two of you can go on a long weekend with your $3,000 share," Smoot prodded. He wanted to postpone disclosing to Lightfoot the unhappy revelation that BioServus was obligated to provide another six torsos in a week.

"Fuck that," Lightfoot sneered. "The longest period of time in the world is the time between when I cum and she goes."

"As you think best, Danny. I simply wanted to show my appreciation for all your hard work."

Lightfoot changed the subject. "I guess I'm drivin' the shit to wherever it's supposed to go tomorrow?"

"Yes. It's a local delivery, so it won't take you very long. I'm sure you'll be there and back before you know it...and $3,000 richer."

"Riiiiiight," Lightfoot retorted. "Spoken like a man who doesn't have to deliver a ton of shit and unload it."

Smoot didn't respond.

***

Gwen sat on the edge of the travel trailer's sofa. Henry was in the flimsy chair, facing her.

"There's an old industrial park on 51st Avenue and the Lower Rio Parkway. It's about as good a place as any, I guess," Henry remarked. "Out in the middle of nowhere with lots of room for the shit-load of cops that'll be there."

"The delivery needs to arrive at exactly the same moment we do," Gwen reiterated.

"Well, if Lightfoot's in charge of the delivery, good luck with that. I'm not even sure he knows how to tell time."

Gwen laughed. "Maybe he has one of those talking watches!"

"Yeah, maybe. But you're right, he has to get there right when we do...directly into the welcoming embrace of the Phoenix Police Department."

"What time shall I tell them? Smoot and Ortiz, I mean."

Henry reflected before responding.

"I suppose it doesn't really matter," he finally said. "We just need to do everything in our power to minimize the chance that something will go wrong...Murphy's Law, and all that.   But what, exactly, that might be, I have no idea. At the end of the day, Smoot remains the wild card."

"All we can do is the best we can, Lyman. Even if the wheels fall off and everything goes to hell, the worst thing that will happen is that you'll be arrested. But I promise you'll get the best legal representation available in Arizona...I'll call in every favor ever owed to me."

"Great," Henry spiritlessly responded. "I'm not sure that makes me feel a hell of a lot better, but thanks for trying."

"Okay, how about 3:00 tomorrow afternoon? Are you okay with that?" Gwen asked.

"It's about as broad as it is long, so I guess 3:00 will work."

"Lyman, do you still have the money Smoot paid you?"

He pointed to a cabinet. "In there. I'm sure I'll need it, and a pile more, to pay for my defense lawyer."

"I'll call Smoot and Ortiz when I get back to my office. And I'll be here tomorrow at 1:30 to pick you up. That'll give us time to discuss last minute details, if need be." She stood, "Call me tonight if you just want to talk, Lyman."

Henry wearily got to his feet and dragged his chair out of the way.

"Will do."   He stepped toward Gwen and embraced her. "Thank you."

Gwen nodded wordlessly, hoping he didn't see the tear when she turned away.

TWENTY TWO

Lisa was already at the mortuary when Lightfoot arrived. Skinny, frizzy brown hair, too much makeup, bad teeth, multiple tats, and a bull ring piercing the septum of her nose, Lisa chain-smoked while she watched him shove the heavy coolers across the floor.

"What's in those? Beer?" she idly inquired.

"Naw, steaks," he replied. Lightfoot straightened and rubbed his lower back. "Hey, how old are you, anyway?"

"Old enough. What the fuck do you care? I've got a pussy, which is all you give a damn about."

"I was just thinkin' that you might be a little too old for me," he grinned.

"Fuck you," she giggled and took another drag off her cigarette.

Lightfoot heaved the first cooler into the back of the funeral home's windowless van.

"Wanna go for a ride?" he asked.

"Where to?"

He bent and lifted a second cooler into the van, sweating profusely.

"What's it to you? Gotta hot date or something?"

"Yeah, with you," she said. "I suppose I could tag along. But why don't you pinch a few steaks from one of them coolers and we'll cook 'em up later?"

He laughed. "Darlin', I *guarantee* that you don't want what's in these chests."

"Whatever." She lit another cigarette.

It took longer to load the van than Lightfoot anticipated. The coolers were much heavier than he'd expected and his back hurt like hell. Each torso occupied an individual container packed with dry ice, while the internal organs were indiscriminately dumped into heavy plastic trash bags and placed in additional coolers.

Lightfoot glanced at his watch. Plenty of time to get to the old industrial park specified by Smoot.

"Wait here. I've gotta go tell 'em that I'm headin' out," he told Lisa.

"Okie dokie."

Lightfoot entered the funeral home through the rear door and walked to Smoot's office. He rapped on the frame of the open door before entering.

"I'm leavin'," he informed Smoot, who sat behind his desk staring at the computer monitor.

Smoot looked up.

"You wrote the address down?"

Lightfoot nodded. "Yep, it's all good."

"Remember, Danny, you must collect $48,000 in certified funds before relinquishing the product. Understand?"

"Yeah, yeah, I got it. Everything's under control. Be back in a flash."

Smoot smiled wanly. "Good. See you when you get back, Danny."

Lightfoot returned to the van, where he and Lisa clambered into the front seats. He twisted the key and the engine roared to life.

"Care if I smoke?" she asked as she lit a cigarette.

He pushed the transmission lever into 'D' and pulled away from the building.

"Go ahead, it ain't my van," he said.

***

Although just past noon, the industrial park was already brimming with police officers. A dozen police cruisers were positioned out of sight behind various buildings. Ortiz's unmarked Ford Expedition was the only vehicle that was immediately visible. Overhead, a police helicopter noisily churned the air.

The public defender called yesterday with the intelligence that she, with Henry in tow, would arrive at 3:00 that afternoon. Ortiz would believe it when he actually saw them arrive at the industrial park. He walked over to shoot the shit with another cop.

***

Gwen arrived at Henry's trailer at 1:35. Characteristically, he met her outside.

"Hi." He nervously smiled and hugged her.

"Hi, yourself," she said as she reciprocated his embrace.

They entered the trailer, where she sat on the sofa. Henry pulled a chair up and wearily plopped into it.

"I'm gonna call Smoot, just to make sure everything's still a 'go.' Don't say anything," Gwen cautioned. She removed the burner phone from her purse and dialed the funeral home's number. She promptly identified herself and Eileen transferred her call to Smoot.

"So good of you to call," he greeted her. "My associate is en route to you at this moment."

"What?" she blurted. "I won't be there until 3:00. I thought we discussed that already!"

"Yes, yes," the funeral director acknowledged. "We simply wanted to allow sufficient time to get there...traffic accidents, road construction, and the like. He will arrive promptly at 3:00, as agreed."

Gwen silently breathed a sigh of relief.

"You will have full payment with you?"

"Yes, of course," Gwen responded. "That was our agreement, was it not?"

"Indeed, it was, Ms. Clarine."

"I'll call you afterward to confirm that the transaction was satisfactorily completed," she told Smoot.

"Splendid. I'll be here all afternoon and look forward to hearing from you."

Gwen terminated the call and looked at her watch.

"Let's go."

***

The funeral home van approached the industrial park from the east. Lisa leaned forward in the passenger's seat and pointed through the windshield.

"What's with the police helicopter?" she idly asked no one. "It's been there forever."

Lightfoot followed her gaze upward.

"How do you know it's a police helicopter?"

"'Cause it *looks* like one," she emphatically declared. Lisa punched the button to lower the passenger's window and flicked her cigarette butt out.

Lightfoot slowed and eased the van onto the dirt shoulder. Allowing the vehicle to idle, he watched the helicopter through the windshield.

"Prob'ly nuthin'," he finally concluded.

"Yeah, prob'ly," she agreed. "Let's go." She rolled her window up and lit another cigarette.

Lightfoot glanced at his watch: 2:50. Close enough. He took his foot off the brake and guided the van back onto the tarmac.

***

Gwen looked over at Henry. "You doin' okay?"

"Never better," he lied.

She looked at the dashboard clock.

"We'll be there in ten minutes, Lyman. Hang in there." She reached over to pat his leg.

He grasped her hand and held it.

***

Aside from the helicopter circling overhead, the only vehicle Gwen discerned when she pulled into the industrial park was an idling, dark blue SUV. She recognized Detective Ortiz in the driver's seat. The moment he spotted Gwen's Sentra, he flung the door open and stepped from the Expedition.

She pulled abreast of the detective's vehicle, put the Nissan's transmission in 'park', and switched the engine off.

Scarcely one block away, as he proceeded west on Lower Rio Parkway, Lightfoot watched as a red rice-burner pulled into the industrial park and drove slowly toward a stationary SUV. He knew he had the correct address and surmised the two vehicles were associated with the buyer he was supposed to rendezvous with. Like fuckin' Grand Central Station, he thought as he approached the turn-in and tapped the van's brake pedal.

***

Ortiz reached back inside the Expedition and grabbed the handset of his police radio. He depressed the button on the side of the microphone.

"Now!" he shouted into the handset.

A dozen police cruisers instantly shot from as many concealed positions to encircle Gwen's Sentra in a cloud of dust.

Ortiz whipped his service automatic from his waistband and pointed it at the Nissan.

"Get the fuck out with your hands where I can see them!" he screamed.

***

"What the fuck?" Lightfoot cried.

Although he had no idea why cops were swarming all over the place, all hell appeared to be breaking loose only fifty yards from his van full of human remains. He had to get the hell out of there before becoming accidentally embroiled in the developing chaos. The cops might think he was somehow involved in whatever was happening around him and the last thing Lightfoot needed was for the oinkers to take a squint inside his coolers. Lightfoot slammed the brakes on and the van slid to a stop.

A cop looked up, directly at him, clearly surprised by the van's unexpected arrival.

"We gotta get outta here!" Lightfoot barked.

"What the hell are ya doin'?" Lisa demanded. "It's a fuckin' pigapalooza! I got a coupla eight balls of meth on me! Crank this bitch around, man! Bounce!"

Lightfoot gunned the engine and flung the van's steering wheel hard to the right as he fishtailed away from the pandemonium playing out in front of them.

"Goose it!" Lisa shrieked over the rising bedlam.

***

Gwen and Henry opened their respective doors and slowly emerged from vehicle, hands first.

"I'm Gwen Harp..." she began.

"Shut up!" Ortiz barked. "Get over there." He nodded to one side with his head, his pistol never wavering. "You!" he shouted at Henry over the roof of the Nissan, "on the ground, spread eagle."

Henry sank to his knees with his hands still in the air then fell forward onto the cracked blacktop. The police officer closest to him intentionally drove his knee into Henry's back as he dropped on top of him, wrenched Henry's wrists behind his back, and snapped handcuffs on him. The cop then rolled the prostrate prisoner onto his back, more than a dozen police weapons trained on him.

"Detective!" Gwen pleaded. "Mr. Henry is not resisting!   But Daniel Lightfoot is driving that van, which contains evidence of multiple felonies.   You must intercept him!"

Ortiz looked away from Henry long enough to see the funeral van race from the industrial park.

"Please!" Gwen importuned. "Please, detective!"

"Stop that van!" he reluctantly ordered the officer nearest him. "Go!"

Two cops holstered their weapons and sprinted to the nearest police cruiser. The driver gunned the engine and squealed from the parking lot while his passenger was still in the process of slamming shut his door.

Satisfied that Henry was fully subdued, Ortiz quickly ordered a second police car to follow.

***

Lightfoot glanced into his rearview mirror. Two police cars were less than 100 yards behind them, hauling ass and rapidly gaining. Although he floored the accelerator, the van labored due to the heavy load it carried. The overburdened coolers in the back slid about, further rendering the lumbering vehicle difficult to control on the potholed street.

"Punch it, for Christ's sake!" Lisa screeched. She spontaneously reached over and grabbed the steering wheel. Lightfoot slapped her hands away.

"Fuck you!" he shouted. "Keep your fuckin' hands away!"

"Fuck you, you prick!" she bawled.

In an effort to halt its mad flight, one of the trailing police cars drew abreast of the escaping van and attempted to force it onto the shoulder of the road. Lightfoot countered by cranking the van's steering wheel hard to the left. The police cruiser slammed its brakes to avert a collision.

Lightfoot overcorrected.

Punctuated by Lisa's screams, the funeral van spun across the roadway. Although Lightfoot attempted to maintain control, the vehicle flipped and rolled 60 yards down the asphalt, ultimately sliding to rest on its side. The van's rear doors sprang open as it bounced, ejecting some of the coolers inside. The plastic bags they contained burst when they struck the tarmac, spewing their bloody contents pell-mell.

Lightfoot was hurled through the windshield and lay akimbo on the ground in front of the twisted van. Lisa caromed around the interior like a ragdoll but was not ejected.

His face-first exit through the van's windshield nicked Lightfoot's carotid artery. Gouts of dark blood pumped into the dirt where his head lay, turning it into sticky mud. He was very nearly exsanguinated by the time the first two cops leapt from their vehicle and sprinted to the wreckage. One knelt by Lightfoot's inert body while his partner climbed gingerly into the rear of the wrecked van. The trailing cruiser slid to a stop 100 feet away.

"Paramedics are on the way," the cop told Lightfoot. In order to assess the severity of his injury, he extended his hand and gently tried to turn Lightfoot's head to one side.

Lightfoot resisted.

"I'm fuckin' dead," he croaked.

"Well, it sure doesn't look too good, partner," the cop stoically concurred. The howl of approaching sirens could be heard in the distance.

The cop roughly shook Lightfoot's shoulder in an effort to keep him awake and focused until the arrival of an ambulance. With his thumb, he gestured vaguely over his shoulder as the third police officer approached.

"What's with all the guts?"

A muffled voice emerged from inside the van.

"Hey, there's a chick in here!"

"Alive?"

"Yeah, but pretty messed up."

"As long as she's breathin', don't move her until the para's get here. Anybody else inside?"

"Nobody who's alive...just a bunch of ice chests with cut-up bodies and shit. Jesus, it looks like a slaughterhouse in here!"

The cop turned his attention back to Lightfoot, who was sliding into shock.

"Hey!" he shouted. He vigorously shook the dying man, indifferent to his suffering. "Stay with me! Tell me about the ice chests!"

"Blow me," Lightfoot rasped.

"Where were you taking the stuff in the van?"

Inexplicably, Lightfoot attempted a feeble smile. A rattle emanated from deep within his chest and frothy blood bubbled from his mouth. He coughed weakly.

"Ask Smoot."

The cop shook Lightfoot again.

"Hey! Don't die yet, partner. What's with the stuff in the van?"

"Smoot," Lightfoot repeated, barely audible.

His jaw slackened and, though his lacerated head was turned toward his interrogator, his glassy eyes focused on nothing. Blood abruptly ceased pumping from the wound in his neck, the flow immediately reduced to a languorous drip.

"That's it," the other cop said without emotion. He stood behind his colleague, looking down at the dead man. "Who's 'Smoot'?"

The kneeling police officer rose to his feet. "Beats me...the girl probably knows, provided she doesn't die, too."

The cop pointed to the demolished van, where they could hear their colleague struggling to move about its interior.

"Pretty nice set of wheels for a couple of low-lifes." He gestured toward the roadway they had just traversed. "The paras are gonna think there were multiple fatals 'cause of all the guts scattered from hell to breakfast."

His companion nodded wordlessly.

***

Lightfoot's body was transported to the coroner. Despite the absence of ID, his criminal history made it easy to establish Lightfoot's identity once his finger prints were rolled at the morgue. The owner of the demolished van was rapidly determined simply by running its plates. They'd have to wait until the female regained consciousness to figure out who she was, as her fingerprints drew a blank.

Lisa suffered a concussion, three broken ribs, and a shattered wrist. Once the paramedics stabilized her, they automatically shunted her to the county hospital. Because Lisa had neither identification nor money on her person, no private medical facility would accept her as a patient. The cops wouldn't be able to interview her until the following day, however, following surgery to pin her wrist. Her broken ribs would simply be taped until they healed. No matter. They had a lot to work with in the meantime.

***

"Daniel Lightfoot," muttered Detective Ortiz to himself. "The guy reminds me of that old movie where the main character always seemed to be everywhere at once. What was the name of that movie?"

"'Gay Boys in Bondage'," responded the other detective without looking up.

Ortiz looked over at him. "No, I'm serious. Lightfoot's like that kid in high school that everybody claimed to know or, if they didn't, *wanted* to know. But nobody ever actually *saw* the guy...he went clear through high school and nobody ever laid eyes on him, yet everybody talked about him.   That's Danny Lightfoot. I been lookin' for Lightfoot for weeks and he ends up drivin' right up to me. What are the odds?"

"Well, you found your guy, all right, but he's dead. I guess you got half a loaf," the other detective said. "Congratulations."

"Why do you suppose Lightfoot was drivin' a van that belonged to the mortician he worked for, loaded to the gills with body parts?"

"Who cares? What else would be in a van owned by a mortician? Egg nog? Just be glad that you finally found the bastard and that he's fuckin' dead."

TWENTY THREE

"Why were you with Danny Lightfoot?"

"Who?"

"Daniel Lightfoot. The guy you were with in the van."

Lisa shrugged. "Oh. I didn't know that was his name."

Ortiz stood at Lisa's bedside in the county hospital. Although a sheet covered the lower half of her body, the upper half was a patchwork of bruises. Lisa's left forearm, which lay across her stomach, was in a cast extending from the palm of her hand to her elbow. Her fingers, swollen like sausages, protruded from the cast.

"Were you guys friends?"

Lisa laughed weakly. "Fuck no. I barely knew him."

"In that case, I guess you won't be too broken up to learn that he's dead."

"Why should I be?" she pointedly responded. "Like I said, I didn't even know the dude's name until just now."

"Then explain to me why you were in the van with him."

"Some old dude paid me to have sex with him," she apathetically replied.

"Who?"

"I dunno. He said he found me on Craig's List."

"How'd he contact you?"

"Cell phone...how else do you contact anyone?"

"How much did he pay you?"

"$250."

"Where'd you rendezvous with Lightfoot?"

"Huh?"

Ortiz rephrased the question. "Where did you and Danny Lightfoot hook up?"

Lisa shifted in bed as she tried, unsuccessfully, to ameliorate her increasing pain.

"The old guy picked me up in a Lexus and drove me to a fuckin' funeral parlor. Danny, or whatever his name was, was loadin' ice chests into a van there."

"What'd the guy look like?"

"Who?"

"The old guy who picked you up," Ortiz impatiently responded.

Lisa frowned as she tried to recall.

"Short, fat, balding, wearin' a suit and a pinkie ring...looked like Elmer Fudd."

"And he never told you his name?"

"Nope. He had cash, which is all I cared about."

"Where was the funeral home?"

"Central and Fell. *That* I remember 'cause it looked like something out of a goddamned magazine...big green lawn and shit."

"You know the name of it?"

Lisa shook her head as she shifted position again. "Ya know, I'm really enjoying our little chat but I'm in a lot of pain here."

"Yeah, that must really suck," Ortiz said without a modicum of sympathy. "But I'm not going anywhere until you answer my questions."

"What the fuck else do you want to know?" she retorted. "I was in a van with some dude that wrecked. He bought it and here I am in the fuckin' hospital...what the fuck else can I tell you, man?"

"Well, you could start with the meth we found in your pocket," Ortiz suggested.

"I don't know nuthin' about meth," she sullenly replied. "You or one of your little besties musta put it there."

"Yeah, I guess that's possible," Ortiz conceded. "But how'd my besties manage to put meth in your blood? That would be a lot trickier, don't you think?"

"I don't feel like thinkin'. I'm in pain. What do you want from me, huh?"

"Look, Lisa," Ortiz said, "I'm gonna tell you how the cow ate the cabbage. I don't give a crap about you *or* Danny Lightfoot. You're a fucked-up junkie runaway and he's dead. The guy I want is the guy who paid you the $250...he's the *jefe*, not two losers like you and Lightfoot."

"So?"

"So, if you help me, the meth problem goes away. Poof!"

She winced as she adjusted positions again.

"Help you how?"

"Tell a judge about your conversation with Elmer Fudd and what you agreed to do for the $250."

Lisa shrugged. "I agreed to fuck the dead guy. Big deal."

"See? Easy as fallin' off a log," said Ortiz with a cold smile.

***

Ortiz arrived at the funeral home with a uniformed police officer in tow.

"Detective," Eileen greeted them uneasily. "I didn't realize you had an appointment today. Is it about the accident?" she nervously probed.

Immediately after the wreck, Phoenix PD telephoned the funeral home to advise that one of its vans had been involved in a crash and was towed to a city impound yard. The department provided no additional information regarding the vehicle's occupants, nor of their fate.

The fact that no subsequent communication from either Lightfoot or Gwen Clarine had been forthcoming was, however, unsettling. Despite his anxieties, Smoot decided that it was vital to project an air of normalcy around the funeral home until he could initiate damage control.

"Smoot in?" Ortiz brusquely asked.

"Yes, let me buzz him for you." Eileen reached for the telephone on her desk.

"No!" he barked. "Don't touch the phone. Take us to Smoot's office. Now."

Ortiz gestured for Eileen to lead; she unhappily complied with the two men following close behind. As they approached the open doorway to Smoot's office, Ortiz pushed Eileen aside and stepped around her.

Smoot, wearing a pastel blue suit, sat at his desk intently writing on a yellow legal pad.

"What is it?" he crossly asked without looking up.

She started to answer but Ortiz cut her off.

"Williams Smoot, stop what you're doing, place your hands flat on the surface of your desk, palms down, and stand. You're under arrest for solicitation, sexual contact with a minor, attempted sexual assault, child molesting, kidnapping, conspiracy to commit statutory rape, providing false statements to a law enforcement officer, and first-degree murder."

Smoot's head snapped up. His jaw literally dropped when he saw the two cops with their service pistols trained on him. Eileen cowered to one side, pressed against the doorframe, her eyes wide with fright.

"What is the meaning of this?" Smoot bleated, his watery eyes darting from Ortiz to Eileen and back again.

"Stand! Now!" Ortiz again commanded. "If you don't, I'll put you on the floor and handcuff you myself!"

The funeral director's pen fell from his trembling hand onto the legal pad. He pressed his plump hands onto the top of his desk and slowly rose. The uniformed cop darted behind him.

"Put your hands behind your back," he instructed.

"Detective Ortiz, there must be some mistake," Smoot whined in a high voice as the cop snapped handcuffs around his thick wrists. "I have no idea what you're talking about...I've done none of those things." He looked at Eileen pleadingly, though she remained mute.

The funeral director began crying. "Please, detective," he blubbered in a tremulous voice.

As Ortiz recited Smoot's Fifth Amendment rights his words were rendered nearly inaudible by the latter's heaving sobs.

TWENTY FOUR

Gwen gave Henry the news when she went to visit him in the county jail. Danny Lightfoot was dead. Lisa was alive and expected to make a full recovery.

"What about Smoot?" he asked.

"I have some good news and some better news," she smiled.

"I'll start with the good news."

"The good news is that they raided the funeral home and Smoot's residence. In the funeral home and offsite, they found all kinds of body parts in freezers: limbs, brains, livers, kidneys, Tupperware containers full of blood, disarticulated joints, you name it. They're gonna try to use DNA to identify as many of the remains as they can. Maybe we can find out whether some of them are Max's, Lyman."

He listened intently.

"In both the funeral home and Smoot's house they found account books, logs, inventories, ledgers, and client lists. The DOJ, IRS, CDC, DEA, FDA, everybody and his brother is involved. Smoot and Eileen have already been arrested and I'm sure that more arrests are in the pipeline. Eileen has already turned on Smoot and is spilling her guts..." Gwen paused. "Is 'spilling her guts' an appropriate expression under the circumstances?"

"Seems about right," Henry chuckled.

She resumed. "Eileen is spilling her guts about Smoot...she knows where all the bodies are buried. Literally."

"So, they're gonna be able to bust Smoot for what? Operating an unlicensed, unsanitary tissue bank? Or mistreating corpses? Meanwhile, here I am, awaiting trial for killing Freddie Smoot."

"That's where the better news comes in," Gwen beamed.

"Okay, I'm sitting down. Lay it on me."

"Arizona Revised Statute 13-1105(A)(2)," she proudly said.

"I'll bite: what the hell is that?"

"Arizona's felony murder statute."

"Go on, please."

"Under Arizona law," she explained, "if you commit a felony and somebody ends up dying in the process, even if it's just by accident, you're legally responsible for his death. For example, if you rob a bank and a customer has a heart attack and dies as a result, you'll be charged with bank robbery *and* first-degree murder. You might as well have taken a gun and personally shot the guy in the head."

Henry looked at her blankly.

"Gwen, I'm not following you. You and I both know that Smoot killed people, including his own son and probably Max, but the chances of ever proving it in court are about nil. So how does that help anything?"

She began to laugh merrily.

"No, Lyman, listen! We don't have to prove that Smoot killed Freddie or Max...the important thing is that Lisa is only 14."

"So?"

"She's a minor. When Smoot paid Lisa to have sex with Danny, Smoot *ipso facto* became a party to conspiracy to commit child molesting, child rape, and sexual assault, all of which are felonies. Smoot, through Danny, was also guilty of kidnapping because 'kidnapping' means placing somebody in apprehension of imminent physical injury. In other words, the out-of-control van. On top of everything else, Danny was engaged in felonious unlawful flight when the van crashed. When Danny died in the wreck, his death was *automatically* attributed to Smoot because of Arizona's felony murder statute. Don't you see, Lyman? We don't *have* to prove that Smoot actually killed Freddie, or Max, or anybody else. We just have to show that Danny's death, even though unintended, was the culmination of a series of felonies relative to which Smoot was an active participant...conspiracy to commit statutory rape, for instance. Smoot's hands are covered in blood because Arizona's felony murder statute makes him responsible for Danny's death! Like I said, Smoot may just as well have taken a gun and shot Danny in the head." Gwen paused to catch her breath. "The bottom line, Lyman, is that Smoot became guilty of first-degree murder the moment Danny died in the crash."

"Well, I'll be damned," Henry grinned, though he was almost afraid to believe Gwen's words.

"Wait, I'm not finished," Gwen continued. "Between Eileen ratting him out and Arizona's felony murder statute, Smoot has already agreed to plead guilty to conspiracy in Freddie's murder, hoping to dodge the death penalty! But, Freddie's murder aside, once they really start digging into Smoot's operation they'll undoubtedly find evidence of more murders that they'll be able to hang on him, too. Smoot is toast, Lyman."

"So that means...."

"That means you'll be outta here sooner, rather than later! I've already got calls in to both the state's attorney and the presiding judge, Lyman!"

Henry didn't know whether to laugh, cry, dance, or hug Gwen. He felt like doing all of them simultaneously

"Well, I'll be damned," he repeated.

***

Gwen met Lyman at his apartment.

"The manager was very understanding when I explained to her why the cops trashed my apartment and why I didn't pay rent for the past two months: I was a fugitive from justice, fleeing a first-degree murder rap." He handed her a glass of moscato.

"I'm certain she was quite sympathetic," Gwen commented. She patted the space on the couch next to her.

"Very. Fortunately, we were able to come to an understanding over the awkward matter of my unpaid rent." Henry sat and held his glass aloft. "To life."

"To life," she repeated. They touched glasses and sipped their wine in contemplative silence.

"Ya know," Henry suddenly interjected, "I've got a bottle of *Flor de Caña* rum that I've been saving for a special occasion.   I wouldn't mind putting some flowers on Freddie Smoot's grave tomorrow and breaking open the *Flor*. I'd like to dedicate a toast to Max. If you have nothing better to do, what do you think about joining me?"

"I think I'd like that very much."

Gwen placed her wine glass on the coffee table, leaned over, and kissed Lyman Henry.

The End

TERMS OF USE

The author gratefully acknowledges the copyrighted or trademarked status and trademark owners of the following mentioned in this work of fiction: Agent Orange, Best Buy, Cabela's, Cadillac, Camel, Church's Fried Chicken, Craig's List, Denny's, Diet Coke, Dodge Coronet, eBay, Elmer Fudd, Facebook, Flor de Caña, Ford Expedition, Ford LTD, Google, Harbor Freight Tools, Home Depot, Hublot, Hyundai, Kool, Lexus, Linked In, Magnum PI, Marlboro, Nissan Sentra, Pop Tarts, Reuters, Rockford Files, Safeway, Sawzall, Styrofoam, Tesla, Tupperware, Uber

Also available from

WF Waldrip

 **great novel!**

What a wonderful novel! The author drew very vivid pictures of the characters and events. What a riveting book! A fascinating read !

Published on June 3, 2014 by Vincent R. Mayr

Find more at www.amazon.com

Also available from

WF Waldrip

☆☆☆☆☆ **An Excellant Sequel**

By michael caburis on October 12, 2014

Format: Kindle Edition   Verified Purchase

A riviting sequel to The Guards Themselves .
i hope another by the author is forthcoming
WF Waldrip is a must read author

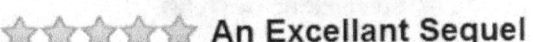

Find more at www.amazon.com

Also available from

WF Waldrip

☆☆☆☆☆ **Steven King can relax**

By Doug T. on March 14, 2018

Format: Paperback   Verified Purchase

Steven King can rest easy and retire knowing Wade Waldrip can carry the torch and scare the wits out of people.

Find more at www.amazon.com

ABOUT THE AUTHOR

WF WALDRIP is a widely traveled author, and Arizona native.

His writing style is true to life, bypassing the 'Politically Correct."

www.ingramcontent.com/pod-product-compliance
Lightning Source LLC
Chambersburg PA
CBHW062120170626
46813CB00002B/521